Crows Go
Wild

Crows Go Wild

GORDON OFFIN-AMANIAMPONG

TATE PUBLISHING
AND ENTERPRISES, LLC

Published by Tate Publishing & Enterprises, LLC
127 E. Trade Center Terrace | Mustang, Oklahoma 73064 USA
1.888.361.9473 | www.tatepublishing.com

Tate Publishing is committed to excellence in the publishing industry. The company reflects the philosophy established by the founders, based on Psalm 68:11,
"The Lord gave the word and great was the company of those who published it."

Published in the United States of America
ISBN: 978-1-62510-380-2
1. Fiction / General
2. Fiction / Action & Adventure
14.02.05

Acknowledgments

Thank you to my beloved children, Jeffrey Kyei Baffour Offin-Amaniampong, Joel Agyeman Wadie Offin-Amaniampong and Nana Adwoa Dufie.

I love you Thelma for your steadfast prayers.

Kate Reynolds, book project manager, and the entire editorial, designing and marketing team of Tate Publishing & Enterprise, LLC in Mustang, Oklahoma, U.S.A, kudos for a good job done.

And last but not least, Ma'am Earlean Jones, Jessie Freeman, Mr. Robert Thomas, Charles/Carole Duarte, Mr. and Mrs. John & Jane Muguku, Tammy Eckler, Tiffany Dempsey and Peter staff, US Bank (TCC Branch Tacoma), Frank Malone, Deacon Telfare and David Lind in Tacoma/Puyallup/Gig Harbor of Washington State in the United States and all the good friends out there.

Preface

It remained a jigsaw puzzle. It bred anxiety, disappointment, frustration, and incompetence. Decades went by. Lead after lead yielded no positive results. As files gathered dust, hopes evaporated into thin air. The mysterious assassination of the heir apparent to the Ashanti Golden Stool had become an old, cold case.

And it would take no mean a person other than the deceased's own son.

Indomitable Captain Crow delighted many in Kumasi and beyond when he brought the killers of his father, Barima Adom Yiadom, to justice almost three decades later. He set up his own undercover agency, Big Eye, to unravel the mystery death and had the mission accomplished.

Obliquely, the ubiquitous investigator had his daring personnel infiltrated the inner circle of the country's intelligence body, the Bureau of National Intelligence (BNI).

One of the protagonist's (Crow's) inexorable staff was the slick Hawa Owoahene Ogede, nicknamed Lady Dynamite, who often made her victims piss in their underwear during interrogations.

Having served five years in the US Marine Corps as an undercover agent, ten years with MI6 in the UK Intelligence

Agency and worked as a pilot for the German national carrier, Lufthansa Airlines, for two years, the seasoned detective brought her influence to bear on the spying agency.

Already in tango with the police chief of Kumasi, uncompromisingly snooping into all the old, cold dirt files at the Criminal Investigation Department (CID) headquarters, she had the chief's office bugged, and every conversation that took place at the office was captured.

In the heartland of Kumasi, the spying group occupied the fiftieth floor of the Pyramid Buildings that literally dwarfed the tiny pre-colonial police post opposite her.

From this prominent height, Captain Crow and his team could survey all the land. Accurately, they knew who was frequenting the police chief's office and, perhaps, their day-to-day activities. The veteran detective and his squad would spread their wings as wide as the North American XB-70 Valkyrie and, like a shaft of light, parachute deep into the dark belly of Mother Earth, where the assassins of his slain father had sought unholy refuge.

However, the captain's reputation as a civil rights icon was hugely bruised following the never-ending pursuit of one of the runaway fugitives Tweneboa Kodua, who was believed to be the chief architect of the heir's assassination.

In the course of the frenetic hunt, Kodua killed himself after sensing danger of his imminent capture. Unfortunately, the hunter was hunted. Captain Crow was wrongfully charged with manslaughter and attempted mutiny to dethrone the Ashanti king. Consequently, he would serve nearly thirty years concurrently on the two separate counts at Graceland's worse penitentiary, Apollonia, and the Firestone *(Ogyakrom)* prison in Gloryland for a crime he never committed.

His agonies deepened while still serving term in prison. Captain Crow lost his mother. Ama Samanhyia, his longtime wife, was disgustingly gang-raped by four masquerading men.

And several of his inmates died, as a result of wanton police brutality. Miraculously, he survived the carnage!

By mid-eighties, he had become the greatest civil rights icon across the globe and began travelling places: notably the former Soviet Union (USSR), the United Kingdom, France, and the People's Republic of China, giving public lectures and speeches. Blacks in diaspora including whites and yellow people caught what many called the *'crowmania syndrome'*——winning a number of disciples into the comradeship.

Finally, the maverick and his colleagues docked at the New World, where he recalibrated his activism machinery and planned to push the barometer of freedom, justice, and equality to the top rung of the ladder.

But much to his incredulity, it turned out that injustice abounds everywhere, inequality knows no borders, and discrimination transcends all frontiers. Paul Cook one of the 'latter day' saints who joined the Walatu-Walasa group during their tour in North America went to jail for civil disobedience even in the Free State. So how did Captain Crow and his Walatu-Walasa Operation team have the job done in such an admirable fashion?

Well, the secret to their successful act in the exhilarating novel was due in part to the zeal the squad attached to the exercise. Their artful modus operandi could be cited as another. They carried out their duties as night watchmen, bar attendants, Susu collectors, and palm-wine tappers, and sometimes as advertising/marketing agents.

Chapter I

"Somber Summer!" screamed the *Frontline*, a local tabloid.

At its head office in Ash Town, a suburb of Kumasi, many swarmed a newsstand across the street like bees to catch a glimpse of the mystery headline.

Nana Dufie, the tabloid's editor, couldn't hold her breath.

"I've never covered anything like this before. And never has this paper received such an outpouring of goodwill and condolence messages from people of all walks of life. I certainly don't remember," she editorialized.

"At least not for the last half a century—seeing a whole city turned upside down with its adults and aged slumping on the ground like poisoned horses."

Evidently, the early-morning sun that breathed on Kumasi (the ancient powerful city of the Ashanti kingdom) with its sensual golden rays on July 24 didn't bring good news. It was gloomy news—a mighty tree (*odupon*) had fallen.

One of her illustrious sons, Barima Adom Yiadom, heir apparent to the enviable Golden Stool, had been assassinated. The tragedy had scared many town folks out of their wits.

By far, it was seen as the goriest ever committed on the empire's soil and the first in a century that the monarchy had witnessed. But by who, residents didn't know, and whereabouts of his body they couldn't tell.

Absolute grief had gripped the nerves of the entire kingdom. Kumasi was in tears. Her heart had been broken. Men, women, and even children mourned (*mometwe*) like doves for their slain royal. And it seemed every living soul in the historic city felt the seismic shock. Dirges were heard at every quarter and gown of the capital, while the widow woman underwent significant funeral rituals.

Undoubtedly, the benign Garden City had been thrown into fright and bewilderment. On the main streets of the capital, Fear (in his combative fearsome gear) walked as bold as the atrocious and giant Goliath—flaunting his deadly weapon, threatening the city's inhabitants, and plunging them to their beds as though they were under a curfew.

Approximately four miles away from the chaotic scene was another site of magnetism—the once-peaceful home of the would-be king had been besieged by sympathizers and mourners. And like wildfire, the news of the terrible death spread its long fang across and beyond the borders of the empire.

As the news traveled outside her boundaries, the residents also poured their hearts out at home. "Asase Yaa di ade," a mourner intoned. (Mother Earth is at feast.)

The rear-guard chief of Manhyia Osabarima Atakora Amaniampong (Kyidomhene) noted in his condolence message to the bereaved family: "Truth be told, death is unkind and unfaithful."

"Owuo nim Odehyee," noted the home-guard chief (Ankobeahene) Kwadwo Bonsu. (Death is not a respecter of royal.)

In twos, threes, fours, and tens, mourners gathered to discuss the gripping news at every street corner.

"This is unbelievable," said Kofi Aggrey, a mechanic who lived close by the residence of the heir. He continued, "I think I saw him less than a week ago. He was coming out from his vintage jeep."

"Unlike many royals," Kofi Aggrey further stated, "Barima was such an honest and down-to-earth man, charming and adorable."

Elsewhere, in a little ramshackle beer bar at Adum, the heartland of Kumasi, speculation had hit peak level. And the tittle-tattle bells would continue to ring for months and would even morphed into years.

"I suspect this must be an inside job," Yaw Preko, a World War I veteran, whispered into the ears of Jomo while the two shared a bottle of *akpeteshie* (strong local gin) together.

"Jomo, let me state it unequivocally to you, royals don't vanish like that. I am an old dog in the block. I have almost lived seventy years of my entire life in this kingdom... This is unheard of; this is totally outrageous.

Barima's death must have been engineered by someone from within. Trust me."

"You mean from Manhyia?" Jomo queried.

"I bet you," he replied.

"Where else do you think it originated from?"

"Is it from my mother's kitchen or your father's farmland?"

"Tell me if you know of any other place beside the palace."

"I don't doubt your claim, old soldier. Certainly, the people at the palace aren't immune from this unfathomable saga. There is no smoke without fire, the old sages say."

"I think we all need to be more careful and cautious nowadays. Nobody's safe in this kingdom," Jomo submitted.

From one after the other, the verbal assaults continued; and without even looking over shoulders, some angry folks launched whatever scathing remarks they had on their minds—like this young man, Kwadwo Kanawu.

"Those responsible for the heinous crime will one day pay the price. I don't think one person could have executed this nefarious act," he told a group of persons who were engrossed in his thoughts.

"I also don't care where these goons live either from inside or outside the palace. Their cups will be full. The killers will be smoked out from their hideouts," he snapped.

In the meantime, Manhyia, the symbol of power and residence for Ashanti kings, had officially been briefed about the inexplicable disappearance of the heir. An emergency meeting comprising the sitting Asantehene (uncle to Barima Adom Yiadom), rear-guard chief (*kyidomhene*), home-guard chief (*Ankobeahene*), the queen mother, and other prominent figures followed shortly afterward. The crisis gathering was preceded by a poignant prayer from chief linguist Okyeame Odei Ampofo.

Symbolically, the official notification also marked the slaughter of twelve sheep, three fatling cows, and pouring of libation— Gordon's Dry Gin *(broni nsa)* as appeasement to the gods and ancestors of the land to ward off any future calamities.

In the aftermath of this ritual, a kind of rogue-style raids were carried out across the main streets of the township, as any domestic animals—thus sheep, goats, fowls, dogs, and the like— found were butchered.

Per custom, the widow walked barefooted, clad in all black (*birisie*), and was accordingly forbidden to eat any food considered heavy. Relatives close to the deceased also observed the ancient customary. During the forty-day period of the ritual, they were all given hairless cut, symbolic of the loss of a departed relation.

At the forecourt of the ancient palace, the red flags flew at half-mast, and two weeks of state mourning was declared, amid sea of red banners, red armbands, red headgears, and red clothes.

There was also *kuntunkuni*, the traditional black cloth clad by the old guards and the elderly, with green leaves protruding their mouths, signifying a great loss.

It was a huge loss of course, a protégé that citizens of Asanteman would have loved to see become their next king. Indeed, Asanteman would have preferred to see Barima go to the grave at his complete age as a shock of corn in its full season, but death struck him with its venomous pointed tooth.

Without a doubt, Ashantis had been mourning not just an ordinary person but also one stately viewed as the legitimate successor to the coveted Golden Stool.

Nearly one month after the disaster, the king and elders of Manhyia, having diligently followed all protocol to the letter, held a grandiose funeral rite for the slain royal.

The venue was the Jackson Park. And the afternoon had enough to swallow. It was a scene that by far outdid the word mournful, amid color and energy. At the fully packed funeral grounds, the Ashanti Dance Ensemble, the Adowa Dancers, the Kete Group, the Asafo Company, the Densuom Group, and the Nnwomkoro Troupe from Mampong had all been called into action to showcase the dynamic root culture of the people and, more importantly, bade final farewells to an empty coffin draped in red.

When the sun began to wind down its hard day's activity, the home-guard chief signaled that it was time to send Nana home. The pallbearers were closely trailed by a retinue of royals, executioners, traditionalists, and firecrackers.

While the mourners wailed and wept hysterically, the enigmatic horns (*mmentia*) from the *ahenfie* (palace) buzzed onomatopoeically, conveying pity, empathy, and sympathy: "Damirifa due! Damirifa due! Due! Due! Nana due."

Barima's soul would have been restless had his most-liked choral music group from Cape Coast (the people with the queen's accent) not been there to unleash their harmonic repertoire. He loved not only choral music but also patriotic songs. The song "Asem Yi Di Ka," written by the late emeritus Dr. Ephraim Kwadwo Amu, was his most preferred.

Alas, all the necessary rituals had been performed! And weeks after the elaborate funeral ceremony, Akua Akyeampoma, the deceased's wife, would be left in perpetual brooding.

"When I wake up and I don't see the sun, it seems to me the heavens are mourning. It reminds me that Mother Earth is also grieving in eternal pain. And the whole world is experiencing an uneasy calm. Ever since Barima disappeared, my whole world appears to be shattering," she told her sister Yaa Asantewaa.

"Yaa, it hasn't been easy at all for me. It's been absolutely tough over the past few days, and I know it's going to be a long healing process."

"You couldn't put it better, sister; it is a long healing process. Remember sickness comes in a moment, but it takes days, weeks, months, at times years before it goes away. Nonetheless, I trust the good Lord will make amends. He will recompense you; so take heart and focus on Him."

"The heartaches and the pains would last long—that I can vouch for."

Sleepless nights, nightmarish dreams, and weird thoughts seem to eclipse my mind, because anytime I turn to the other side of my bed, I feel his presence—notwithstanding the fact that he is gone forever. Yes, the glowing sun that hitherto lit the heavens has now disappeared into the dark clouds, holding him captive. But above all, time never seems to be on my side."

As Akua Akyeampoma gabbed back and forth, Yaa, her sister, repeatedly urged her to stand firm and be of good courage.

But moments later, the widowed woman walked straight up to the windows facing east as though someone had gestured at her to come, while Yaa looked on in perplexity.

"Maybe one day, we will meet again. Maybe someday, Barima and I will recall the fond memories we shared together. Maybe he will show up one day, unexpectedly. Anything is possible. But death indeed is a wicked somebody. Somebody we don't see but we fear most. Because when he wraps his icy hands around you, it's a foregone conclusion till 'thy kingdom come.'"

Meantime, there still remained many unanswered questions: Where was the body of the slain heir? Who killed him, why was he assassinated, where was he murdered?

Chapter 2

Forty days after Barima's assassination, his survived wife Akua Akyeampoma, a well-bred woman, had a baby. It was a rainy and breezy Friday. The time was exactly nine o'clock in the morning, and the Mack truck that smacked into Jack Shadrack's home a fortnight ago, along the dirt road nearby, had just passed by.

That sight had resurrected dreadful memories. Jack, a distant cousin of the widowed woman, was killed instantly. In a sequel, that horrific incident would arouse funny feelings, sending shockwaves into the abdomen of the pregnant woman.

The sensational emotion, she recalled, "was like butterflies in my stomach. For once I couldn't figure out what I was going through. I felt like caving in, so I fell on my knees." She narrated, "Praying to God for his protection and guidance. Heavenly Father, let nothing happen to me and this baby. Even though I don't know what I'm going to have, I know for sure everything good comes from you. And I will accept gracefully whatever you blessed me with.'"

Over by the undulating knoll of the wonderful, flowery banks of the Offin River in Graceland, the expectant mother had had a lifeline bouncing baby boy.

Earlier, a teenage girl named Akuaba dressed in *kaba* and a piece of Holland cloth wrapped around her waist, who'd recently gone through puberty rite initiation, heard Akua Akyeampoma groaning in the shrubbery.

As she walked closer to the direction towards home, the wailing sound intensified.

"This must be a woman's voice," she conjectured.

Quickly the young girl realized that the woman was in labor. So she ran to the town and relayed the information to the village's traditional birth attendant.

It wouldn't take Maame Ama Korkor the midwife minutes to answer the emergency call. Like a jet plane she glided to the house grabbed her toolbox and put her white headgear on. Off to the 'labor ward'——-where the young woman, Akua Akyeampoma twice struck by pain within a month, writhed on the ground in an attempt to have her first child.

Amazingly, moments before she got there, the laboring mother had already broken the water without any inducement, and in less than thirty minutes, the seasoned midwife also broke the frontline of the enemy. She picked up the battle from there.

"Pushhhh, puuusshhhhh. Don't give up; you can do it, a little harder." The midwife told the birthing mom.

As the fetus showed its head, sweat poured down Akua Akyeampoma amid irrepressible wailings and wriggling. Her eyes rolled back and forth like a dice. She screamed and squealed harder, looking helpless and totally worn-out. But repeatedly the midwife urged the laboring mom to give it all as she reeled in pain.

Sweetie push harder now. Don't give up," the nurse wheedled her the more. Sooner than later she would successfully have her first Captain Crow *(Osahene)* traditionally named Kofi Antobam.

"Congratulations, my daughter," She said. "Bravo!"

Initially, it had appeared impossible, but she managed to deliver the hefty baby who weighed over fifteen pounds.

With clenched fist and a big head, he landed like an eagle from the fresh womb that bore the future king, civil rights icon, and an alleged mutineer. On a piece of blood-soaked cloth, the new baby lay recoiled and motionless while his fatigued mom heaved a deep sigh of relief.

But she was concerned about the strange muteness of her baby.

"He is not crying. Why?" Akua Akyeampoma asked the traditional nurse.

"Don't worry, he is okay. Babies behave differently," she assured her.

The nurse was right!

Shortly afterward, the baby began to cry so loud and so shrilly as though he had been pinched. Ama Korkor (a widow herself who lost her husband through alcohol poisoning) was the village's only traditional nurse. The midwife had been doing this job since the Mosaic period, and she did it all with such adroitness.

She reached out for her toolbox, picked up the scissors and the blades to begin yet another delicate clinical task—natal operation. Meticulously, the midwife had the umbilical cord severed, tidied up the little boy, and buried the placenta.

"We're good to go now," she told the nursing mother.

Sheathed in a piece of cloth called *kyenkye bi adi ma wu* and held closely to the chest of the midwife amid the gusty wind, they turtled through the craggy footpath and made it home safely. But the aftermath of that successful birth was wrought by mixed feelings. The door to that womb was shut forever after bearing that fruit.

In the intervention time, goodwill messages poured in from far and near the kingdom. Friends and loved ones saluted the nursing mother.

Undeniably, she merited *ayekoo* (congratulations). She had cinched victory. Birthing is nerve-wracking, and pregnancy is nauseating.

However, some men (husbands) don't even appreciate that. They obviously have no clue as to the excruciating pain these mothers go through during childbirths.

In short, they had been lucky. Lucky because most men get dehorned by *wanzams* (circumcisers) at infantile stage, except those who let theirs overgrow like backyard bushes and get sheared during adolescent period—that experience minor pain.

That notwithstanding, many young kids, particularly the uncuts, dread the *wanzams*.

Several days after the birth of Kofi Antobam, congratulatory messages continued to pour into the residence of the royals.

"Welcome home, our newborn king," they said.

"Oh, look at him; he's cute!" Adwoa Dua, Crow's paternal grandmother, said.

"Who do you think he resembles?" the Granny asked Crow's mom.

"Well, I think he looks just like Barima...he has his forehead and firm cheeks." Akua Akyeampoma replied.

"You're absolutely right." Ama Fordjour, a relative, interrupted. "He's just a carbon copy of his father. He will be tall and strong," she added. "However, I think he has his mother's striking nose," she remarked. "Not as prominent as Barima's. And not only that, his pollinated eyebrow inherited from his mother is another distinguished feature."

Indeed, the birth of the future king would also culminate several rituals that took place at the Manhyia Palace following the strange disappearance of his father. It additionally meant that an equally important custom was about to take place. Like most Akan kids, Captain Crow would be circumcised at his infantile stage as pointed out earlier.

Circumcision, which dates back the Abrahamic age, is viewed by Akans as a sacred practice. Therefore, the young royal, like many male children born in Ghana, particularly Akans, would be put on the knife-edge. Traditionally, the Akans count their days from the very day one was/is born. It defied the conventional seven-day count.

So, on the eighth day (*nnawotwe*), exactly a week after his birth, Papa Wanzam showed up at the nursing mother's home. Dressed in long garb and his left hand holding on to an old, tiny, leather, bronzed bag that housed his blades, knives, and other stuff, which included herbs and bandages, Papa Wanzam sat on a small stool outside the courtyard and asked that the baby be brought to him.

"I can't watch this," Captain Crow's mother remarked. "I pray he doesn't bleed like some babies do."

That's true. There were times the 'cut man,' or the circumciser, misjudged his gauge and cut the foreskin of the penis deeper. Amid chewing of kola nuts (wearing red-colored teeth), the man with northern extraction began proceedings. Within minutes, the newly born baby had been circumcised. Luckily, Captain Crow didn't bleed much, and he did not cry as his mom feared.

This ceremony was dovetailed by an outdooring, or baby shower, two weeks afterward.

The skyline at the little town was fine, bright, and beautiful enough for the family of Captain Crow to wine, dine, and make merry and herald his arrival. As anticipated, the event was attended by a cavalcade of family relatives, loved ones, and neighbors. Attendees showered assorted gifts on the little boy as a symbolic gesture.

Even though the ceremony was marked with joy, at the same time, it brought back fresh memories of a departed kinsman, a husband, a father, a brother, an uncle, and a friend—Barima Adom Yiadom, a royal from the Oyoko family and a prominent businessman (a timber contractor), who had been tragically murdered by unknown assailants just five weeks before his son's birth, hence the name Antobam—because he did not meet his father.

Across the kingdom, the birth of the young royal had been greeted with absolute joy amid strong belief that Barima had reincarnated. This view gained more currency, particularly among the indigenes at Mogyabiyedom, the traditional homeland of the royals. And strangely, Captain Crow had a birthmark on his right upper arm, the same as his dad carried.

Besides, the dark-skinned, broad-faced, handsome-looking boy had six toes—a thing hitherto considered a stigma among Akans in Ghana. Deformity, ailment, financial insolvency, any criminal or immoral act like murder, theft, homosexuality, incest, etc., at the time and even today Ghana could possibly ruin one's chances of becoming a king.

What would the soothsayers and palmists say about him?

Captain Crow was destined to become a prominent figure in the future.

❧

Five years later, the little noble and the mother visited Mogyabiyedom where he was introduced to the family members, as well as kingmakers in the native land. This was in keeping with tradition.

But heaven had no clue what the protégé had under his sleeves and what might befall the celebrated Manhyia Palace—the seat of the occupant of the Golden Stool, in the years that would follow.

Absolutely, no one had a wind of what was to come, when then beautiful five-foot-ten tall, twenty-five-year-old Akua Akyeampoma (a royal from the Ekoana clan), gave birth to Captain Crow several years ago. He was a royal-royal, in view of the fact that his mom was later enstooled as queen mother, and his dad an heir apparent to the Golden Stool.

Understandably, with the departure of her great husband, it naturally became imperative for the widowed woman to raise the little boy singlehandedly. Nonetheless, as required by tradition of the land, the prince or royal occasionally would pay visits to his uncles' and granduncles' homes where he would be taught the rudiments of kingship, rules, and ordinances.

Chapter 3

Captain Crow's deceased dad Barima used to pay courtesy visits to his close friend, Nana Kwame Gyetuah, and other relatives, too. The two even had what they termed as *'our reciprocated'* gestures. Three times every fortnightly at least the two friends visited each other.

"Honey, could you pass me the old newspaper I hauled out from the cabinet yesterday?"

Nana Gyetuah the maternal granduncle of Captain Crow asked his wife.

"You bet." Yaa Amponsah replied as she readily handed him the tabloid.

"I want to show it to Barima; he must be here in a few minutes time...See I told you, talk of the good Angel... there he comes. He does not play with his time at all. Did you see his vehicle turned around the corner?"

"Where...?" His wife enquired craning her neck.

"Oh I see him now," Yaa Amponsah stated. "He just pulled over by the courtyard."

Barima had on a white T-shirt, tanned baggy-shorts, and *'Ahenema'* traditional footwear for royals.

"Good afternoon!" He said. "How is everybody doing?"

"We're doing great today." Nana Gyetuah replied. "Not as bad as it was yesterday…. Thought I caught a slight flu; I am not sure, but I woke up today with new energy and new strength like never before. On top of that, Yaa, my better half, is as ever vivacious as Grandma Eve."

"That's God's favor," Yaa Amponsah interjected.

"By the way, how are you and my niece——-your wife?" Nana Gyetuah asked Barima.

"We're both doing very well. She says hi to the family."

"We appreciate that; she is such a lovely lady," Yaa Amponsah remarked. "I might stop by tomorrow to see her…the thing is getting bigger and bigger. I suppose you're very excited aren't you?"

"Yes I am," Barima replied. "Auntie,"—referring to Nana Gyetuah's wife—"you're looking gorgeous this afternoon."

"Thank you Barima," she responded with a blissful smile as she excused herself to attend to other chores.

"I like this nook chair (Akentennwa)," Barima commented. "It's really beautiful. Very natural!"

"Where did you buy it from?" He asked.

"I bought it from the Asafo market. The guy who makes them, though, doesn't live here in Kumasi. He told me he comes from a village near Offinso," his uncle-in-law responded.

"So how do I get one? Do you have any idea?"

"See, I told Yaa that Barima might like this chair. I know you. You like crafts and stuff such as this."

"Anyway, I remember he said he comes once every other week, but at times it takes more than a month I've observed. Depending on the market's prospects and perhaps other unforeseen contingencies…."

"You know how it is here. People don't like locally-made goods. They prefer *'painte ma mento'* from China or the West and other western products. But take a look at this nook; very durable and portable, isn't it?"

"I can see that, that's why I'm hankering to get one."

"Don't worry since you're a busy bee I will ask Mensa my grandson to go with me. I think this Thursday will be a month since I got mine. Pray we find luck, though!"

"Thank you, I appreciate that. You might've seated yourself a little earlier today; waiting for me huh?" Barima asked.

"Right on!" He responded.

"Here, Barima let me share this with you before we proceed on." Nana Gyetuah said. "My father told me this when I was a little boy..."always get your house ready for your guest. In other words, put it in order."

"That's right!" Barima interjected. "You know at times we gloss over certain social values. Invariably, we assume they aren't relevant—values that our elders have jealously guarded against."

In the course of their discussion, the two also briefly talked about the rumor making rounds at the time in relation to the health status of his maternal uncle the Asantehene. And the prospects of him becoming the successor (in case the great king dies) even came to the fore in their conversation. It's often said; when the elders meet obviously bottles must crack open.

Both men liked Jonnie Walker the Scottish brand whisky; so while sitting at the balcony they enjoyed themselves with a few glasses of the gin. Like the former colonial secretary, Barima occasionally invited family members to his residence and had conversation with them.

But little did he know that that Sunday's evening meeting, which probably occurred on July 19, five days before his inexplicable disappearance with the man he referred to as his bosom friend at his Ahodwo residence in Kumasi, would be the last.

As they continued to relish themselves with the Scottish marque at the terrace, few nutcrackers flew in to perch on the shady 'Fram' trees flapping their leaves like the lilies of the valley, giving stress-free breeze in front of Nana Gyetuah's beautiful compound.

"Are those crows?" Pointing to the direction where the birds were perching.

"What do they want here?" Barima asked.

"Yes, they are. I haven't seen them here for a while now," Nana Gyetuah replied.

"I thought they weren't coming back again. Maybe they went for a sabbatical leave… I'm just assuming," he said.

"You know Barima, the crows are like vultures, not in features, but they have good sense of smell. I call them detectives. Listen to them moaning, they must be hungry. Here, one moment."

The aristocrat handed Barima the tabloid—'*Pioneer*'—to browse through while he rushed to the kitchen to get the birds some food.

"Ah… there they go," '*Kwaakwaa*' with their usual croaky tone.

"Have you checked the back page stories yet?"

"No, I'm about to," Barima replied.

"Please do. I wanted to show you something before I ran to the kitchen."

"Ah…..journalists and their sensational headlines: There they go again. "THE DISGRACED WAYO!"

"Who is this Wayo? Is he the doctor at Ash Town?" Barima enquired.

"No. He is the baldheaded old man, the one who owns the transports."

"Oh, I think I know him."

"Yeah, he is getting older now," Nana Gyetuah said. "He used to be another controversial figure in town. Lots of people in the metropolis remember him for two things. First as the alleged murderer of his wife, and secondly, his epic gaffe at a Town Hall meeting when he vied for the mayoral position in Kumasi over two decades ago. He lost anyway."

"Let me start with the booboo," Nana Gyetuah told Barima. "I suppose you're familiar with this popular Akan proverb: *Koto didi a n'aye Aponkyereni ya.* Literally translated, 'a wealthy crab is not loved by the frog.' In other words, the frog goes livid when he finds the crab eating."

"Well, Wayo got it all rumbled. He said: "*Opete* (vulture) instead of crab and also confused frog with *kraman* (dog)."

"Did they forgive him?" Barima asked.

"Where, here in Kumasi (*'Nya asem whe'*) get into trouble and you'll know your friends. I remember very well, Wayo had returned from the former Soviet Union. He'd studied Mechanical Engineering after a decade or so....In part that was the reason: mixing his English with the Twi language. Political pundits and pollsters had put him ahead of his opponents even in the midst of the goof.

"But his waterloo was near if he thought the storm was over. His detractors seized upon that blunder. They ridiculed him and labeled him as unfit, uncouth and un-nurtured for the job. In a nutshell, they sank his political boat.

"And had he won, he would have been the youngest mayor ever elected by the metropolis." Nana Gyetuah underscored. "However, as the dust of the historic gaffe began to settle another disaster reared its foul head—the alleged murder of his wife."

"Incredible." Barima remarked. "And how did the murder story end?"

"Well as you might've read already, about two weeks before the election he was arrested and charged for the killing of his newly wedded wife. The businessman turned politician was subsequently found guilty and sentenced for five years.

Luckily, for him, two years into his sentence the security agents nabbed a young man thought to be the deceased's ex-boyfriend. Upon a tip-off, detectives recovered the murder weapon, and later the suspect told the police that he was hired by one Kodua who would later become the king's chief Butler to kill Wayo's wife. So that was how he got his freedom."

"Did Wayo go back into politics after his release?"

"Not at all," Nana Gyetuah explained. "He expended his energy and time on his transport business, which he still runs today."

✼

Indeed, that Sunday meeting would also mark the end of all visitations between the two. Barima often spoke highly of the man he regarded as his father.

"The old man is intelligent and articulate," he told his wife.

Neighbors in this calm suburb called Barima "Baricash," thus a wealthy man. The businessman also earned the name Stanley Baldwin (former British prime minister in the 1920s) because of his seemingly British accent. He was very affable and easily approachable.

Throughout their happy marriage, the widowed woman knew Barima admired and respected Nana Kwame Gyetuah very much, and therefore, it wasn't out of place to let her beloved son Kofi Antobam (Captain Crow) understudy him.

And so for more than fifteen years of his juvenile upbringing, Captain Crow went through what would be described as regimental exercise like learning and seasoning himself with the kingly norms and ordinances of the native land.

Several of his relatives like his uncles and granduncles helped in that direction. But Nana Gyetuah, the family head of the Ekoana clan (Abusua Panin), became a character symbol and a great pillar in the life of the young royal.

Under his conventional tutelage, Captain Crow would grow to become the greatest orator who ever lived in the history of the powerful Ashanti empire. Generally known for his aptitude for precision and articulation, he would earn the respect of the entire community and beyond.

In fact, Nana Gyetuah was a walking historian; his whole mind was history. His depth of knowledge of the Ashanti history filtered through the borders of the Bonos, the Akwamus, and the Ga Adangmes to the Moshies, as well as Dagombas, to the Abudus, and the Andanis.

It even extended beyond former Trans Volta Togoland (the Ewelands) boundaries to Dahomey (today Republic of Benin), the land of snakes and haven for voodooism, to Ille Ife, and up to the topmost part of Anago-Maiduguri.

Knowledge acquired, especially customs, norms, and traditions, he opined, "must be shared with one another so that there wouldn't be a generational gap. Pass it on." Diligently, Nana Gyetuah extolled that mantra and passed on the richly packed repository of wisdom to his grandnephew by oral tradition or by word of mouth.

Beyond those sterling qualities, the role model and exemplar's whole persona was cut for mentorship and leadership.

The mentor loved Captain Crow so dearly. And he never called him by his preferred name. Instead, he called him Kofi all the time. During one of their usual meetings, he told the then twelve-year-old royal, "You are as beautiful as your mom, as tall and bold as your father, and of course, as intelligent as me, your granduncle," educing sidesplitting laughter from the young prince.

"Today, we're going to talk about the Akan clans," he told Captain Crow. "These clans symbolically define the members of all the nine clans in this ethnic grouping. They include the Aduana, Agona, Asakyire, Asona, Bretuo, Ekoona, and Oyooko. Each clan has a stool or throne and a totem."

"What is a totem, Granduncle?"

"Good question. It is something kingly related. Mostly, clans, families, group, lineage, or tribe adopt a personal spirit animal helper which has a special meaning to them. This is what we refer to as totem.

"Just to give you a quick rundown, not in any perking order though, the talkative parrot [*akoo kasatenten*] represents the Agona clan, whiles the vulture and the yellow snake are symbols for the Asakyire and Asona clan, respectively.

"Interestingly, the Aduana clan has fire, not an animal, as their totem. History has it that the survivability of this clan during the historic journey from the old Ghana empire across the Sahara to modern Ghana was hugely dependent on a small fire the forebears chanced upon.

"Last, but not least, the Bretuo, Ekoona, and Oyooko clans have the tiger, the buffalo, and the hawk as their totems."

"Pardon me, Nana, what did the tiger do for the Bretuo clan?"

"Mmmm good you asked! Hard to believe it Kofi, the tiger was understood to have protected the Bretuo people. He didn't harm them instead the predatory animal according to legend made the arduous journey with the clan to their final destination, ensuring that no wild animal attacked them."

"That's awesome, Nana," Captain Crow exclaimed

"Now the buffalo and the hawk too, that piques my interest. Would you tell me more about these two totems, Nana?"

"Yes, I will. The buffalo is one of the strongest animals in the forest with exquisite horns, depicting elegance and strength of the Ekoona people also known as the *ahene* [the kings].

"On the other hand, the hawk [*akoroma*] is a powerful bird that stalks the streets and trees for its preys. From the sky, he usually hawks around, waiting for his victim. When the hawk captures a prey, he displays its victim up in the sky, as if to say, 'I am the conqueror.'"

"So what I gather is that these two animals, the buffalo and hawk, have power. They both have strength. Am I right, Nana?"

"Yes, you're absolutely right."

"But, I think the buffalo is far bigger than the hawk. Isn't that right as well?"

"Correct."

"In contrast, the hawk is perhaps faster than the buffalo. I assume that is also a fact. How then did the Oyookos end up becoming the legitimate occupants of the Golden Stool?"

"That's another brilliant question, Kofi. I wish time would allow me to go into the matrix of that. The devil is often said to be in the details. But the psychology of the human mind is an impermeable perimeter. To cut a long story short here is the gist.

"Perhaps at the end of the seventeenth century [roughly three hundred years ago], the legitimate occupants of the Ashanti throne were the Ekoona people. From time immemorial, the Ekoonas had been the rightful inheritors of the Ashanti monarchy.

"The last Ekoona king whose reign marked the end of their succession to the dynasty was the magnanimous Nana Obiri Yeboah, who mentored and adopted Osei Tutu as his nephew. According to myth, Nana Obiri Yeboah had no nephew born to him by his blood sister[s].

"Osei Tutu, an Oyooko, would later become the first Oyooko royal to ascend the coveted throne. That paradigm shift evidently was the smoking gun that sank the Ekoona lineage to the Ashanti stool…"

"Nana, what really happened?"

"Something happened but again, I don't think time is on our side. Probably we can do that on your next visit here. It is getting late I suppose. We can possibly make it next week if you don't mind, my sweet grandnephew. Is that fine with you?"

"I really want to know it now, Nana," he interjected.

"What time is it?"

He seemed to have been softened by the little boy's incessant plea.

Captain Crow giraffed his neck to check the black Kit-Cat wall clock.

"It is half past the hour four. Mom is not home yet. Probably, we can use the next half hour to wrap up things. And what does the adage say, when the music is nice you play it twice? Isn't that true?"

"What was the question again?" he asked his grandson.

"How did King Osei Tutu get to the throne if it were for the Ekoona clan?"

"Oh, you've really turned my wheels now. That's a deadly question...Anyway, there once lived a powerful, fetish priest named Komfo Anokye. You may remember I talked about him briefly during our last conversation.

"He hailed from Awukugwa in the eastern region. The duo had met at Abankesieso in Denkyira. At the time, the Denkyira kingdom was the super power. Osei Tutu had been sent there by Nana Obiri Yeboah to learn the tradition and norms. This was a normal practice back then, nothing unconventional.

"But I must point out, at the height of the never-ending tribal wars, states paid homage to the ruling empire rather than the ruled referred to as vassal state [state subordinate to another]. Again, being a vassal implied providing military assistance to the sovereign state when requested to do so, and any kind of support the dominant state might demand from the vassal.

"Such demands, I should add also included the provision of human heads to the sovereign state upon the transition of its king. Sounds weird, isn't it?" he rhetorically asked Captain Crow.

"So in effect, if I understood you, Nana, Osei Tutu was being groomed to become the next king after Nana Obiri Yeboah.

"You're right."

"And what happened next?"

"Ah! When Osei Tutu and Anokye met at Abankessieso, they became good friends. Legend has it that Anokye asked Osei Tutu to call on him, rain or shine. And when the need arose, he didn't renege on his promise. Anokye would later lend his unalloyed support to Osei Tutu to defeat the Denkyiras."

"That seems like backstabbing to me. Why did he turn against the Denkyiras after being friends with then Denkyira King Ntim Gyakari and his people?"

"Kofi, that is another lethal question. Well, the elders say you'll never know the efficacy of the *nunum* [herb], until and unless you stir it up. So let's stir it up. Myth has it that Anokye once asked the Denkyira king to offer a severed head of an old woman to perform black power what is known in Ghanaian parlance as juju for the Denkyiras so that they would remain the only super power at the time.

"It turned out they provided the powerful fetish priest's own biological mother's head, according to legend. This act, it is believed, angered Anokye. He cursed the Denkyira people and from thereon, swore to pitch camp with his newfound friend Osei Tutu and the Ashantis.

"Osei Tutu's return to his homeland culminated an intense tribal war that involved two Akan tribes who one could call them cousins—the Ashantis and the Dormaa people.

"His ageing uncle, Obiri Yeboah, had become frail and could hardly marshal his people to fight the enemies. Therefore, Osei Tutu rallied the able men as well as the women, and they defeated the enemy.

"With the battle against the Denkyiras, he realized that they [Ashantis] could lose the battle if Anokye's support wasn't sought after urgently."

"Sorry for the interruption, Nana. Did you mean women at the time also fought alongside men?"

"Right. Let me digress a bit here. Between 1900 and 1901, the Ashantis fought the British under the aegis of then Queen Mother of Ejisu, Yaa Asantewaa."

"Wow, I'm surprise to learn women played such militant role, fought battles in those years, and even commandeered a whole ground force," Captain Crow exclaimed.

"Yes, militancy, politics, and kingship functions had never been a preserve of men among the Akan milieu and today Ghana in general. A classical example is the selection and installation of a king. The queen mother plays a pivotal role in this facet of kingship: without her input and blessing, there will be no king. So you see, we respect our mothers, sisters, and wives."

He checked the clock.

"I guess we still have time to finish the Ashanti-Denkyira battle," remarked Nana Gyetuah.

"So, as I said earlier, Osei Tutu fell on his bosom and longtime friend. And the powerful, fearsome, spiritual leader heeded the distressed call. The result was triumphant! The two pugnacious tribes fought two terrible battles. The Battle of Feyiase as it was called took many lives, but in the end, the Ashantis crashed the mighty Denkyiras in one of the fiercest wars ever fought in the annals of the Akan history. And that marked Osei Tutu's ascension to the throne. He also won many battles and annexed many states during his reign under the guidance of Anokye."

"From the foregoing, Nana, would it be right to say that Osei Tutu's ascension to the Golden Stool was ably aided by his longtime friend Anokye, much as his adoptive uncle Obiri Yeboah also played a doyen role in delegitimizing the Ekoana clan from the distinguished dynasty."

"I couldn't agree with you more on that, Kofi. Both personalities played a major role in that flagellation. That notwithstanding, Osei Tutu was also a shrewd young man.

"Actually, in fairness, with all apologies to the elders I should say it was Boa-Siako who signed his own death warrant."

"Oh, Nana, you've cracked me up, 'death warrant'!"

"Yes, of course. It was nothing but signing his obvious death warrant. Anyway, there was supposed to be a permanent swap after Osei Tutu's reign, but that never happened till now. So that wraps up today's segment."

"Wow! Thank you very much, Nana, I really do appreciate your generous time and profundity of knowledge of the history of our forebears. I'm always humbled to have you as my granduncle and mentor. I know many of my peers today would have loved or wished to have somebody like you to share information like this."

"Unfortunately, such expectation has remained a mirage to them."

"Brilliant boy, you're—!" Nana Gyetuah remarked.

"Thanks for the compliments. It's now time for you to go. Your mom should be home by now. I think we've been able to do justice to that subject. Oh, lest I forget, remember to read the good book every day, especially the book of Proverbs. It's very interesting. I can tell you, Kofi, many seek wisdom every day, but they blatantly ignore to fall on the Holy Book."

"It is no doubt the reservoir of wisdom. You know, if wisdom were to be marked down [*donkomi*], in other words put on 'clearance' at any supermall, say Tesco or Wal-Mart, I guarantee the poor, the weak, and the downtrodden would have gone home with nothing but bruises on their faces.

"After all, life in our world will be worth living if mankind will surrender to the Heavenly Father, and let him take the wheel."

"You're right, Nana. See you tomorrow, God willing. Bye."

Chapter 4

His eyes tailed Captain Crow while he stood at the terrace. He leaned over a broken-dead 1844 antique piano (George Fergurson, an English catechist, gave this to him) to fetch his tobacco smoking pipe from a small locker fitted to the sunburned patio wall.

"Smart kid," Nana Gyetuah said under his breath.

"Yaa Amponsah,' he called out his wife from the kitchen.

"Just a moment honey," she responded. The ideal woman was making a hotchpotch soup (Abunu-abunu) for the old man. In less than a minute she showed up with watery eyes and runny nose.

"You see what the smoke and the onions have done to me; trying to fix for you your most wanted," she told her husband amid laughter.

"Anyway, what is it?"

"What do you think about Kofi, my grandnephew?"

"Oh that chap is smart and very courteous, if he stays like this, I'm sure he will be a prominent figure someday. He always reminds me of his father, just like him," she said.

"You're right honey; I see that in him, too."

"Anything else, my Love?" she enquired.

"No that's about it; I am not going to bother you anymore. Thanks for coming," he said.

Moments later, Nana Gyetuah lit his tobacco while the beautiful woman dashed back to the kitchen.

Gently and delightfully, he inhaled the fumes of the burning leaves (*tawa*) and released palls of smoke that streamed out from his nostrils and mouth. He still gazed beyond the street corner to catch a glimpse of his beloved grandnephew.

It didn't take Captain Crow minutes to get to their upper-middle-class suburban home. The terrazzo concrete, gated reticent residence nudged in the attractive Graceland district, frequently baked by the mid-morning sunrise, gave its glassy windows (facing eastward) a rainbow outlook.

Acacia and cedar trees lined neatly on her paved but narrow streets; highlighted by modern and historic monuments. Several great men and women had once lived here. They included Oburumankoma, Odapagyan, and Osono; their long historic journey pre-dated the fall of the old Ghana Empire—from the Upper Volta (now Burkina Faso) all the way to Techiman in the Bonoland, where, according to history, they first established. Years later, this threesome of powerful leaders would blaze the trail and settled at today Fanteland.

Contrasting many suburbs in the Garden City, the streetlights in this affluent locale thrust darkness into mere oblivion and sparkled like a refined diamond at daybreak.

Graceland's magnificent milieu was by far the magnet that hauled the aristocrats and the wealthy. Nonetheless, she blended upper-class with middle- to low-income dwellers. It was here that Captain Crow grew and blew hundreds of thousands minds away with his enduring charisma.

The agile youngster with long props zoomed through the familiar neighborhood blocks like a cheetah. "Better late than never," he told his classmates at college. He was used to running, which happened to be one of his desired sporting disciplines, deeply rooted in the family genes.

Akua Akyeampoma, his adored mother, was in the kitchen busily fixing dinner and humming a lullaby. It is understood that good mothers never forget what they used to do best for their adorable babies or young kids.

Obviously, once in a while, like pop-up ads on computer screens, they hum good old lullabies as though they're still nursing a new crop.

Captain Crow darted into the living room, changed his clothes, and went to the kitchen.

"Hi, ma'am," rubbing his big head against his mother's curvy, tender shoulders.

"Where from this sweats and the wheezing—did you run here?" she asked.

"Yes, I did."

"You must be hungry, I guess."

"You're always right, ma'am."

"Kofi, I was thinking of you just awhile ago. The weather has changed, and I fear it might start to pour soon like it did last night."

"By the way, did you have something to eat at your granduncle's house?"

"Yes, I did."

"What did you have?

"A bottle of Fanta and tuna pie, but I am still hungry."

"Well, take it easy. Don't freak out. Food will be ready soon."

"What are you cooking?

"It is your favorite meal," she said.

"You mean rice and spinach sauce with fried plantain and charcoal-grilled tilapia aside?"

"You bet!"

"Mmm, sounds yummy! I love it," he said with such an impeccable smile.

Pretty soon, food would be ready.

"I know what you like, son," she told him.

"Did you enjoy your time with Granduncle?"

"Yes, it was superb. Oh, ma'am…"

"What is it?"

"Do you know what Fanta means?"

"Naughty boy, I'm not ready for your quiz now."

"Oh please…"

"Fanta you said? It is a brand of soda or soft drink."

"No, that isn't the correct answer."

"What is it then?"

"It means for all nonsense, take *akpeteshie*—fanta."

"Who told you this? Was it Granduncle Kwame Gyetuah?"

"Who else, ma'am? I nearly had my enzymes spilled out."

"He is a funny old man with earthy sense of humor."

"Lest I forget, Granduncle says hi to you. And he asked me to read the book of Proverbs."

"Thanks for telling me. That's an interesting book. I like it."

"Yes, he said so."

"Oh, look here. Hurry up and get the clothes out of the line. Tonight, I will tell you some folklore stories Grandma told me growing up.

"What is it about, Ma'am?"

"No, I'm not going to tell it now. Remember, what did I say?"

"You said tonight."

"That's right! This will be after dinner, okay? Perhaps it would serve as dessert."

"Sounds good Ma'am… Oh, I can't wait."

"C'mon, dash up; do you see how fast the clouds are gathering?"

And when you're done, go take your bath. It is drizzling now. It might start to pour in a few moments.

"I like it when it rains in the night. I sleep better," Captain Crow told his mother.

"Do you?"

"Yes, I do, ma'am."

"Why?"

"Because the room gets cool...But I don't like the accompanying thunderstorm, it makes me freak out. It reminds me of the death of our neighbor's daughter, Akosua Puni."

"Oh, Akosua," Captain Crow's mother interrupted. "She was such a sweet little girl. Very playful and kind. Akosua would have been twelve years old and perhaps being in the same grade as you had she lived."

"Anyway, how was your time with Nana? I guess you learned a lot today, you didn't want to come home."

"You guessed right, ma'am, Granduncle can talk, and he likes oxymoron. He said Paa Joe is the only honest thief in this town. And I asked him why he thinks so. He burst into hilarious laughter and remarked, 'Because he's a damn criminal. Paa Joe is dyslexic too. In other words, he's suffering from dyslexia—difficulty in learning, reading, and spelling.' This one isn't funny because it is disability."

"There was another one he told me... gosh, I've forgotten it; I will tell you when I remember. Ma'am, that was funnier."

"I guarantee it must be," Crow's mom interjected.

"Uncle Kwame Gyetuah has always been like that, and many in the town love him for his earthy sense of humor. My mom, your granny, used to tell me how smart he was as a little kid. His command over the Akan language and the infusion of linguistic terms in his statements always made him outstanding communicator decades back. Did he mention to you his days with the Freedom Party?

"He was a staunch member and became what was known at the time as DC [district commissioner], championed many meetings, protestations and had a few brushes with then colonial masters."

"Ma'am, what role did the DC play?"

"The DC reported directly to the colonial governor under the British rule at the time in a system called indirect rule. He was responsible for carrying out the policies of the imperialists at the grass roots level and ensured that they were well executed.

"As a political conduit, if you like, between the colonial master and his own people, the DC wielded enough influence and used the political capital effectively. The chiefs did not like the DCs because they were perceived as power usurpers.

"How did this system of Indirect Rule help or hurt our people, Ma'am?"

"First of all, I will have to say that power was decentralized, thus from the governor's office down to the District Commissioner. The DC had opinion leaders (most of them teachers) who supported him in the day-to-day activities. Hitherto, power resided only at the palaces. Again, that explains why the traditional rulers became so livid and disliked the DCs.

"The system also helped put up many infrastructure developments in the country, i.e. schools and colleges, hospitals and clinics, roads and bridges, pipe-borne water, electricity etc. In addition to this, manufacturing industries were built to help process some of the raw materials we produced locally, which in no small way enhanced job opportunities.

"Furthermore, most of our men and women were blessed with formal schooling, which was principally a British education. By this development, the seed of Britishness, so to speak, was planted on the soil of the Gold Coast. Our cousins or neighbors in Nigeria, Sierra Leone, and the Gambia had same policies implemented there.

"From coast to coast, the Union Jack Flag jogged from the Sub Sahara to Central Africa, through Eastern and Southern Africa, up to the Northern part of the continent. But keep in mind, son, that man makes policies and therefore this imperialist policy (Indirect Rule system) like many or all plans also has its downside. Particularly in the Gold Coast at the time, Indirect Rule created division and mistrust amongst the people, pitting brother against brother and parents against their own children.

Besides, respect for traditional rulers by their subjects declined to the lowest ebb, thereby deepening the enmity between the DCs and the chiefs.

"Maybe one of these days, he will tell you about his life. He may even tell you the policies of Assimilation and Association, which the French also introduced in the French-speaking countries in West Africa. Without a doubt, his pioneering role during the struggle for self rule in the pre-colonial era earned him a great deal of respect among the entire populace."

"Oh I see. I'm sort of wondering, ma'am…"

"Wondering about what?"

"Nana likes smoking tobacco. Could his long flirtation with the white man account for this craze or something else?"

"Interesting question, Kofi, but I dare say no because tobacco smoking in the Gold Coast, particularly among older Akan folks, predates the advent of the Europeans—the Portuguese in 1482 or the English in 1553—in the fifteenth century.

"Actually, these pipes were the clay bowls, frequently ornamented with precious stones unlike the modern ones you see around."

She searched his eyes as the little boy swung his feet in a lazy armchair, uncharacteristically quiet.

"Are you still wondering or you're now satisfied?"

"I'm deeply satisfied, ma'am. You know I like history," Captain Crow said with a smile.

❈

Right after dinner, mother and son exhausted, played an hour of *ludo*, a simple board game, while the monsoon winds accompanied by the torrential rains pounded the roof of their concrete-gated house.

The next day, they would learn the rainstorm had been unkind to folks in the outlying suburbs of Kumasi and lives and property had been lost.

Meanwhile, the entire villa had been enlivened as a cool breeze ambled into their cozy living room. The four walls of the setting were lined with photographs of her deceased husband, Barima Adom Yiadom. At the left top corner of the wall to the master-bedroom hanged a portrait of the heir and his uncle Nana Sir Agyeman Prempeh I who was captured and sent to the Seychelles Islands by the British during the 1900–1901 Anglo-Ashanti wars.

In like manner, the window panel to the right side of the sitting room had a collage of photographs of Nana Yaa Asantewaa, Osagyefo Kwame Nkrumah, Okyemnana JB Danquah, business magnate, Paa Grant, and Sir Gordon Guggisberg, former governor of the Gold Coast.

There were other visual rendering that added interior décor to their plush living room. They included figurines of Jesus's twelve apostles at the Last Supper, a china doll, and other collectibles.

As the night wore down, mother and son teasingly rolled the dice one after the other from the start to the finish and then drifted into another discipline—traditional pep talk, which had become an integral part of their daily chores.

But sooner than later, that segment would also give way to an emotional subject matter before they would even retire to bed later that night. It was an uncomfortable subject, the age old multibillion cedi question: Who killed the heir apparent?

Incredibly, if anyone thought that the demise of Barima was the end of his influential figure, they might as well be prepared to face what was to unfold in the aftermath.

Barima's ghost was coming back to haunt many across the kingdom. It didn't die a natural death. Instead, it resurrected more than a decade later with wide horns and wide eyes. And the questioner was no mean a person other than the deceased's own offspring. The irony is, not all coming events cast their own shadows. Moments ago, the widowed woman didn't anticipate such a bombshell from her young chap. She certainly had no clue!

But the young boy had located his mother's Achilles' heels. Captain Crow looked the mother in the eyes and threw the jab, and obviously such question would bring back agonizing memories, as well as worry to the person being questioned.

It opened old wounds and bled profusely like fresh cuts, but sometimes it brought spiritual alongside emotional healing.

The questioner Captain Crow also got his fair share of the hare's meat—surprise, sorrow, apprehension, and perhaps, the quest to payback.

"How did Dad die?" he asked his mother again.

Already, she seemed to have been carried away by dropping inadvertently that melancholic event during the pep talk segment. Back then, it was unthinkable to reveal to young kids about the death of their parent(s), particularly tragic deaths, because it was believed they would be haunted by the spirit of the dead. And most likely die as a result of such revelations. Notwithstanding, Akua Akyeampoma would break the jinx for the first time in more than a decade to tell it all to her loving son.

Her voice cracked up intermittently, still contemplating.

Must she tell the young boy the horrific story now or sometime in future?

Or would it be too late or too soon?

Salty, tasty tears streamed down her luscious face decorated by two bubbly dimples, while Captain Crow clutched her like a kangaroo mother and her joeys.

She firmly wrapped her arms around him, planted a kiss on the head. A sob followed and cupped it all with another kiss on the head. "It shall be well," she said amid sporadic sobs.

"I am hopeful we will get over this someday," Akua Akyeampoma gave the assurance to her big-eyed son.

It appeared she wasn't ready to divulge the grotesque murder but those soothing words couldn't soothe him. Captain Crow pressed harder.

"What happened to him, ma'am, I would like to know," he pestered her.

"Your father went to work in the morning of July 23, and never returned home that night," she said loosely.

"What do you mean he never returned? Did he elope like Ms. Havisham's supposed groom, Compeyson, in Charles Dickens's novel *Great Expectations?*"

"No, not at all. Your dad was a loving man, kind, and genteel. He wasn't a fraudster like that gold digger."

"He never returned, you said, and what happened? Did he come home the following day or days after?"

"No, that was the end of him," she replied. "You know, Kofi, as a timber contractor, your dad used to get many contracts from within, and sometimes, outside the kingdom. Barima was prospecting a new indenture at a village called Sowoboduam in the Bonoland. He revealed this to me during our last conversations a few days before his disappearance," she narrated.

"'Honey, you know I don't usually do this, I like springing up surprises,' he said to me. 'A bird is only yours when you have her in your hand, not when it is gallivanting in the bushes.' That deal, as I was well aware, hadn't been sealed yet. 'Supposedly, a Manhyia staff was fronting [liaison officer sort of] the said timber concession,' he told me.

"So I waited for him almost the whole evening thinking. Oh, he will be coming home soon. Literally, I kept looking through the windows every second amid expectation that he was going to show up in the next twenty minutes or thirty minutes"

"A Manhyia staff? Who is this Manhyia person, ma'am?"

"He is the king's chief butler, Tweneboa Kodua," she said.

"Was this man questioned?"

"Yes, he was interrogated by the police, but he claimed he knew nothing about the said business. Perhaps, his denial marked the end of the whole police investigations of your father's disappearance."

"Did Daddy call you that fateful day?"

"No, he didn't."

"What was your first instinct, ma'am?"

"I still had the strong feeling that he was going to come home. But I was daydreaming."

"Was he killed in a car crash, by a lone assassin, or assassins?"

"Perhaps, the latter," she replied.

"I became a bit apprehensive when it was about ten o'clock in the night, and he had still not returned home. He was usually at home by six in the evening. About half past nine, I called Mr. Asante Gyeabour, his close friend, to enquire if he had perchance stopped by his house. But I knew that was unlikely."

"No," he answered.

"At this point, my mind was racing like a horse. I'd called the office of Manhyia to enquire if by chance he was there for the supposed meeting. The response from the palace secretary was much the same as I got earlier.

"I didn't stop it there, I called the police.

"Two officers from Bantama Divisional Police Command came over shortly and asked me a few questions regarding his disappearance. And according to the command, they were dispatching immediately a patrol team in and outside the metropolis to search for him. They also promised to launch a full-scale investigation into the whole issue.

"The next day, I was called in at the police headquarters for questioning by officers at the CID. There, I wrote a statement and was tape recorded as well. This was followed by a thorough interrogation, and much to my disbelief, the police no longer viewed me as a witness but a 'suspect.' That statement didn't sit down well with me.

"How could I kill my own husband? But I had to resentfully reason with them. That's how they [investigators and police] are trained to do. Sometimes, they ask foolish questions, and sometimes, they can make you feel like a buffoon—a block and senseless *Homo sapiens*. They actually can be very mean sometimes.

"The irony is, this man was my soul mate, the flesh of my flesh, and bone of my bone. He loved me so dearly, and I loved him back, perhaps more than I loved myself. I still love him, and will always love him. So I consider that argument as baseless. I can't ever imagine conceiving the idea, let alone plotting this wicked action—killing my own beloved husband. Above all else, I probably have less than a month to deliver our first child, you, Kofi."

"'Madam,' said the police, 'I do understand your point, but in this age of our time, crimes have become increasingly sophisticated. Hitherto, we used to give spouses the benefit of the doubt. In other words treat such cases with kids' cloves, but not so today. Things have changed. Studies have shown that crimes such as these are likely to be committed by either of the spouse. In fact, almost all the cases we get here concerning spousal deaths, according to the studies one out of five turns out to be the culprit.'

"'Which explains why,' the officer continued, 'we treat everybody as suspect and meticulously take them through all this drill and grill. We know it is frustrating and unbearable, especially in times like this. Nonetheless, suspects are not guilty until the court of law proves so or otherwise.'"

"Did they buy your explanation?"

"No, son. Tried as I did to convince them and prove my innocence, the police wouldn't budge. Instead, I was put under intense pressure during this stressful period at least for the next three years or so. Ironically, they couldn't arrest the perpetrators, neither were they able to put a finger nor link anybody to the crime.

"However, I remember a day after the incident a witness called in at the Criminal Investigation Department (CID) office to report about a vintage Land Rover residents had sighted at a village near Abrepor junction, a detective told me. For a moment, we all thought that could be a good clue to unravel the mystery. Conversely, it turned out to be another chimera.

"According to detectives, the said vehicle had been burnt almost beyond recognition, ostensibly to destroy any alibi that might lead to the apprehension of the crooks. Though the description suggested it was your father's vehicle, the ultimate finding never got any better. And the case would remain unsolved, unfinished, and unpursued up to date.

"In the end, I was left with pain and misery. Incontrovertibly, I was left with many unanswered questions that seemed so absurd and so irrelevant to me. I knew he was dead. But how did he die, who killed him, where was he killed and why would someone kill a man of such caliber? How could the eternal death be so callous to me, leave me in a solitary state, wrap me in a mournful cloth, and feed me with sour grapes and scorpions?

"I remember when Friar Margaret Kojo Bonsu and some leaders of the church visited me a day afterward.

"'Weep no more woman, shed no tears,' the man of God told me."

"'God gives, and he takes away',", the priest added.

"'Really, '*Osofo*' (man of God), you mean I should shed no tears for my husband? Wait till the log falls on your roof,' I told him. How on Earth can I suppress these tears....these tears for my loved one?"

"Later that evening, the Asantehene sent a delegation here to express his heartfelt condolence to me and the entire family for the huge loss."

"Did the police question Manhyia?"

"Yes, they did. But as I noted earlier, they still were unable to place a finger on A or B or connect the dots. Nonetheless, let me underscore here that even when they did have eyes set on a few persons, nothing concrete came out of it.

Perhaps, that was too much a dose for the young boy, but like bitter pill, he cringed to swallow it. With chin still cupped in his hand, Captain Crow (exhibiting a patent strength) assured his mom that the killers of his dad would face justice someday.

"Mom, the wheels of justice, I'm told, grind slowly, nevertheless, I believe the assassins of my father would be captured and brought to book someday. The wicked shall surely fall, and the minnows will trample upon them."

Chapter 5

As it happened, the *Frontline* chronicled the whole mystery saga.

Investigations began a day after the incident. However, the public had not been enthused about the entire operation, arousing street protests and fueling the familiar blame game.

First on the chopping block was the police. Many had blamed them for slapdash investigative work.

James Addison deputy commander of CID at the police headquarters responded to the public outcry. The police capo had questioned the justification in the uproar and urged the public to exercise restraint.

"At times I wonder," Mr. Addison said, "whether police officers all over the world have friends at all."

"Do people hate or dislike us because of the nature of our profession. Or just because some citizens assume the police have become so corrupt, bias and forgotten its core duties?" the under pressure police officer wondered.

Throughout Kumasi and beyond, many thought the law enforcement agents weren't sophisticated enough in terms of logistics to handle such high crime. While others also believed that, the police had condoned and connived with the killers to cover up their trails.

And still, a good number of citizens across the kingdom held the view that perhaps there could be an insider's plot which evidently begged the question.

Chronologically, what appeared as a twenty-first-century movie with all its attendant mystery and confusion to the putative queen mother began on Friday, July 23. Her husband, Barima Yiadom, a corporate lawyer and timber contractor, left home that morning for work. He was supposed to visit the logging sites at Mampong, and thereon head down to Sowoboduam and Jacobu. Investigators couldn't say whether he went to any of these sites.

But where did he go that he couldn't make it home at his usual time—8:00 p.m. and even beyond. As the minute and the hour fingers of the old-fashioned mantel wall clock in their lavish living room *ticktocked* slowly past the expected time, the wife reeled in perpetual pain.

At 9:00 p.m., she (Madam Akyeampoma) called Mr. Asante Gyeabour (a family friend) to ask him if her husband was at his residence. She got a no answer from him. Mr. Gyeabour and his wife followed up the call a few minutes later. They visited the distressed woman to give her moral support.

The Gyeabour family waited for a little over half hour to see if Barima would return home but to no avail. Their fear was becoming a reality. They would urge Captain Crow's mother to have steadfast fortitude in the wake of the misfortune.

"We've got your back, sister. Your family has always been there for us and we will do likewise for you." Mr. Gyeabour gave the assurance.

From thereon, his surviving wife, Akua Akyeampoma called the police at 10:00 p.m.

Two burly plainclothes officers (one clutching a Motorola) were detailed to the victim's home at about 10:30 p.m. and did some interrogations.

The wife would visit the Criminal Investigation Department for further questioning on Saturday morning, July 24.

Earlier that Friday night at quarter past ten, she had called Barima's mother.

And the unusual scene would soon attract neighbors, family members, and loved ones in and around the vicinity.

As of midnight, there was still no sign of the heir. Fears and anxiety had become reality.

On Saturday, July 24, an eyewitness called the police to report of a burnt car (in a narrow ditch) he had sighted at the outskirts of a village near Abrepor junction. The tipster claimed he had seen the debris in the early hours of Saturday morning; a day after the incident was reported.

Police went to the supposed crime scene and cordoned the entire perimeters in the hope that they would be able to gather some evidential proof. The officers discovered the said scalded car. Though it had been burnt almost beyond recognition, the chassis number revealed a 1935-make Land Rover.

The owner was Barima Adom Yiadom, Vehicle and Licensing Authority (VLA) records showed.

"If true, where were his remains?" a detective asked.

None of the forensic tests conducted by the detectives and experts at the country's apex lab at the CID suggested that there was/were any occupants on the car, according to the police.

Day 3, Sunday, July 25. Manhyia sent a high-powered delegation comprising the Mankrado, Abusuapanin, and the Akyempimhene to console the victim's wife.

On the same day, as expected, the monarchy issued a well-crafted press release to debunk the allegations that it had a hand in the assassination. It went on to say the following:

> The palace is deeply saddened by the loss of *his* kinsman, Barima Adom Yiadom, whose sudden death occurred on July 23.

The royalty would like to state categorically that Manhyia had no hand in the assassination of one of its own kinsman.

We are profoundly saddened and shocked at the alleged slain of Barima the heir apparent and we hereby promise to cooperate with the police in their investigations; adding the throne condemns the act and promises to help and collaborate with the police as it begins its investigative work.

Otumfuo, the Asantehene therefore urges all and sundry in the metropolis to remain calm, and engage their day-to-day activities while the police carry on its operations.

Day 4, July 26. The decomposed body found in River Subin.

According to the police boss, his office and the CID department had been inundated with calls regarding the said floating body. Residents at Asafo and Adum had sighted the remains around morning in the Subin River at the railway station. Several thousands of people thronged the area to catch the scene. But it doubled down to be same old story as autopsy test on Monday, July 27 (day 5), revealed otherwise.

The said body, the police claimed, was that of a lunatic who used to hang out around the locality.

"We sent men there to retrieve the corpse in the hope that it was that of the heir, but it turned out again to be one of the many unsuccessful pursuits," the police said.

Almost a month later, the metropolitan police chief officially declared Barima dead but not without strong misgivings.

Three conspiracy theories were assigned to his death. The first suggested Barima might have been killed in a car accident on his way to the Manhyia Palace as he was supposed to attend an important meeting.

A further theory believed he perhaps didn't make it to Manhyia after all. Because Manhyia claimed it called off the scheduled meeting.

But at what time was the said meeting cancelled?

Did Barima know about the cancellation and didn't tell his wife? And was there an alibi or substantial evidence to exonerate the royalty whose integrity at the time had dominated the headlines?

And yet there was another pejorative conspiracy theory being bandied around.

Investigators believed Akua Akyeampoma might have hired thugs to kill her own husband. But, the multi-billion-cedi question remained: How can an almost eight-month-pregnant woman kill her husband and later called the police to inform them about the tragedy?

These questions would send tongues wagging for a long time, perhaps decades that followed, as the case was declared cold, and the mystery hanged over the necks of the good people of this ancient powerful state.

❧

In the wake of all this, the police chief called for public collaboration to help arrest the killers, but the search remained a wild goose chase. No one could tell the mystery that surrounded the assassination of the royal.

Paradoxically, the investigation that began with full vigor at the onset would end abruptly roughly in a month's time with no headway. Akin to many cases in the history of the kingdom, it had become a nine-day wonder. Must have been dead at the time and possibly forgotten by many, but time would silhouette its destiny later.

They say he that smoothes with his hammer strikes the anvil. And like the goldsmith, the widowed mother would hammer home the facts and possibly the truths of the whole case to her only son. She would psyche him up, as well as tell the young boy how great and awesome the father was, the things they used to do, and the huge thoughts he had for him while he was in the mother's womb.

This boy would remain her greatest companion, confidant, and a close friend even though she had a few friends in town.

"Your father and I never had any plans of parting company. No not this early. Our marriage was embedded on a solid rock until death struck our door. We understood each other and loved ourselves. There are certain things in our lives we cannot control, especially death. And in the case of your dad's, I can't tell whether it was premonition or tragic. It came unannounced and stole him away from me. I think of him almost every day as if he was alive because of the way we lived our lives together. The same way that I want you to treat the woman you would marry in future."

❈

"Once upon a time," she recounted, "I really don't know where this thought came from. The sun had barely gone to sleep. We were taking a stroll up the hills over by the Presbyterian Church. And I asked Barima if he still had his gauge on the coveted throne.

"He replied affirmatively. 'It's interesting you asked me this question today, honey.' He said. 'I've been pondering over it lately, for the reason I don't know. But I think the stakes are high and personally have no doubts about my prospects. They're all aware that I am the putative heir rising.'

"Still curious, I asked him how he was dealing with the whole rumor in town that his other brothers and cousins had their eyes set on the throne, explaining to him that things could get nastier in the run-up to the selection.

"'Well, honey, that's the beauty of our system of democracy. It's not so much like that of modern day democracy, which the ancient Greeks gave birth to centuries ago and was later popularized by the Americans.

In our system, as you know, the kingmakers would have all the interested candidates or cards on their selection table, but would in the end settle on the prominent and the most fitting one.

"'You may be right, but do not rule out any kind of machinations and underhand dealings. Don't treat this issue with kids' gloves. We aren't kids in this kingdom. History has good lesson for us and posterity. I am not against the idea of them showing interest. I like competition, but unbridled competition usually breeds animosity. It breeds civil and political upheaval. That is what I detest, hence my fret.

"'Can you believe, the other day, I overheard Kwame Awuah the older son of Atta Agyeman tell his friends that his father would by hook or crook means to be the successor after the ailing king Nana Poku Sei passes away?

"'I don't dispute the fact that men of his caliber would do everything necessary to win power. However, God makes kings. He made David a king, when he was viewed by many as the underdog or the least favorite. So I roll that burden unto him. I'm well aware there had been power struggle in the past. But I am not going to get into that quagmire—

God forbid!'

"He looked at me with heavenly smile and asked, 'Who has won the debate honey?'

"'We're both winners,' he replied immediately, not allowing me to speak. In effect, the healthy debate that evening ended amid the conviction that if he was destined to be the next successor, it will surely be.

"Unbelievably, that was another side of your father. His absolute faith in God and letting things take their natural course. He wore a beautiful silver hair—even at twenty-eight, he sported it all over. I loved it, but he didn't.

"There was one afternoon—another story, huh?" she quizzed with a lovely smile. "I remember very well. He had gotten himself a haircut, and I said to him admiringly, 'You're looking good. Did you get yourself a haircut?'

"'Um yep, I cut the grays.'

"'What do you mean?'

"'I've given all the black to age. There's no time for style anymore.'

"'C'mon, hubby, gray doesn't necessarily mean ugliness or ageing. Don't you see young folks today wearing grays?'

"'What does that mean to you?'

"'Well, I love you for who you are regardless, so stop being naughty and sarcastic.'

"'I also love you, Akua,' he told me.

"Later that evening, he shared with me an interesting story his grandfather told him when he was about thirteen years old.

"'Marry a woman whose candle never goes off by night,' he quoted that wise saying from the book of Proverbs.

"'Tell your mother too to read Proverbs 31:29.'

"And guess what I discovered there. 'Many daughters have done virtuously but thou excellest them all...'

"Barima had good sense of humor. He told me a story about a man who forgot the well-known manners bit at a dinner. He didn't leave even a morsel in the bowl when he visited his in-laws at the village. Alone in the guestroom, the man attempted to escape through a narrow window of the house but broke his nose in the process, thereby facing more embarrassment.

"Therefore, don't forget the manners bit whenever you go somewhere as a guest. Okay, son?

"And then he asked me, 'Why do you like your sweatpants hanging on you?'

"'Oh, you want to know?' I enquired. 'I just like it baggy on me because I can't trust men anymore. Lately, some guys are behaving like animals. They just get ticked off merely seeing the curves of women in their dresses. If you can't stand the heat, you better back off.'

"I've admired Grandpa Adam for the good example or the foundation he set during the creation in the garden of Eden. The old man asked God to give him a partner. He saw what the other animals were doing.

"So if you're a man and you can't zip up or keep your *langaga* in between your thighs, find a woman. In other words, marry and stop the numerous traffic infractions.

"Anyway, your father was a disciplinarian and a very responsible man. Though you didn't live to see him, I'll ensure that you fulfill his dreams and live an exemplary life. He used to tell me his thoughts about this great kingdom, with huge opportunities, yet many still live miserably in abject poverty due to injustice and discrimination.

"It had been his avowed dream to fight the good fight, straighten the crooked paths, and right the wrongs in our society. Sad though, he never lived to fulfill this dream.

"Possibly one day, you will live to realize your father's unaccomplished dream. It is the expectation of every parent to see his/her children live a good life, chart a good course, and make a remarkable dream.

At about 10:30pm, when Captain Crow's mother peeked outside their burglarproof windows, the rains were still pouring amid lighting and thunder. She had preempted her son that they go to bed.

But that idea would not sink into the ears of the young royal until his mother had told the story she promised him before dinner. He loved folklore stories, so he wouldn't let that opportunity slip him by.

"Well, Kofi, before I draw the curtain down, let me tell you something our family has been able to hold on to over the years: our strong faith in God and willingness to listen to the advice of the elders. This element has in no small way made us who we are today. I met my seventh generation grandparents when I was 12. They were all Christians and never stopped worshipping and serving God diligently. The people in this community respect us; not because of our wealth or standing in the society, but principally because of our devotion to the service to humankind and, more importantly, to God.

"It is like a race baton——passed on from the seventh to the sixth and the fifth to my generation and this is something I will seriously guard against, ensuring that you'll always stay close to your maker."

"Well, Ma'am, I won't disappoint you. I'll also surely pass it on to the next generation."

"That's right!"

"Also, being born a man means additional responsibility. Therefore, heed my advice, and lean on God for direction all the time. See you are now a boy, but time changes. There will come a time that I won't be providing your needs. I won't be fixing breakfast or lunch for you. You will pay your own bills, buy your own clothes, build your own home, and be your own man. At that stage, you'd need a woman in your life, and when you get married, you become a husband and, later, a father. These are realities that humanity all over the world has been dealing with since creation."

"Understandably, life is how one makes it, and ultimately, the end justifies the means. Along the life road, you'd hit the bumps and the rumps, but never give up for there is no price or reward for the wimp. I know Satan operates daily and his aim is to destroy God's children; there's no question about that. But I don't blame him for all my woes—like problems that I have power and control over.

"For instance, why should I have ten children when I know I don't have the means to educate them, pay for their medical bills, clothes, and other stuff? Therefore, son, remember to make the right choices and the right decisions all the time.

"The world is not the same as it was twenty or fifty years ago, when probably seventy-five pesewas could fill petrol tank in a car, a whole month rent was $10, and some parts even less. Successful life has its own secret; if you know the rules, you play by the rules. You don't just decide to produce many children because your neighbor has ten.

"It is a lost gamble. In that, the moment you sow that seed you create space for Satan to come in. Already, due to your inability to take care of your children and your wife, everything begins to turn upside down. The next flag you see is marked danger; your wife has fallen through the cracks; she is gone, because you have lost your rented apartment and your ten children are scattered like troubled sheep. Obviously, a broken home breeds drug and sexual addiction, alcoholism, and all the junks, you name it. It takes one's joy and happiness away and replaces it with depression and sorrow.

"I'm sure you might've read the accident that occurred on the Volta Lake last week. I understood the boat was supposed to take forty passengers. Yet the operator decided to pack up. What I learned was a wretched boat and it drowned all the seventy-five lives he had on the ferry. This to me is human negligence and not an act of Satan. It's purely an act of laxity and care free attitude of some folks. Just like the other motor accident. The driver, I'm told, was drunk and the passengers also urged him on to speed up so that they could get to Accra as early as possible. And they got there, right? Sadly, they never got to Accra; the foolish driver had sacrificed all those souls to Satan.

"In this society today, we blame Satan for our failing finances; when the bad guy is perhaps trying to run away from the arch Angles because they're waging war against him. So, Young man, learn to cut your coat according to your size. Don't engage in stuff that would ruin your finances."

"How can one stay away from these dangers, Ma'am, and/or not be tempted by Satan?"

"Kofi, the truth is Satan would even try to tempt the righteous. But staying on God's word, being prayerful, and making the right decisions could help. Be wary of the young ladies you take out;

don't smoke, and don't leash debts over your head. And I want you to get this: Remember Satan is not God. He is not Omnipotent, Omniscient, and Omnipresent. Therefore, he can't be blamed for everything that happens to humankind. We fault him for our failed marriages, we fault him for our promiscuous behaviors, we fault him for our binge drinking (alcoholism), and we even fault him for our hatred against others.

"Now consider this; if the boat operator wasn't selfish and greedy, perhaps that Volta disaster would not have occurred at all. The same applies to the drunk driver. Police officers arrest law breakers and not the law-abiding citizens. In the same vein, soldiers don't fight when there is no war."

"That's absolutely true, Ma'am," said Captain Crow.

"In a nutshell Satan strikes when we create openings in our lives. Until such avenues are created which eventually might become so deep seated; believe me you the bad guy has no power to drive you and me crazy.

"The reason is God is ever-present and He always has His arm of protection around you. At the same time He has given you choice. Your choice can make or break you: Remember he (Satan) asked permission from God before he could torture Job and deprived him of everything he owned...

"You may fall today but you will rise or get back on your feet tomorrow.

By the way, Job recovered all his lost treasure. The Great Man who helped him (Job) to recover all his lost asserts still does His wonderful work, and He will help you if you allow Him.

"I'm about wrapping up, but I cannot forget to hammer home this salient point. Learn to save and don't depend on credit cards. This is what my Grandpa told my father, 'Son,' he said, 'Save like the ants so that you'll always have plenty even when there is financial drought.'

"I'm hopeful you'll grow to take boldly the challenges of life rather than flee from it; for he who cuts the tree by the riverside without uprooting it comes back later to deal with the same problem. So remember to take the tree by the 'horns.'"

As the years rolled on, Captain Crow's mother relocated to Adum, a suburb of Kumasi, but still in strong ties with her brothers, uncles, and family members. She managed to raise, nurture, and groom the future civil rights icon. Barima, his slain father was a well-to-do man. He owned several companies across the kingdom, though over time, some of them would become distressed.

Still, the industrious widow would strive hard to make ends meet, uphold the well-known family values of the royalty to take care of themselves, as the extended maternal family also remained supportive concerning the upbringing of the future king.

Chapter 6

Nearly a decade later, at the age of fourteen, Captain Crow traveled alone to Mogyabiyedom, their native homeland for Easter holidays with his cousins and aunt.

Easter is not as huge as Christmas is, but still an occasion many Ghanaians take pleasure in. But among the Kwahus in eastern region of Ghana (another Akan tribe), Easter is viewed as the biggest reunion event for families and friends.

The festivity which usually attracts musicians, actors and actresses across the nation sparks anxiety among revelers. And already caught by the fervor Captain Crow on Wednesday April 15 began preparation. He had told some of his friends about the trip and his mother as usual had given him some briefings.

"Make sure you pack all the clothes, in one suitcase. And put your shoes, tennis shoes and slippers in the polythene bag, Captain Crow's Mom told him."

"Also don't forget the gifts you bought for your cousins. I know they (especially Ama) will love the original Ghanaian chocolates and the candies.

I've already put your auntie's cloth, shoes and the ear rings in the suitcase. Whiles there you know what to do, help your aunt with the chores and be nice to everyone in the village as you typically do."

"Ma'am I think they would need some soaps too. Don't you think so?"

"Good you reminded me Kofi, here check the drawer, I think I've a bar of key soap and three tablets of sunlight stashed in there."

"Did you find them?"

"Yes, I did."

"Alright, wrap it all nicely and place it at the bottom of the polythene bag."

Last but not least wish everyone a Happy Easter celebration for me and tell them I love everybody. Remember, everybody is somebody."

By mid-day Thursday all the roads leading to Kwahu Mountains, were saturated with cars, vehicles and motorbikes. The road to the Bonoland and beyond wasn't different: That of Takoradi to Nzemaland through to neighboring Ivory Coast was busy as well.

The Ejisu-Nkawkaw road to Ga Adamgme across Mount Djebubu in the Volta region were equally searing with vehicular traffic. And from Kumasi to the town where historically royals had been nurtured and groomed for centuries, Captain Crow would for the first time in almost ten years meet his kindred and the people who had long desired to see their future king

Mogyabiyedom, the ancient village is the traditional habitat for the Ekoana royals. It is also the birthplace of the maverick's maternal great-grandmother Obaahemaa Yaa Afriyie Ampem II and has the royal mausoleum—a historic site that has over the years attracted an overwhelming number of people across the kingdom and the neighboring countries.

Swarmed by the virgin forest in the Kontanase range and endowed with natural resources such as gold, diamond, and iron ore, Mogyabiyedom offers its visitors a good toast in all weather.

Captain Crow was visiting his aunt Akua Adutwumwaa, a teacher and mother of four. Two of the children were twins (a boy and a girl), about the same age as the future king. The other siblings (both males) were nine and seven years old, respectively.

Like several of the villages in the enclave the historic town on the eve of the festivities was bursting at the seams——with visitors including natives from the cities. From Accra, Kumasi, Takoradi, Tamale and even Abidjan they had all come to reunite with their loved ones.

But among its overwhelming crowd was none other than their adorable future king. The handsome teenager sporting his beautiful Ghanaian Woodin shirt, blue jeans and black leather shoes had returned to his native homeland. He was immediately escorted into the palace to meet with his relations and the elders.

Walls indeed have ears; the news had reached the four corners of Mogyabiyedom. And within minutes the whole town would besiege the palace. Young and old, women and children, rich and poor they all thronged the royal house to catch a glimpse of the would-be king.

In a brief message Captain Crow thanked his people and wished them a Happy Easter: "I'm deeply humbled and I'd like to thank everyone here present for coming. I wish you all a Happy Easter and God bless you!"

"He was quite bashful then," said his auntie. "But I think he additionally surprised the elders in that there was no such plan like that. I mean speaking to the crowd."

"The kingmakers were stunned by the multitude and therefore asked him to say a word or two to them as a sign of respect, which he did graciously. And everyone liked it and they were all happy."

"Very tall, handsome, and sturdy…He stood unafraid"

"All in all, I think he enjoyed the visit. It was a fascinating experience for him, and real return to his native land," she told one of the kingmakers at the palace.

Royals, customarily and historically, are required to pay visits to the native lands of their forbears, meet with folks in the village, as well as learn more about core tradition of the clan. As his granduncle Kwame Gyetuah did whenever he visited him at his residence in Kumasi, uncles and relatives in this small village would do likewise.

In the midst of these pleasantries and warm welcome, it dawned on the young royal that sooner than later, he could be crowned as the next king. Even though Captain Crow had been musing on this for years, the pressure had not been so telling and so daunting until he made the historic visit to his native land.

However, he knew he carried a stigma, an indelible mark that had remained an open secret in his mind: A mark, which had the potential to sink his futuristic dream. First of all, he knew the traditional nurse Maame Ama Korkor was aware of the shame he bore from birth which presupposed that it was no longer a secret.

He also knew that that shame could impede his prospects, if he really wanted to be king one day. But he had no authority over deformity. Neither did he have any idea nor hands-on answers as to how to deal with the obvious conundrum.

Obviously, growing up as an adult with six toes could be anybody's nemesis. But it would perhaps be more of a headache if you were a kid as well as royal and lived in a close-knit neighborhood.

Yet the young prince was facing another significant problem that had to do with lineage.

Though Captain Crow's father was an heir to the Ashanti Oyoko dynasty, tradition bars paternal offspring to ascend the throne.

In other words, by virtue of his maternal ancestry, as in the case of all Akan kingship or chieftaincy institution, a prince born to say an Oyoko or Agona father cannot inherit him. This however, contrasts the chieftaincy practice in northern Ghana, where enskinment is inherited through paternal line.

Traditionally, deformity or any acts of criminality apart from the criteria above-mentioned debars any royal to hold himself as a king. It doesn't matter how thoroughbred or full-blooded one might be.

So this was the situation Captain Crow found himself. He had to battle all fronts to save his dignity if he had any at the time. Simply put, he could count himself out, when the trumpet sounds.

Nonetheless, destiny would shape the life of Kofi Antobam who once thought doom hanged over his neck. Something unnatural happened. Something bizarre and frightening was about to happen at Mogyabiyedom.

There was a *Fofie*, a Friday observed by the natives as sacred. Fofie was and perhaps still is one of Akans most sacrosanct day.

It was taboo to go to farm or perform any sort of activity near the Goro River, which shares tributary with river Alomo. From the Kintampo range up to the middle belt of Ghana, Goro empties into the Tano River, the longest in the West African country.

The Goro River, which lies roughly two miles away in the Reserved Forest from the historic town, is gifted with beautiful flora and fauna.

It was a Black Friday (*Fofie*) also known as '*Dabone*' among the natives as already indicated. It was a forbidding day. Apart from the prospect of being fined when caught working, there was also the ominous danger that trespassers could incur the wrath of the river god and the earth goddess, '*Asaase Yaa*'. Myth has it that the river god would unleash a bad omen upon the norm breaker, which might result in lunacy, epilepsy, or even death.

Moreover, it is believed that this bad omen could be passed on to the next generation of the family. A generational curse they call it.

Unfortunately or fortunately, they (Captain Crow's relatives) forgot to brief him about the Fofie taboo.

And oblivious to the status quo, the young boy went to the bush alone.

It was an absolute dead silence that very day. The crickets were not chirping, likewise the birds. Eerily, all the sounds of the universe had gone to sleep.

With a well-sharpened machete amid whispers of songs, Captain Crow began the day's activity. And moments afterward, he narrated, "I had this funny feeling, as though I had contracted cold. It was a feverish feeling. Then there was a bizarre noise that sounded like a roaring lion. I couldn't figure out what exactly it was and therefore didn't pay much attention to it. That weird sound would soon be tailed by a weirder noise, a loud sneeze, and then a cough, which seemed much closer to me. My first instinct was to run away but with no destination in mind.

"I got frightened the more as my heart sank deep into my knee. The sparse hairs on my forearms stood up. They stood still. And from the depth of my sole up to my crown, I felt my whole frame had been clothed with goose pimples like mushrooms sprouted on a mound.

"I literally made a 360-degree turn, yet I couldn't find anyone.

"'What is going on?' I cried.

"It resonated with me then that disaster was indeed at hand. But again, I had no solution to the unfolding episode. To run or not to run.

"Suddenly, the bright, sunny day had melted away, and in its place was this strong whirlwind, which violently grabbed all the weeds around the place where I stood. My entire being had completely been consumed by fright at this time. And as though I were in the Arctic region skating on tiny ice surface, I developed a terrible cold feet. I could feel these icy long arms wrapped around my body. Paradoxically, there was no one to be seen.

"I had prayed the hardest prayer in my whole life ever, seeking God's immediate intervention. While my eyes remained tightly closed, afraid to see what was to come next.

"'Kofi,' a deep voice howled my name. Stubbornly, I blocked my ears refusing to hear the deafening noise. The unknown instructed, 'Kofi, take off your right boot and look behind you toward the riverside.'

"I unwillingly obeyed. Turned 180 degrees this time, and opened my eyes. Upstream, there emerged a huge creature like a yacht splashing the water at both faces of the riverbank moving toward my direction. Her sharp shining, hawkish eye emitted perpetual lights. And her tongue was as large as a barge!

"She stevedored half of her giant seemingly slimy, glossy body to the riverbank, amid glowing fire spewing from her gaping mouth. I couldn't figure out exactly what kind of mammal it was.

"The terrestrial voice demanded I shoved the six-toe foot into the yawning jaws of the wild beast. I hesitated awhile because I feared I could be swallowed up like biblical Jonah and probably not benefit the proverbial second chance. I would have loved to be spewed out at the coast of Nineveh—in my case at Mogyabeyedom."

"'Hey, Kofi, I say thrust your right foot into the mouth of the animal.'

"I trembled vigorously! Absolutely, no word could surpass trembling. I obliged to the command, though with utmost caution and much trepidation. I could feel the warmth in the beast's mouth, throbbing energetically. The three minutes or so episode seemed like a two-hour horror movie, completely sitting on tenterhooks.

"The voice spoke again, 'Take your foot off from the mammal's mouth and put on your boot. You're not supposed to work here today, go home immediately. Don't look back.'

"I realized momentarily that my sixth toe has gone. Is this a dream or reality? I wondered.

"I double-checked and noticed it was real. Without any further hesitance, I gathered all the strength left in my tank. For a moment, it was difficult to take a step forward as I dawdled around a bit. The motion was slow at first; I then began to run as fast as I could like the ancient Greek marathon runner Pheidippides.

"Miraculously, I made it home safely.

"Except for the fact that I was dog tired, within a couple of hours or so, chicken pox disease grew all over my body. The nightmares that followed hours later were so dreadful. I had wild dreams. Inexplicable dreams that appeared to revive the frightening day's episode accompanied by creepy images sleeting through the dreams.

"In the process, I saw thick darkness walk into my room stealthily and, moments later, fill the entire space. So terrifying and so consuming, he was as thick as bitumen. I could feel his huge presence, but my sharp eyes could no longer penetrate through his dense figure. Not a silver lining could be spotted even at the doors and windows. As if to help me speak, he touched my golden tulip lip with his thick finger; that made me feel like I was running a cross-country race around the city of Dearborn. After awful twists and turns for several times on my bunk bed, Mother Nature grudgingly loaned me a sleep.

"I woke up the next morning with one rigid resolution: I'm not going to disclose this encounter at the bush to anyone here, not even my aunt, I said to myself convincingly. To the surprise of my relatives in the village, I had decided to go back to Kumasi. Of course, my aunt wouldn't have allowed me to leave had it not been the eerie disease I contracted."

Auntie Akua was as tough as my Mom. I have no idea where they got that from. Maybe it's an Ekoana thing."

So, Captain Crow was returning to Kumasi a day after his strange encounter with the unknown. His departure that morning was preceded by a powerful prayer. Nana Kwaku Boafo a kingmaker and Tufuhene Osabarima Kofi Ntim had both prayed for their kinsman asking the good Lord to grant him His traveling mercies and safe journey home.

Suffice to say that, Captain Crow was feeling a little better a day after the out of the ordinary encounter. The chicken pox bug had disappeared. However, he'd missed his mother so soon just a week and a half. And he would take bag and baggage, cutting short his three-week vacation at Mgyabiyedom.

In the meantime, Auntie Adutwumwaa had telephoned her sister (Captain Crow's mother) in Kumasi to inform her that he was returning home.

"He is quite unwell," she reported.

"Is it the food, the water or mosquito bites?" Captain Crow's mom enquired.

"None of those Sister; he had this strange rashes all over his body yesterday. Thankfully, he is feeling better today... There is absolutely no cause for alarm. Honestly, I was a bit worried initially but we woke up this morning to see a miracle. All the rashes are gone.

"I'd wanted to accompany him, but I've a special class today with the senior citizens. It isn't serious though. I believe it is children's thing, feeling nostalgic. He'll be okay," she gave her the assurance.

Captain Crow's mom felt a little uneasy after hearing the news. But she believed her sister. Auntie Adutwumwaa always told the story as it happened. She disliked hyperbole—embellishing matters or exaggerating them just to cause panic and distress.

By two o'clock in the afternoon, he had arrived in Kumasi, and his mother was already at the Graceland lorry station to take him home.

"Aw, my sweet son," she gave him a warm hug and welcome.

The teenager looked straight into his mother's eyes while his unsullied handsome face beamed with infectious smiles. He had brought good news from the royal land.

"Are you feeling better now?"

"Yes, ma'am."

"Oh I see', your Auntie was right to paraphrase her; she said you would be very much excited as soon as you see me. So wait till we get home then you'll tell me as to what made you decide to cut short the trip."

But, Captain Crow couldn't wait for a second he whispered into his mother's ear as they were heading home.

"Ma'am my sixth toe is gone..."

"Gone for where?" His mother asked him.

The joy was too much to keep; Captain Crow couldn't wait for a second as he would reveal the whole phenomenal experience to his mom moments after they reached home.

He told his mother what he saw in the bush, the unbelievable miracle, and the aftermath nightmares he faced.

Momentarily, Akua Akyeampoma got frozen. She couldn't believe her ears, let alone wrap her mind around the wonderful story. However, her laughing eyes said it all, and stream tears of joy tumbled down her face.

Indeed, everything is possible at the Royal town; the once ashamed boy would soon become the most venerated in the whole kingdom. And his mother would remain the happiest person on earth.

"Alas the doom is gone, and the unexpected miracle had taken his place," the loving mother said joyfully. She shuttled back and forth in their living room. Sheer joy seemed to have swallowed her up. While she stood totally confused and bemused at the news.

"I never dreamt about this. I never imagined this miraculous thing. I thought my son was going to carry this shame forever. But Providence you are always at my beck and call!"

Relatives at native Mogyabiyedom were also amazed at the news. And that episode would change him forever. He was nothing but a genius and warrior who exuded enormous power, a global icon as the soothsayers said about him when he was born as a little child.

As his popularity soared even at that young age several tales about the future king also made rounds throughout the kingdom. For instance it was even rumored that Captain Crow once killed a crocodile with his bare hands, when the mammal attacked him while fishing with friends.

His huge frame, according to people across the kingdom, was just like the legendary Asebu Amenfi. Though not as gourmand as the legend (who myth said could eat or chew one hundred bags of corn nuts in less than three months), ostensibly because of his undying spirit and charisma.

The maverick demonstrated that in all human endeavors. He enjoyed what very few pupils did in their lifetime in education. Captain Crow did eight years of his elementary school education instead of the normal ten. The young chap had no encounter with stage four. He was jumped from stage three to five and then gained government scholarship in the West African Examination Council (WAEC) at the ninth grade/stage to proceed to one of the country's most prestigious colleges, Mfanstipim, his father's alma mater, where he joined the college's military cadet corps during his sophomore year.

As a versatile figure, he joined several of the college's groups and societies namely: the Rotary Club, the Debating Club, and Give Your Best (GYB), a voluntary organization.

Joe Moshosho, Captain Crow's classmate (himself a cadet) said this: "He was such a brilliant student. Besides, he was very instrumental and disciplined in the cadet corps. In fact you can put me on record; the entire student body liked him for his bravery, as well as his uncompromisingly selfless attitude when it comes to fighting for their rights. He always was there for the students and he fought for their rights. I don't have the words to say it all, but I think he left an ineffaceable mark at the college."

Another former student who also spoke highly of him was a guy nicknamed the 'stubborn cat.' "I remember at a Carol's Night at the Main Cape Coast Methodist Church, the school prefect was supposed to give a speech but, had not dressed up for the occasion. In better translation, he was improperly dressed and the assistant headmaster prevailed on the Captain at a short notice to hold the fort, and boy, he did it impeccably. That was our Captain Crow——that's the guy I'm talking about. There was something about him. Something none of us had at the time and even now."

Additionally, the maverick proved his prowess in the area of sports. He excelled in almost all sporting disciplines like football, table tennis/ping-pong, running, javelin, bowling, badminton, taekwondo, etc. Once touted by his peers as the best debater the college had ever produced since its inception. The clever guy always won the day, a discipline which also shaped his entire persona.

But he surprised thousands of spectators who had thronged the Cape Coast Sports Stadium on May 15 to witness the nation's inter colleges athletic competition. According to his close associates, he won the Boys' Marathon race with a staggering record breaking...

"By the blast of the whistle for the contest I remember," said Archipelago, Captain Crow kept a measured tempo and speed. In between time he appeared to be falling back a little. But perhaps that was his winning strategy."

"And I recollect very well, watching his mother from the VIP's stands cheering and chanting her son's name repeatedly-Kofi-oo, Kofi-oo, Kofi-oo. I think if I'm not mistaken every cheer or chant spawn new energy and pumped up his adrenalin. By the turn of the tenth round, I thought my good friend couldn't finish the race. And if he did at all his position would be eight," Archipelago narrated.

"Surprisingly, at the eleventh round he had pushed himself up to about fifth position.

I said to myself he might settle for that; he cannot push any further. But Mr. Doubter -Good Old Thomas, I would soon eat my humble pie. And then the big cheers from his mother, followed by the blast of the whistle, signifying the final lap of the titanic duel.

Long story short, spurred by the cheers from the mother coupled with his undying spirit the maverick won the race. Perhaps, it was such zeal that made him excel in almost all disciplines at the great college and anywhere he plied his profession and trade."

Two years later, Captain Crow became the Mfanstipim's twenty-fifth captain for the army cadet corps. Obviously, he demonstrated a marked quality and leadership skills to merit the position, often given to well-disciplined, brilliant, and versatile students.

Endurance was also part of his natural psyche. And he did that throughout his life.

Among those he mesmerized with his fortitude spirit was Mfanstipim's Principal, Mr. Archibald Turkson.

"How did you do this when you have a fractured ankle?" The college's principal asked Captain Crow after showing sterling quality and bravery at the Bondase jungle during one of their infantry regiments/drills.

"First of all," Captain Crow replied. "I think I show great interest in whatever goal I set myself up to do. This might sound crazy to many but my commitment to train every single day (sometimes I even find myself running and working in my sleep) coupled with that passion I think does the magic."

I remember when the incident happened in the course of the steeple chase at the base most of my friends thought I was going to give up. I was hurting but my mom usually tells me this: 'drink deep or don't taste it at all.'

"Well, let me tell you this," remarked Mr. Turkson, "that is positive attitude. And I'm really proud of you."

"Now, you've broken the College's over fifty-year splinter and marathon records. Your performance at the regional and national debating competitions is second to none; you topped the West African Examination Council's annual Common Entrance

Exams and today you've added yet another title belt to the hordes of medals you already possess.

So what's next?"

"Thank you Sir," he responded. "I'm pleased and equally humbled by these achievements and I thank all of you for your motivation and support. To your substantive question…I think the sky is the limit Sir…. Records are set to be broken and my main goal is to break the standard records set by my predecessors.

I'm optimistic that with good attitude and good mindset I think I'm all out for that."

"Keep it up son," Mr. Turkson encouraged him.

Indeed, the sterling quality and bravery he showed at the Bondase jungle during one of their infantry drills was no mean a feat. Even though he had fractured his ankle in that event at the training base, he kept his endurance.

Captain Crow's old college buddy Kwaku Badu who; participated in the Bondase jungle exercise also shared similar thought about the legend: "Everyone thought he would throw in the towel, but he kept pressing hard till he reached the finish line."

"Must have been the frequent visits his mother paid him, I guess. He really was born lucky. I haven't seen such motherly love in my life. His mom used to visit him almost every week at the college to see how he was faring.

And she brought him lot of provisions too, which he often gave them away anyway to some of us— the have-nots. See I didn't get that… My parents never visited me at the school."

"I think he was more or less like a husband and a brother to his mom. I always wished I had that same motherly care," Kwaku noted further.

Per his spirit of giving as earlier pointed out by his friend, Captain Crow had always desired to be part of the College's voluntary group, which he later joined.

The main reason, he told his colleagues in the group: "I want to get the opportunity to serve, interact, and share with others."

Moreover, I love to see the country side and the rural poor who in my view are often neglected during the distribution of the national cake."

Fortunately, by the turn of the school's summer vacation that opportunity offered itself. And the young intelligent chap if so purposed would have the chance he had long sought after.

As he walked out from the dining hall earlier that sunny evening Captain Crow met four of his pals. The looks on their faces suggested they had won the mega ball lottery, beaming with indescribable smiles.

"Have you heard the news Captain? Bagbin one of the vociferous students at the campus asked.

"What are you talking about?" Captain Crow enquired.

"I hear d the Canadian High Commission here (in Ghana) is or has sponsored our group," Bagbin gossiped.

"Where did you get this news from?"

Bagbin motioned to Crow to draw closer and he whispered the name into his ears.

"Do you believe that guy...? I'm excited though."

While they proceeded on the untarred pavement behind the college's administrative block towards the residence of the president they got their appetite whetted.

The GYB, the voluntary group courtesy of the Canadian High Commission had been given sponsorship to travel to Tamale. Mr. Stephen Arhin the president had confirmed the report—-calming all shaky nerves.

The summer program takes the volunteers (students) to the northern capital and some of its surrounding villages for a week. Luckily Captain Crow and three other volunteers had been selected to make it to the Savanna city. It had been a long wait for him as selection of the members was usually done by first come first serve basis.

"I'm thrilled to be part of this group," Captain Crow told the Mr. Arhin. "And I am optimistic that together we will be able to bring smiles on the faces of many and change a lot of things."

Chapter 7

The summer vacation trip couldn't have come at a better time; as luck would have it, Captain Crow and three other volunteer-students had been selected to go to Tamale. But he would first have to visit his great mentor. The eighty-nine-year-old man was just a week shy to turn ninety years old, and family members were putting up a grand birthday party for him.

Captain Crow would miss this one, though.

Every year, the young prince and his mother would send presents to Nana Kwame Gyetuah and wish him well. His birthdays normally drew kids in the neighborhood, and family members showed up in their numbers.

He (Captain Crow) had turned up incognito. None of the people in the serene residence of the old man knew he was back from school let alone visiting. He had brought his mentor some gifts: Bonwire *kente* cloth, traditional sandals (*ahenema*), a wristwatch, and a crate of Fanta, which he liked most. That was part of the maverick's trade, springing up surprises.

"It is good to just pop up at the doors of a close neighbor impromptu sometimes," he told his aunt in response to her question as to whether his Granduncle knew he was in town.

"Come on in," cried Auntie Nana Adwoa from the living room after hearing someone knocked on their polished Mahogany door.

"Oh, it's you! I haven't seen you for ages. You've been hiding from me, huh?"

Auntie Nana Adwoa the youngest daughter of Granduncle Kwame Gyetuah was a returnee from Abeokuta State in Nigeria, a banker by profession. She had gotten a new gig—-Deputy Manager Barclays Bank Adum Branch.

And her husband Baba Tunde had just won the gubernatorial race in the Bendel State of Nigeria.

"I heard you're at Mfanstipim College. How's school and studies?"

"Everything is going well," Captain Crow replied.

"That's good to hear."

"Here," she pointed toward the door to the balcony where the old man was rollicking in his chair.

"Do you care for some drink?" she asked.

"Yes, please," Captain Crow replied.

"What do you want?"

"Water please. Thank you." "Boy, you really have good manners. Cool!" She handed him a glass of water.

"How are you?" Nana Gyetuah asked.

"I am fine, Nana."

"Great! Good to see you back. I missed you a lot. How long have you been gone?

"Three months," he said.

"It seemed like a whole year to me. How's your mom too?"

"She's fine."

"You have a wonderful mother. Do you know that?"

"Yes, I do, Nana."

"Her lamp never goes off. She brought me some groceries last week."

"How are you also doing, Nana?"

"Marvelous! Fantastic! Except for the fact that I'm aging now, as you can see. Gray here, gray there, gray everywhere. Hahahaha." He laughed frenziedly. "It's always good to see you, Kofi. Any new things in terms of studies, and what you would like to do in future? Have you decided yet?"

"Something like that."

"Something like what?"

"Call spade a spade, not an implement for digging."

"What do you plan to do in future?"

"Maybe a lawyer...?"

"Have you told your mom about it?"

"Yes."

"Did you get her approval?"

He nodded his head approvingly.

"That's a brilliant idea. Like father like son. Go for it, Mr. Pro."

"Anyway, I have a subject I want us to look into today. Do you know that human beings are like cars/vehicles?"

"Sounds illogical to me, Nana, but you may have a point there."

"All right, let's take the issue to the laboratory and test its strength and soundness. Are you ready?"

"Yes, I am."

"First of all, I believe you don't deny the fact that we're born equal in the eyes of God."

"That's true. I don't dispute it."

"And I am one hundred percent sure you believe there are many inequalities in our physiological makeup. We're different in many perspectives. In other words, there exist among us many disparities.

"For example, our ability to handle stress/shocks, control anger and hunger, or deal with other human emotions differs. Some people wear their anger, envy, etc., on their sleeves. You know that!

"And though as humans, we all have these traits in us. It turns out some are able to control or even tame the lions in them, while others choose to display theirs—throw them the red meat and the upshot is tragedy. Do you agree with me on that claim?"

"Yes, I do."

"Secondly, our strengths, intelligence, thoughts, etc., are perhaps configured like that of vehicles. Agreed?"

"You are right on, Nana."

"Now consider this. Naturally, as humans, we're guided by our two headlights: some as pungent as the owl's binocular eyes. The other guys have two eyes that aid them to run/walk in the nights. In that sense, vehicles that ply nocturnally without their eyes on will get ticketed. Moreover, our Maker is so gracious and so unselfish that he has given us powerful engines. Yes, powerful engines! Vehicles have hearts. Both humans and cars depend on this crucial element for their survival. This implies that a dysfunction heart/engine has no life.

"Vehicles have veins which regularly supply food and water to the various components. Humans on the other hand have wires. And like conduits, they supply petrol, gas, oil, and water to the system to enhance smooth mobility and good health.

"Therefore a vehicle having funny feelings may have to see his doctor for immediate prognosis. In the same vein, a person may visit the auto shop if in doubt of his health status for retrofitting as soon as possible. Further than these commonalities, we have tires, and they have legs. We have trunks, and they have gyrating backs that come in different shapes, shades, and sizes. In a nutshell, always remember that the cheetah is faster than his peer, the tiger. And the tiny ant is smarter and wiser than man."

"Wow, Nana! I think the subject couldn't have been better tested at the 'lab' as you eloquently put it. I am impressed by the way you turned things inside out. It is really true that old soldier never dies. You're turning ninety next week, but you incredibly show no sign of aging in the mind. Your cognitive ability is as sharp as a knife. Sharper than guys of my age."

"Well, I give the credit to my Maker, nobody but him. Besides, I didn't waste my time on alcohol, drugs, and not too much on sex in my youthful days. Don't get me wrong, sex is good, but do it when you're ready to father the goods you'll manufacture in the future, and remember to take care of your wife. So that's food for thought."

"Nana, I must say it's been another wonderful time with you. As usual, you've filled my bowl with juicy stuff. But I hate to say I would like to take leave of you now. That notwithstanding, before I do so, may I please share a thought with you?"

"Go ahead, Kofi."

"The point you made concerning the way we individually handle stress or anger got me thinking as I sat through the entire conversation."

"Really? What was going through your mind?"

"Nana, just take for instance the cat and the dog. The dog will cry wolf and run pell-mell whenever she cites something unusual or scary, as though Satan had lowered a 125-kilogram silver helmet on her head. On the contrary, the cat will handle the same situation coolly, and on top of that, give it a wink. Just a blink does the trick. And I think this goes to buttress and reinforce your earlier argument that our stress levels aren't the same and that might be applicable to all disciplines in our lives as humans."

"Brilliant chap, you got it."

"Thank you so much, Nana, I'm leaving now. God willing, I will travel to Tamale tomorrow and won't return till next week."

"What's going on in Tamale, Kofi?"

"We are undertaking a voluntary exercise there."

"Oh, that sounds good."

"Pardon me, when are you leaving? I lost my mind moments ago, thinking about my lunch."

"It's tomorrow. We are leaving tomorrow."

"All right, have a safe journey, and may the good Lord grant you His travelling mercies."

"Thank you, Nana."

Before he knocked off the door, Captain Crow handed the old man a birthday card, which simply read: "Nana, I'll always love you!"

Chapter 8

On early Thursday morning, Captain Crow and his friends went to the Kejetia Lorry Park. The rowdy lorry station is perched at the heartland of Kumasi, roughly a quarter of a mile at the northwest end to the Komfo Anokye Teaching Hospital (KATH).

"Tamale, Tamale!" a driver's mate yowled repeatedly for passengers.

The Tamale-bound bus was half full. Supposedly, not too many passengers were out in that early morning, or perhaps going that direction. However, the Accra terminal had a sizeable crowd as travelers queued to get tickets. The quartet—Captain Crow, Kofi Koranteng, Omar Bagbin, and Yaa Mansa—got on board the twenty-five-seater bus, sharing good-natured remarks.

And within a few minutes, the mate had gotten far more commuters than the bus's required intake. Crammed together like sardines, the driver set the ball rolling.

By ten o'clock in the morning, they were on the highways cruising across the virgin woodlands of Ahafo Ano, the habitat for the mighty bimbo elephants, the hippos, the friendly Fiema monkeys, and the exotic jaguars who had now faced extinction.

Along the way, the driver made a couple of whistle stops at Sunyani, the Bono capital, and Techiman, a vibrant market hub to give the seemingly tired passengers a respite. Some attended to nature's call, while others had something to eat at Las Palmas, a local restaurant nearby.

The low-lying foliage of the middle belt up to the northern region intrigued Captain Crow. Besides, he realized while sampling the picturesque landscape from the passenger's side of the driver that they were nearing the savanna lands.

At school, they had learnt about the northeast trade winds, also known as the Hamattan. The months of January and February are often not good times to travel here, especially if one isn't used to the unfriendly weather because the dry winds from the Sahel region can unleash hazards, causing discomfort, nosebleeds, crack heels and lips, as well as dry skin.

Already, one of the volunteers, Kofi Koranteng, had vomited on the bus (the contraband goods had soiled the clothes of Omar Bagbin) after complaining of a mild stomach upset. Koranteng would be quarantined later that night, while Bagbin had his dirty linen bagged and binned. And deservedly, Yaa Mansa got massaged by the maverick.

On this stretch of road, it wasn't uncommon for the naked eyes to witness what one would describe as an ugly thing. Checkpoints or barriers manned by police officers added a bit of distress as they dotted around like post marks. Apparently, they're meant to check traffic infractions as well as miscreants. However, there was as an obscure business going on.

Captain Crow observed that whenever they reached a barrier, the driver (perhaps in his twenties) would sneak undisclosed cash into his license book and handed it over to the officers manning the post as though he was a Santa Claus or Father Christmas. And sitting next to him at the front, he couldn't help the sight.

"Why are you doing this, my brother?" he asked the driver politely.

"I have exceeded the passenger capacity, and because of that, I fear I might be arrested or delayed for hours if I fail to give them something," he replied.

"Kind of an obligation, right? Do you have an idea how much you've doled out so far?"

"Perhaps seventy cedis [about sixty dollars]," he said.

"Seventy cedis at seven police check points. That is good amount of cash. You know, we haven't reached Tamale yet, and it seems to me that there might be three or more barriers on the way. Evidently, as you claim you can't deny them your charitable token, it follows that you may give more.

"It is hard to believe that after a hard day's work week after week you would notice that you've absolutely worked for these men on the highways—not for the employer and not for yourself. Perhaps, in the meantime it would be fair to say that you are lucky because some of the passengers had already alighted on the way. Otherwise, you would have doled out more.

"But generally, I think most drivers don't get it. Better translation they have no idea the consequences this practice brings. This trend breeding on our roads and highways has to stop. It must start from you and me, as givers. If you stop giving, they will stop taking. Somebody has to be the rogue student and say for instance, 'Headmaster, yendzeooo yendze.' Meaning, 'We are not going to eat this food [porridge].'"

"My friend," said the driver. "You maybe right on that when it comes to dealing with master-student relationships. But this is a different ballgame. The man in the uniform, by virtue of his position, will do everything within his power to roll you into his dragnet. No matter what you do, they'd find fault on your vehicle and make you pay anyway."

But Captain Crow wouldn't take that.

"I hear this all the time, Mr. Bus Driver—on the Kumasi-Accra highway, the Accra-Cape Coast, and Cape Coast-Takoradi roads—but I disagree. Tell me, did you pay at the last barrier?"

"No."

"Why?"

"I wasn't carrying overload. Besides, several of the passengers had gotten down."

"So would you have continued the unselfish giving if they'd asked for?"

"No, I wasn't going to do that."

"That's right. That's the point," Captain Crow underscored. "Because now you know everything is correct, and you're good to go. Be as it may, I think we're all part of the problem on our roads, thus the rampant accidents and the slaughter of precious lives. That said, what portends to be more troubling and maybe fueling the whole phenomenon is the fact that the blue-black uniformed man, who is supposed to enforce and protect the laws, has joined the fray.

"Corruption no longer sits in the markets and offices. He has apparently found his way into the highways extorting monies from both innocent and culpable drivers. And the bottom line is we are progressively heading down the deep steep."

Even as young as he was at the time, Captain Crow always spoke his mind. He was an opinionated figure and knew when and how to touch the hot button without offending his audience.

Meanwhile, as they navigated through the woodlands and the savanna lands, the two chatted along as though they'd known each other for decades while the sights and sounds of the northern city revealed themselves.

First to welcome them were the sorghum, rice, yams, cowpeas, and maize/millet fields which to date fall away as far as the eyes can see, demonstrating the industrious spirit of the people in the northern region. In Tamale, the nostrils get served with the infectious locally brewed alcoholic drink *pito* (millet wine with 5 percent alcohol content) even before one enjoys the well-known northern congeniality.

The Baobab trees, anthills, and the straws tread along same lines prior to setting forth on Tamale's hot-red soil. It is hotter in Tamale than in Kumasi.

But the Garden City's boisterous rowdy atmosphere contrasts the northern capital's seemingly composed, idle streets. Indeed, Tamale, like most northern cities, is quite tranquil. Not as populous as down south, such as Kumasi, the magnet in the middle belt of Ghana.

Captain Crow was fascinated. The landmark buildings he witnessed here reminded him of the last visit he and his mother made to Paga nearly ten years ago. They were there to see the mysterious crocodiles. And he recalled his joy ride on one of the strange mammals in the Paga Lake.

The group was met on arrival by an official from the Ministry of Local Government at Tamale's main bus station, and from thereon, helped checked them into one of the government's bungalows. The facility was primarily for voluntary organizations or volunteers who visited the region as part of their voluntary activities.

The next day, Captain Crow and his contemporaries hit the ground running.

In Tamale, the group observed that most governments' projects had been abandoned due in part to political instability. Also, children of school-going age were at home, and worse of all, the girl-child had been denied with formal education.

"I think it is about time this tendency was looked into," Captain Crow told his colleagues. A multipronged approach, I suppose. Governments, communities, churches, individuals, including all stakeholders, have to act collectively in this direction to solve the problem. We need to do more to help the people in this part of the country."

The trip also took them to three nearby deprived villages, where they acquainted themselves with rural life. Strikingly, he met a widow at Kpunkurugu-Yooyoo who was brewing *pito*. The hands-on trade caught the interest of the young man, and in his quest to know more about it, he discovered that the woman had lost her husband through murder.

"What happened?" he asked.

"My husband had an altercation with a man who lived across us then."

"You mean the yellow house opposite us?" Captain Crow said, pointing toward the ramshackle home.

"Yes," she replied.

"It was just an argument over a guinea fowl," she said, "and he [the attacker] drew the knife, drove it deep into my husband's belly, and then to his chest, followed it up twice into the tummy again, four times, resulting his untimely death. As I speak to you today, the man still walks on these streets. I don't know how to describe him—a villain or victor? This man was remanded in jail for just two weeks, after which, we never heard anything about the case again," she narrated.

About a quarter of a mile from her house was the clan's cemetery, where she led Captain Crow. "Here," she pointed to a baobab tree that loomed over an unmarked grave of her deceased husband as they stood in the sizzling sun.

"There are other anecdotes like mine," remarked the widow. "I'm not alone in this saga. There are several people who have lost their relatives through shooting or stabbing, but they have had justice denied them. And it grieves my heart everyday to see these wicked men walk on our streets with impunity."

"Mama," Captain Crow called her. "I share your grief and the heartaches. Seventeen years ago my mother lost her husband, a month before she gave birth to me. I truly understand the pain you've been going through over the past years. I bet it's a crimson stain left in the minds and hearts of many folks, not only here but across the country."

Just two miles away, another woman had another harrowing story. Madam Fatima Mahama who lived in this tiny savanna village called Tong, lost her husband. They had been married for over a quarter of a century. Unexpectedly, the peace and quietness enjoyed by residents in this little town had been disturbed, a car-snatching syndicate goon had moved to the closed society, preying on innocent taxi drivers. And sooner than later, he would strike like thunder.

Prowling along the streets of Tong and its environs like a creeping animal, the criminal had already found his victim. His next victim, however, knew not what the future had in stored for him. But it won't be long!

Madam Fatima Mahama told him the story. "At about quarter past five on Sunday morning, my husband told me he was leaving for work. Even though the day was too young, the sun was already emphasizing its presence. Perhaps that sun was my husband smiling to me early to say goodbye. And indeed it was a real good-bye! He was supposed to come back an hour later to have his breakfast, like he usually does, which I was busily fixing. Food was ready. And I waited. And I waited again and again. Then a little later, I heard this bizarre news from a neighbor across.

"They say someone had been shot," the neighbor told me.

"They say someone had been shot," I quipped. "They say, they say. Always they say—the message never comes from them. I was hesitant to ask questions. But the informant claimed the supposed shootout occurred in an affluent neighborhood, Roman Ridge, less than a block behind GNTC building in front of Pawa House."

"But sooner than later, a young guy who told me he witnessed the attack would bring the saddest story home. And it would hit me like a bombshell. Like shrapnel, it would pierce deep into my heart, rock my bone, and thrust me strongly to the ground.

"The young man was a security guard. He had gotten off work that fateful morning. He too, saw the sun like I did earlier in the fresh morning.

"'As soon as I crossed over to the other side of the road,' he told me. 'I heard a shot from a taxicab occupied by two men. I was very close, so I got a clear view of the sordid incident,' he narrated.

"Unfortunately, that victim was my husband, Yakubu Mahama.

"When I raced to the scene to see the fatality for myself, there was Yakubu who lay in a puddle of blood, his attacker had bolted away with the taxi. The young security guard who had a bird's eye view of the whole episode said my husband, struggled with the killer for awhile before he was empowered. A passerby and coconut seller narrowly escaped a gunshot aimed at him as he attempted to impede the murderer from absconding. Passengers onboard a commercial urvan vehicle tailing the taxi said they saw the whole episode as it unfolded. But there was nothing they could do to avert the situation.

"Within minutes, the police arrived, hoisted the body unto an ambulance, and deposited it at the Police Hospital morgue, having armed themselves with pertinent information regarding the registration number, car make/brand, colors, and the possibility that it might have a dented fender on the driver's side.

A community radio station called Asempa FM also reported that the assailant could be heading for the eastern, western, or the southern corridors of the country, urging the police to be on the lookout.

Surprisingly, the suspect managed to get to Kumasi—over 300 kilometers from Tong—but luck eluded him as tippers informed the police in Kumasi that a bullet-riddled taxi had been sighted at Suame Magazine, a suburb of the Garden City for its mechanic proficiency.

The attacker was arrested alongside his accomplices, charged for a first-degree murder and convicted to spend the rest of his life at the Nsawam Medium Prisons. The victim's wife later told me the killer hired her deceased husband at about 5:00 a.m. on Sunday from his residence at Wale, a suburb of Tong, the second in two days.

Unfortunately, he met his untimely death. The murderer, Kofi Atinga, aged twenty-five was believed to be the person behind many taxi snatches in the country.

"Let me share with you, Mama, what my Granduncle always tells me— 'whatever goes around comes around.' Maybe someday, justice would come home and widows like you, like my mother, and like the other ones you mentioned to me would heave a big sigh of relief."

"Oh, what a consolatory message, my son," she remarked. "Thank you, and have a safe trip back home!"

❁

Onboard an STC (State Transport Corporation) bus Tuo Zaafi, (the delicious northern Ghana food), held sway in their entire conversation. They talked about how delicious and nutritious food in Tamale was. The foursome had unquestionably enjoyed their one week visit at the savanna region as they returned to Kumasi with some homemade foods and clothes like summer hats, smocks, sorghum, and millet.

"This had been a fruitful exercise," the young volunteers pointed out. "We will continue to discharge our duties as agents of change and do everything within our power to put smiles on faces of many people in the countryside."

Weeks after, when Captain Crow went back to school, he shared and tutored many of his classmates, as well as teachers, about the things he witnessed up north.

In fact, the Tamale trip would also spawn a new sort of awakening in the young man regarding civil right activism. He spent most of his time during summer vacations to educate and inform the critical rural, as well as urban masses the need to fight for their rights and freedoms.

Apart from his keen interest in activism, the young royal's appetite for academic laureates was incredibly outstanding. He had distinction in the final year Ordinary Level West Africa Examination Council (WAEC) exams.

This phenomenal achievement would be repeated at the advance level and helped him gain admission to the country's premier university, University of Ghana, Legon in Accra as a law student.

From thereon, everything seemed to be in place for the darling boy like some cheerleaders used to call him back then at the university. He had once told Granduncle Kwame Gyetuah his desire to pursue the postgraduate program overseas. And the old man gave him his blessings.

"Kofi, you can do whatever you dream about, and I encourage you to pursue your dream goals and grab the opportunities whenever they show up."

❧

Upon completion of his university education (with first class in LLB at Legon) in Ghana, Captain Crow gained scholarship to study law degree at Cambridge University in the United Kingdom. The daunting challenges he faced initially made his friends to think that he would give up the program.

"I don't fight to quit, I fight to win," he told one of his colleague students who had to drop the course because of many challenges. And while studying at Cambridge, he had his eyes set on one thing—become an accomplished lawyer in the future. That dream goal was realized following the footsteps of his deceased father who was a corporate lawyer. But, he would later veer into journalism and other professions of interest.

During his second year at Cambridge, Captain Crow apprenticed at Cromwell & Cromwell Associates, a prestigious law firm in London where he was subsequently employed as a practitioner for two years.

His superb work ethics and ability to work under stress charmed not only colleagues at the influential legal firm but also its numerous clients.

Intrigued long by detective work, he joined the UK secret service MI6 for two years and secretly worked for the United

States' intelligence agency, the CIA as an undercover agent for a couple of years as well.

However, Crow's avowed desire to return to his motherland Ghana lingered on.

Not even the trappings of good office and the luxuries of the beautiful city could make him rescind his decision.

"I love London. I love this famous city and her good people, but I have a duty at my home country. They need me much as I need them, and I can't help to wind myself down here for another year. It is a hard decision, nonetheless I have to go," Captain Crow told his colleagues.

Indeed, he loved London but memories of yester years, especially school days and old friends at the hood made him homesick all the time. Most importantly, he had left a loving mother home, his father's businesses were crumbling, and his mystery death remained unsolved.

Chapter 9

On Saturday, December 12, before twilight, Captain Crow received a telephone call. There was an abrupt silent. He wondered who the caller might be and what was amiss.

Could it be one of the solicitors or clients or his newly-fangled brunette friend?

It was an international call, and it had come from Ghana. But why the silent he wondered further. Suddenly the person at the other side of the telephone cleared her throat, as though she had been choked by tears.

That was Madam Akua Akyeampoma (Captain Crow's mother). She was carrying harrowing news. She had bad news for her son, Kofi: The news of a loved one who had given up the ghost.

"Hello Ma'am, what's happening?" You don't sound good tonight…Is there a problem?

"Yes, of course son, there's a problem."

"What is it then?"

There was a pause from the opposite end again. A dead silent!

Captain Crow knew his mother well she was always discreet, when it came down to breaking news to him or someone: "Always be circumspect when you're dealing with people at home, your job, school or anywhere," she told him.

Apparently, the man he had long seen as a father, mentor, a friend, and a brother had transitioned. Opanin Kwame Gyetuah had died at a beautiful age of ninety-five. But it was still a deadly blow to his grandnephew, Captain Crow's mother revealed.

His sudden death according to Captain Crow's mom occurred at the Komfo Anokye Teaching Hospital at about 6pm on the Saturday. The nonagenarian had visited the hospital on the Friday morning to see his doctor. He returned home hours later feeling better and stronger.

But then on that drizzling Saturday December morning he complained of a minor chest pains so he decided to go back to the doctor's office. Immediately his doctor advised he stayed at the emergency room for a little over three hours to have a closer look at him.

About three hours later after examining him, the doctor decided the old man passed the night at the hospital since his condition wasn't good.

"Even though your condition is not life-threatening, at the same time it isn't the best that I let you go home this evening," the doctor said.

"But I'm hopeful barring any unforeseen mishaps I can get you out of here by early tomorrow."

Meanwhile, family members as well as loved ones had gathered around the Ex-District Chief's bed praying for his speedy recovery. And he said his rosary as they continued to pray for him.

In the course of time, his temperature had begun fluctuating, and the nurses kept jockeying up and down to steady things. He slept for about half hour and thereafter started to initiate conversation. Laying on the right side of the bed he rolled his big eyes as though he was taking a roll call.

"I knew you were here," he said to his most beloved niece—— Akua Akyeampoma (Crow's mom).

"Have you spoken with my friend (grandnephew Kofi) today, and how is he doing?"

"No not yet," she replied. "But I will call later, maybe tomorrow and let him know you are at the hospital and steadily recuperating."

"Well said, Akua. But anyway tell him to pray for me. Tell him I miss him. And tell him to come home when he is done with his education; because he is needed here more than there," he noted with smiles.

A little while later he adjusted himself turned to his left side then to the right side again and gave a hearty smile to all the relations present.

"Keep praying for me," he asked them.

In between time the nurses showed up again and again to administer service on to him and as the hours rolled on it appeared he was amazingly responding to treatment.

"Akua," he called Captain Crow's mother again. He gazed up the ceiling intently and then remarked:

"Tell Kofi to always remember that the cheetah is faster than his peer tiger. He must show resilience in whatever he does or pursues in life and serve God diligently," his mother would later convey the message to him.

But, shortly after speaking to his niece, at about 8:00pm Nana Gyetuah made a lateral turn to his left side; facing the wall, he gave a deep sigh as if to say goodbye. Indeed it was a Goodbye!

Sadly, another star had fallen from the heavens like an asteroid nearly thirty years ago that Asanteman lost one of her renowned sons. In less than no time, perhaps under three minutes three nurses plus his doctor stormed at Room 97 (where the Ekoana Royal had been admitted) and declared him dead His white-draped body was immediately wheeled across the long hallway to the hospital's morgue, leaving his relations and loved ones perplexed and dejected.

Hours later at about 10:00pm London time (GMT), the gloomy news would slog its way across the airwaves. Captain

Crow's mother had conveyed the sad news to him. The shock, the sadness, the anxiety, and the pain; the news brought that Saturday night was unbearable to the astute lawyer.

It was a deadly blow to him as he spent the rest of the months in London alone, consoling himself for the loss of his beloved Granduncle. Whiles in London he coordinated with the funeral planning committee, ensuring that the family back home accorded his mentor a befitting burial and a welcoming final funeral rite.

Even though he tried to convince the committee to schedule the final interment to coincide his return home the elders wouldn't agree. So, Captain Crow would miss the funeral of his Granduncle. Nonetheless, the fond memories of the deceased and the great things he had done for him (Captain Crow) over the years would forever be unforgettable.

�֍

If the maverick's homecoming was a done deal, the death of his granduncle made it direr. Soon the nostalgic feelings would be gone and his beloved mom will have him by her side.

A year before he returned to his motherland, Captain Crow remembered: "Anytime my mom called me; the first question that mostly came out from her mouth was…

"When are you coming home Kofi, are you coming this Christmas or the Easter or the next one?"

"When, don't you know?"

I'll surely be home soon mom, I would tell her.

"How sure are you son?"

"Don't you know yet, which month or day are you coming?"

"What's holding you up?"

".….And more and more," Captain Crow noted.

All came down to nothing but sheer love. A mother's unbridled love for her only child. And incredibly, Akua Akyeampoma wouldn't stop her importunate calls to that child of her who had successfully accomplished his dream of becoming a lawyer.

In a chat with an old friend, Captain Crow revealed that his mom's persistence call at times made him feel like he was uncaring or wasn't willing to return home...

"But far from that," he recalled. "I could feel my mom's sense of desperation and I could tell how deep he cared for me." He told George Owusu.

"Did her calls bother you in any way?" George asked.

"No, I never felt bothered."

"Admittedly, I think I misjudged her some times, because whenever I assumed she was done with her barrage questions; mom would leave me with something like this:

"Don't forget Kofi that you were born and bred here. Remember you're my only child."

"And those punch lines often got me thinking. *Mom I promise you, I will be home..*,

But I knew she didn't like my responses."

Eventually, that time showed up. For the first time in about three years, the British-trained lawyer gave a timeline.

"Mom, I will be home by the next six months," he assured her.

It was a great delight for his mother who hadn't seen her only child for more than five years.

Despite their frequent communications, Captain Crow's mother wanted the young man returned home to find someone to marry. "Time is running out, son," she told him. "Most of your peers—Yaw Asante, Kwabena Ebo, and Kofi Boakye—have all given their mothers grandkids, and I can't wait to see mine too."

"Don't worry, ma'am," Captain Crow replied. "It won't be long. God willing, you'll see me. I love you, and I miss you every passing day, can't wait to come home and grant you your request," he said with laughter.

Perhaps, travelers only know the mess and the curse they've encountered in the course of their labyrinth journey. Tell friends, and even loved ones sometimes, about the realities on the ground, and they think you're just making up one of the famous fables.

Captain Crow, like many foreign students who studied abroad, had to swallow the proverbial bitter pill. He had dated a Londoner for eight months, and they married later.

Sussex Boaz—a blue-eyed brunette, attractive, and somehow a sophisticated lass from a middle-class family—had finished from the London School of Commerce same year as the maverick.

In contrast, Ms. Boaz majored in journalism and joined Heartbeat, a local FM station in London.

"By the way, that was a marriage of convenience," Captain Crow disclosed to his friends, Sarkodie and Afrifa.

"How did you make it work? I'm told it's kind of complex stuff," Sarkodie enquired.

"Well, you're quite right on that, but we followed the due process. I mean, nothing was shady on its face value, except the fact that we'd both agreed on that common principle."

"Though I didn't intend to stay longer in overseas, at the same time, I felt like doing it in case the unforeseen occurs. We had a joint account at Barclays Bank, and little did I know that she'd secretly emptied the entire account. Worse of it all, there were overdrafts. I felt being stupid, not only betrayed by someone I trusted," Captain Crow explained.

"Did you ask Sussex? And what was her reaction?" Afrifa asked him.

"She flared up," Captain Crow said, "when I confronted her one evening at dinner because I'd asked her to show me the overdraft documents."

"And was she able to provide you the documents?'

"Nope, that was the end. She eloped the next day. Evidently, she left no footprints that could help me trace her whereabouts. She was gone, Sussex was gone! Dead or alive I have no clue.

"Who knows," Crow jokingly said to his friends, "I might have stayed in London longer had that marriage worked out. Everything works for good. But all said and done it was that incident that broke the camel's back."

Chapter 10

After months of homesickness and sleepless nights, the barriers that held up passage to Ghana were cleared. It paved way for Captain Crow's much-anticipated homeward bound.

But as a typical Akan man, rooted in tradition, he knew going home meant he had to buy clothes, shoes, necklaces, drinks, and anything under the sun for friends and family members. Cash is most preferred. Expectation back home is normally huge. Everybody needs something from you. Cash or no cash, you are supposed to squeeze water from the rocks.

Back then and even today the term *burger* used for overseas travelers evokes prestige. One would be labeled a nonentity if he returned home without fleet of cars, build mansions, or satisfy everybody who matters, and that includes the entire extended family. Even those he had never met would show up upon his arrival.

They used to say "may your road be rough" when one was embarking a trip abroad. That philosophical statement like the former carried so much weight, and served as a watchword for many travelers. Unlike Asians, particularly Chinese, many African travelers are often reluctant to go back home after study. Basically, the aforementioned unnecessary pressure plays a major role.

They'd be likely to regularize their stay as a means to better their fortunes rather than return home to be tagged as a "lazy brute" or a "nonentity."

To most, or some people, returning home after school is regarded as suicidal because the great continent has suffered and continues to put up with many brutal assaults, natural and man-made.

Yet Captain Crow had given up all the largesse he enjoyed in the UK. Though he lived in cosmopolitan London, the Cambridge graduate didn't allow London to consume his thoughts.

The young African scholar and the astute corporate lawyer, who had the magic wand in his hand and the touch of business magnate Asuma Banda, was returning home.

Indeed, the royal was heading home.

Ghana was welcoming home one of her numerous illustrious citizens who left her shores several years ago to study abroad. The post-independence fever had caught up with many of her children in the diaspora. And the influx had been astronomical.

The time had come for them to go back to help build their homeland. She would open her well-known hospitable gate for the prodigious son. The ideal woman had from time immemorial opened her warm doors to many, including strangers. She is the gateway for *Abibiman* (Africa).

But above all, Ghana had found black gold. Prospects were high and expatriates had turned their eagle eyes back to the region once described as the Dark Continent.

In the middle of the early morning snowy storm, Captain Crow sporting a blue-black jacket with spotless Italian leather moccasin, headed to Heathrow, UK's biggest airport. Heathrow still bustles. It's so real, nothing unusual about her boisterous around- the-clock business activity. The peopling of breeds of all demographic shades makes one wonder how she gets such traction all year round.

Unquestionably, the human traffic at the airport that wintery Thursday was so striking!

Amidst the insane scene, the sky was also saturated with thick flakes. Everything looked whitish. Flights were either delayed or cancelled because of poor visibility.

On the tarmac were many airplanes that hobbled around. Some revved their engines, while others taxied, readying to be given the green light to fly across the Far East, Asia Pacific, and North America, or to the Caribbean Islands.

In front of Gate 15, to the North End of cosmopolitan London, stood two airplanes, British Airways and one of Ghana's flying birds DC10. Captain Crow was heading home with his preferred flight, DC10. He understood domestication.

Earlier, he had checked out his flight schedule from a monitor fixed close to the ceiling of the building. His course mate, Akwasi Afrifa Amankwaa, was also going home.

The two talked about life in the yester years back home in Ghana.

"I wake up everyday with fond memories of my father. It is sad the way I sometimes talk about him as though I knew or ever met him. Going home today to meet Mom and friends is absolutely uplifting. But it would have been more joyous to meet both Mom and Dad, having been away from them for the past six years," Captain Crow told Afrifa.

The announcer bell had rung twice. It was boarding time for passengers travelling to Accra Ghana via Lagos Nigeria. What is joy?

The airplane was fully packed, and the atmosphere at the economy class was just breathtaking. Lost friends and old buddies had suddenly met for the first time in several years; for some it was decades.

While some passengers slipped into sleep, possibly due to jet lag, Captain Crow and his pal, Akwasi Afrifa, continued to muse over the past and talked about what was at stake in the future.

And in midair, they could glimpse and feel a few thousand miles away the hot sweaty tropical weather of the sub-Saharan country. Sooner than expected, the seemingly ice in their bodies and jackets would be melted away.

Meanwhile, DC10 had briefly transited in Nigeria to offload her Lagosian passengers at about 3:30 p.m. And less than an hour time, the flying bird made the second and the final touchdown in Accra.

When Captain Crow stepped out of the airplane, he immediately kissed the ground and made the sign of the cross. "Once a Catholic, always a Catholic," he told his buddy Afrifa.

The huge billboard at the Kotoka International Airport with the inscription "AKWAABA," the effigies of the forebears overlooking the airport city and the traditional Ghanaian clothes (nothing non-Ghanaian) displayed at the arrival hall quickly brought back fond memories.

"This is the land of our birth," Captain Crow told Afrifa. "The land our forebears gallantly fought and defended against the enemies. They toiled and shared their priceless blood in the course of fighting for self-rule and freedom. We must also do our best to help put her at the top rung of the ladder."

And truly, the astute lawyer turned detective never reneged on that avowed promise. The maverick lived it. Later in the evening, at around 9:00 p.m., he arrived in Kumasi to a celebratory welcome from his mother, aunties, cousins, uncles, and friends. From Mogyabiyedom, Hweehwee to Mampong, and Obuasi, they had all come to see the future king.

"I am exhausted, ma'am. You won't believe we've spent almost five hours on this Accra-Kumasi road, a distance which could have been covered in three-and-half hours or at most four hours. Why so?" Captain Crow wondered.

"Was the driver an amateur?" One of his aunties asked.

"No, Auntie, it wasn't the driver, but the poor state of the road.

"Did you think you were in London? You're back in Ghana. Nothing much has changed. The value is the same," they laughed at him.

Old friends, they say are the best. He had already reactivated his social networks, connecting with guys and gals in the neighborhood. But he had a big plan to accomplish.

His immediate goal was to find a wife and give his mother a grandchild. Procreation is very important in the Akan social setting and Ghana as a whole. It is regarded as one of man's natural legacies bequeathed to him by God with emphasis on His command in the Old Testament to "fill the earth."

The next mission was to find the assassins of his slain father, Barima Adom Yiadom—whose bizarre death still remained a jigsaw puzzle among citizens of Asanteman—and haul them before the law courts of the land.

To this end, Captain Crow set up his own secrete agency, Big Eye, headquartered in the plush Pyramid buildings in the heartland of Kumasi. The high rising edifice also housed a newspaper company, a radio station, a law firm and other business entities, all owned by the successful young man.

Within a period of five years, Captain Crow had also revamped his father's beleaguered timber firm, road construction company, the estate developing enterprise, the salt industry at Komenda, the meat factory at Pwalugu, and the local shoe manufacturing factory at Ahinsan in Kumasi.

Of course who else could tell the story better than the Captain himself——having broken the backbone of the well-known red-tape at the country's Registrar General's Department. The maverick told the director of National Communication Authority (NCA) to go to hell when he was asked to go and see the minister of so and so. ...

He met the obstacles and hit the snags but Crow never gave up his avowed objective of setting up his own business and revamping his dad's. The young man didn't have it rosy.

"The frustration and the disappointment I had to face on week-by-week basis, trekking the corridors of these ministries, to say the least, were worrisome. Imagine being asked to go and see the minister of sea, minister of forest, minister of water, or the minister of moon, when you know in your right mind that these guys are fooling you," The London returnee told Afrifa.

"You're funny, Captain," Afrifa said. "But I believe you. I know them. They're like weasels always displaying opportunistic streaks against prospective investors. Obviously it is an understatement to call it frustrating, but I think the earlier it is nipped in the bud, the better."

"Yep, you hit the nail right on the head, buddy," he noted.

"As I was saying, getting these crippling industries back on track was as hard as anybody's guess," Captain Crow disclosed.

"For example squatters had taken over the shoe factory at Ahinsan. And it took a combined team of police and military personnel to get them out of the place."

"I was wondering," Afrifa said. "How did you get it all done in such urgency?"

"The banks, my brother…the banks helped me." Crow replied. "Relatives and good friends also came to my aid. I must add that manpower support from the community was huge."

Besides, I had good collaterals and on top of that I persevered."

"Bravo bro! Very few people can do this."

"Thank you!" he said.

"But as I said earlier," Captain Crow underscored. "It wasn't easy revamping them. I had to pump in lots of money particularly into those three distressed companies—the salt, meat and the shoe. I'm excited to see them back on their feet today."

Can't thank my mom and dad enough for what they've done for me. I'm so indebted to them. My mom kept everything in place for me—-the will and any documents that mattered. That to me also made the task less cumbersome."

"Well kudos once again my friend for a job well done." Afrifa patted him on the back.

Paradoxically, despite his tight business schedule, roughly six months on his return, the brilliant lawyer-cum-investigator met a charming lady, Ama Samanhyia, a fashion designer; and the two lovebirds would have a memorable marriage in the years to come.

✂

Valentine's Day February 14, would also shape the future and the lifestyle of the royal.

Captain Crow and his cronies, Sundiata Gbewaa, Marijata Beyeeman, and Ghanatta Kwabena Sokoto went to Adehye Spot located at the west end of Manhyia Palace. The love fever had held captive the city's over one million young and adult populations as they busily browsed shopping malls to get their love ones gift cards, flowers, candies, Ghana chocolates, and other presents. The four musketeers had had to endure hours in a bleeding vehicular traffic around the Kejetia vicinity, an area noted for its business vibrancy and atypical hustles. Amazingly, St Valentine's Day, which perhaps decades ago wasn't known among many, has become part and parcel of Ghanaian culture today.

"I think today is unusual," said Ghanatta. "I've lived here all my life, but I haven't seen this streaming crowd. Well, I think the night promises to be a good one and we would swing in it," he noted.

"There he goes. I believe you," Marijata chipped in.

And to ensure they avoided the usual stampede that often greets the city's liveliest taverns, the quartet zoomed straight to the hottest base in town. They'd earlier sampled some of the metropolis' bars. Finally, they decided to pitch tent at the pub nicknamed the Royal Base, Adehye where the four converged at a round table and helped themselves with six sweaty, big bottles of Gulder beer, Guinness, and Alomo bitters.

"Guys, I am yet to see," said Captain Crow. "If indeed the saying a breast in hand is worth more than two in a bra."

"Hey, wait a minute. What did you just say?" Sundiatta asked.

The maverick had good sense of humor; he'd tickled the guys bursting into hilarious laughter as they killed the night off with their chilled beers and hot, tasty kebab.

"Actually, I can't wait to find myself someone who would bring back my lost joy and happiness after my first unsuccessful marriage."

Tipsy Crow still lecturing: "I have huge backing from my mom, and I know she would be glad to see me get married soon to a good woman. You know, it's good to get married. However, if luck eludes you and you get *alomo gyata*, I mean lion! Then, you're more than a dead man."

"Hey, you cracked me up again," remarked Sundiatta.

"First, you said a breast in hand is worth more than two in a bra and now, this *alomo gyata*."

"Do you want to smith your own idioms?" Sundiatta butted in.

"Why not? Variety is good that's why we've different brand of goods clothes, etc.," Captain Crow responded.

"Well, that isn't a bad idea, I think the more vocabs we have the better, and the richer our language becomes," Sundiata filled in again.

"Remember Kojo Antwi's album *Densu* and *Dadee Anoma*?" Captain Crow asked.

"Yes," said Marijata, who appeared to be quiet the whole night, something uncharacteristic of him. And like his buddy, Ghanatta, another vociferous guy hadn't spoken yet. It is good to listen sometimes.

"I love Kojo Antwi's songs—so metaphorical and so rhythmic. One white friend of mine calls him Kojo Ant-we. These days, you hardly get served with such hodgepodge songs laced with rich idioms and tropes. He buries lyrics, considered profane in his songs, and weaves them like *kente* fabric."

"That's absolutely true, Captain," said Ghanatta. "It's hard to think through sometimes, the way he does it so musically and shrewdly."

"Listening to his songs faraway in London," Captain Crow remembered, "made me felt quite nostalgic—always wishing to come home. Life abroad is full of uncertainties."

There was an interlude silence. Sundiatta dropped another cigarette butt into the ashtray nearby. He then plunged his hand into the breast pocket, pulled an Embassy pack, fished through it, but all were gone in that spell of moment. All done!

The tavern didn't prohibit smoking inside; however, Sundiatta preferred to step away and smoked himself out.

"I don't have any more sticks," he remarked.

"Better." said Marijata "You can now pin your small butts down on that splendid basket nook chair."

The spot had begun bouncing, and the crowd swarmed in. It was a crowd that cut across all demographic status, gender, age, and religious persuasions. Young and old, big and small they feted themselves with *Azonto*—a popular Ghanaian dance.

"*Massa boho bio,*" the crowd asked the DJ to repeat the dose.

As the evening swam into night, the eyes caught nothing but beauty, and the mind settled on zero except fantasy.

Meanwhile, those who didn't feel comfortable staying inside the pub swilled their beers outside, enjoying the night's comfy breeze.

Captain Crow's buddies are frequent patrons of Adehye. They're familiar with the regular faces and some in names. Yet four of her regular clientele, the Ginger girls had still not shown up. They were the city's glamorous, well-known, well-mannered, and beautiful. The quartet captured eyes wherever they stormed, and ravers at the Royal Base wouldn't be denied with that air of elegance and charm.

Great expectations, suspense, and anxiety seemed to have swept the frenzied guys to the fringes of the pub.

"I don't want to wait in vain," Crow told his friends.

"Chill, bro, the night's still young," Sundiata looked at his authentic Audemars Piguet leather wristwatch. "It is just ten o'clock," he snapped.

Soon, the group of four—Ama Samanhyia, Abena Asor, Yaa Afriyie, and Hawa Owoahene Ogede—entered, immediately catching all eyes at the bar. They reached the V-shaped counter to be served and coincidently took seats opposite Captain Crow and his pals.

The glitzy disco lights spanned around, and the merrymakers grooved on, while the disc jockey dished out the crowd's most wanted song, *"Bome Nkomo De,"* by living legend, Kwadwo Antwi.

Feelings had already hit the ceilings, and as the guys started to talk about the gals the bevy across the aisle did same.

Who will fire first?

Supposedly the guys…but for a while the hunters had failed to pull the trigger as they remained glued to their seats people-watching; prompting Sundiatta to offer some advice.

"Hey folks let's rev ourselves up for the night, lest we will be beaten to it."

Ironically, no one had heard his wake-up call. The message hadn't sunk into their heads yet. As for their buddy Captain Crow his eyes still relished the sumptuous feast.

"Are these ladies from here? Thought Sussex had it all but these gals are incredibly beautiful."

"Well we told you," Ghanatta interjected. "You better brace yourself for the next battle. You know what I mean; how to initiate the right moves."

"Who told you I can't strike the hot iron?" Captain Crow said. "Seriously I don't mind at all approaching any one of them, but my concern is, whether these ladies aren't high maintenance. I hope we don't get carried away by their appearance. That's my worry," Captain Crow explained.

"I do reason with you Captain but how would you know if they're none of what we assume." Ghanatta argued.

"That's right," Sundiata concurred.

Anyway we would have to get you hooked-up first, since you're just comin' from the cold Europe," Marijata said.

And they all agreed with him.

As though they were destined to meet, Captain Crow told his buddies about his feelings for Ama. They encouraged him to give it a shot.

"Go, Crow, go," they urged him on.

He tapped his feet, snapped his fingers and stepped up to the dancing floor. His first two moves had drawn thunderous applauds from a section of the crowd. The maverick was a good dancer. Aside Azonto he could dance Tango, Waltz, Breaks and many other dance genre.

And the girls watching the London returnee from their cliquey corner had equally been swayed by his different strokes.

He looked up and beckoned Ama to join him. And she warmly accepted his invitation.

"My name is Kofi Antobam, nicknamed Captain Crow."

"Do you mind if I call you Captain?"

"Not at all, beautiful lady."

"I'm Ama. Ama Samanhyia," she emphasized.

"On the mean streets, they call me, 'uh-oh, here she comes.' You know, the elders say, *'Omama hoye ahi.'* People would simply hate you for your greatness and charm. They will caricature you as a prostitute because you go to the bars and the pubs. Or they make you feel uncounted. In short, this is who I am, love me or hate me."

"I am already mesmerized, Ama, by your charm, earthy humor, and frankness," Captain Crow said. "Indeed, you're superbly gorgeous, and I can't resist telling you I'll be more than happy to have you as a great friend, if you don't mind."

He then mouthed into the ears of the beautiful lady. "The likes of you are few."

She smiled delightfully and took a close peek into the eyes of her soon-to-be friend as if to say, *I am Ama and I approve this proposition.*

"Well, thank you, for your kind compliment."

"It's nice to meet you, Ama," Captain Crow noted pleasingly.

"The pleasure is mine," she replied.

Amazingly, the spoils were shared. Ghanatta got hooked-up with slick Hawa Owoahene Ogede, who would later be nicknamed Lady Dynamite, Sundiatta befriended Abena Asor, and smooth-talking Marijata endeared his heart with Yaa Afriyie.

Chapter 11

Certainly, when two lovebirds with striking chemistry meet, they leave heart prints and unforgettable imprints. The Adehye spot hosted two of the Garden City's finest, Ama Samanhyia and Captain Crow one month ago. But like sweet music, the duo had the opportunity to meet again. It was time for them to put fingers on the tabs.

Even though they had a night one might describe as groovy and stimulating, that wasn't enough to solidify the real intent and purpose of the hungry he-bird who yearned to spend another moment with his newly found friend. Perhaps, it was time to do the real talk and walk. And, of course, that chance would also afford the smart lady to do some probing.

Since that superb jam, it appeared almost all their correspondences had been on the telephone. There was need to switch gears, and someone would have to take the initiative.

So Kofi set a date! The best place to kill a lion is in the bush.

Ama knew she'd a gig with him. So she wasn't going to the gym that special day and wouldn't stay late at her office either.

They were meeting at another respectable place in town—at the Caprice Restaurant, tourists called it. The indigenes called it *Bobea or Suban.*

Caprice rested on the hills of the most affluent and gated community at Graceland in Kumasi.

Both were time conscious, and so by 5:00 p.m., Captain Crow had already pulled up at the packing bay of the popular spot. And even before he stepped out from his C-Class Benz, the Garden City's breathalyzer a.k.a Koforidua Flower had emerged.

She packed her flashy Rolls-Royce car right by Kofi's.

"I never knew you're that punctual." He said amid giggles. "That's good of you, Ama."

"Thanks for the kind remarks. You're punctual as well."

"How was your day?"

"It was okay!"

"Just okay, you meant?"

"No, it was superbly good."

"Voilà! That's what I want to hear. Always be positive-minded. See, with our powers combined, like the TV character Captain Planet, we can do incredible things in this world," Captain Crow declared.

She was breathtaking as usual. She was incredibly gorgeous in her slick sleeveless blue blouse with a blue Ryder jean, sending her newfound friend openmouthed as never before. Hand in hand, they walked grandly into the restaurant.

There weren't many people. It got crowded at times, particularly late in the evenings during summer. Most tourists liked Caprice because of its serene outlook, first-rate cuisine, and live band stand that occasionally played at the upper deck. The two love birds got themselves perched at a table affixed to a corner, trying to be somewhat sneaky at least for the meantime.

The paparazzi liked Caprice too. They usually come here disguised to get exclusive photographs of celebs who patronize her. And then the tabloids would splash them on their front pages, probably the reason why Kofi and Ama were so tactful.

While they scanned the menu, an elegantly dressed waitress (a "starlet"), fair in complexion, probably seventeen, stole a look at Captain Crow before offering them drink.

Kofi preferred water to soda. And in just a nick of time, their meal was ready.

Diagonally facing Captain Crow were three young ladies dressed in stupendous bare back clothes and eye-popping skimpy skirts who occupied two seats adjacent.

They were very loud, probably a ploy to draw attention. However, Kofi would not have that opportunity to steal glances, let alone look at their direction.

"Okay, so I'm kind of troubled by some things I mentioned to you earlier on our telephone chats." Ama opened the dialogue. That was a smart move to diffuse any obstructions and unknowns.

"What exactly?" Kofi asked gently. She shrugged her shoulders, "In a sense, I'm fine because I was honest with you about me being a brat at times, but I'm hesitant and almost wishing I didn't say it because when you're trying to get to know someone, you want to put your best foot forward, and I think I should have maybe eased into my flaws.

"Although I regret a little, you should know, I like being told the truth, so in retrospect, if I enjoy the truth, I should produce honesty as well. This is what makes up me, though— my composition—everyone's unique with their own quirks. Isn't that true?'

"You're absolutely right," said Captain Crow.

"Simple issue, I know," she continued, "I'm just hoping my honesty didn't put you off. Funny isn't it? You won't believe it, that I've been brooding over this for the past three days, wondering how and what you would read into the whole small matter. But I hope you'll understand me."

"Ama, to be honest with you, I admire people who speak their minds. I think it helps a lot in friendship and relationship. And, personally, I think this is nothing that can rock the boat on the high seas. It will have a smooth sail, so don't worry. You know, I'm a brat too. Call me a stubborn cat. As you eloquently put it, we all have our quirks."

She was her mom's baby girl, the youngest of three girls and two boys in a wealthy family. When Captain Crow stopped by their magnificent home at Gloryland one evening to give her Shakespeare's novel *Romeo and Juliet*, he spotted his would-be mother-in-law eavesdropping.

"You made me laugh when you talked about my mom standing ten yards away. I'm her baby, the youngest of her five children. I guess it was just her natural instinct to want to be close and check on me and make sure I'm all right. And by the way, you're absolutely right, I'm sure my mom was sizing you up too! No worries though, you gave a good first impression. I suspect your parents would do the same too?"

"Certainly so," Kofi replied.

"Anyway, what made you stop and talk to me almost two weeks after meeting at the pub?"

"I guess that's my trademark, at least allowing some breathing space to let things pan out."

"But before talking to me, you wouldn't have known I was 'refreshing,' as you put it. So what made you be like, 'I should talk to her'?"

"Curiosity, anxiety, and perhaps the possibility of getting to knowing you better. I suppose I stated it eloquently."

"Are you really sure?"

"Yes, I am. But just in case you've doubts about my submission, then let me put it this way. It wasn't as though I was trying to flex my muscles if that was your thoughts. I think it is a gentleman's thing. Not a chronic disease, but a temporary flu."

"Hahaha," she laughed hysterically. "You have great sense of humor."

"Thank you," Captain Crow said.

"I figure you're doing massive workout."

"Oh, you could tell I've lost weight, huh?"

"Yes."

"Wow, thanks, because I can't tell yet. I'm doing it more so to remain less stressed and for weight loss. You saw my mom, right? She's quite big, and my dad is big as well."

"And what do two big parents produce?"

"An obviously big offspring!"

"But somehow, nature has been so good to me, because I ain't as big as my mom. I find myself in between. I don't have a small frame. Neither do I have a big one. But I could slim down a bit. Generally, I am how God intended to create me. Anyway, thanks for noticing, I appreciate it."

"You're welcome, Ama."

"That really gave me a little motivation to work a little harder next time at the gym. Any comments?" she enquired.

"Ama, it is fascinating listening to you talked about yourself. You really touched on so many things, and I will try my possible best to do justice to them. First of all, I have seen two dwarfs produced a giant. What may seem impossible though is a giraffe procreating a bird. So it doesn't challenge conventional wisdom or logic for two heavyset parents to beget a carbon copy offspring like my beautiful Ama, an image, well-bred, and carefully nurtured. Besides, I've seen two dwarfs produce a child of normal height too," Captain Crow noted.

"Are you referring to the Television Show *Little People Big World*?" Ama asked.

"No," replied Captain Crow.

"Okay, because that's where I saw that. A bird and a giraffe... You're funny and full of them!" Ama said.

"Anyway, how was your workout today?" Captain Crow asked.

"It was all right. I don't know. I just wasn't really feeling it today. Sometimes, it's like that. Thanks for all the compliments, and I appreciate it."

"Well, I'm glad you'd an above average workout today. Tomorrow will be better. I can guarantee you. I'd like you to stay fit, stay strong, and stay healthy."

So far so good. First date had gone pretty well, and so, two weeks afterward, the lady decided to take the wheel. Ama asked they travel to the Volta region for a cruise on Dodi Islands, and it was all fun and a great joy. They also visited the Akosombo dam, the largest man-made lake in the world and wound down later that afternoon at the cozy Aburi Gardens in the Eastern region.

"I forgot to ask you a fortnight ago about what you do to relieve tension," Ama Samanhyia asked. "But I think I did a few days later. Remember I asked you?"

"For me, I do a lot of exercising, praying, and talking. Crying is also one of my de-stressors. Life is full of many complications at times. So tell me about yours."

"Hmm!" Captain Crow sighed. "I should say prayer and writing help a lot. Besides, I've developed a stubborn attitude: An attitude that tends to believe that I'm a superman of a kind. So no matter the enormity of the problem, I have the conviction that I can surmount it, like a stubborn cat. Sorry though, I got the puzzle wrong. I thought it was love. But I fell flat. I had no idea where that thought came from. I just flopped. However, it doesn't make me a loser though. Does it?"

Thanks for tickling my imagination. I couldn't stop giggling at the opposite end of the line."

"What was the answer to the riddle again?"

"The question was: 'What comes once in a minute, twice in a moment, but never in a thousand years?'" Is…is…you ready? Drum roll please…a moment!

"I had no clue. That's a nice one."

"So you're a stubborn one, huh?" she asked him.

"Yes, I am. And I think we're both on the same wavelength when it comes to being stubborn."

"Oh, I strongly agree with you on that," replied Ama. "I think everyone can be stubborn to an extent. I wouldn't so much say I'm stubborn more than I'd say I'm spoiled. If you recall, I've told you before that I'm the baby of the family, and you know how babies can be at times, they want things when they want them. I guess you could say I'm a brat at times, but I've gotten a lot better with age. Growing up teaches one so much. I still like things my way sometimes, but on the contrary, I'm a very selfless person.

"It's funny speaking to you so formally. Normally, when I chat with friends, I'm a lot more lax. So what brought you back home, Captain? Because many youngsters here yearn to go abroad, especially to London in the UK, and in the United States?"

"Well, it had always been my desire to return home as a proud son of this great nation. A learned friend of mine expressively states, 'If you learn, teach, and if you get, share.' I believe nation building hinges on pooling resources both natural and human. That way, we can have a more stable and sustainable economy. Beyond that, I have a beloved mother who means a lot to me. She has been a great companion, a mentor, a sister. In fact, she means everything to me. And I am hopeful that the woman who would be in my life someday will love her as she will do to me."

"Oh, that sounds great. And you're the only son of your mom, right?"

"Yes, I am. She is my sweet mother, and I will do anything for her. She was there for me when I was a kid and has remained my benefactress. Not many young ones growing up enjoyed the life I got from my mother to this day."

"Wow!" Ama exclaimed, as they end their trip to the picturesque Islands.

Six months later, Captain Crow's friendship with Ama Samanhyia turned into courtship, and he introduced her to his mother. Normally among Akans in Sikaman, this is the time when parents of both parties try to know a little, perhaps more, about the would-be bride and groom. However, Ama had no clue whatsoever, that that day, Kofi's mom would push the drill button.

"Who are your parents?" Captain Crow's mom asked.

"Mr. and Mrs. Samanhyia," she replied.

"Which of the Samanhyias? Is it the maverick lawyer or the medical doctor?"

"He is the medical doctor. The one who owns the clinic at Dekyemso."

"Oh, I see. I think I know him. So how long have you known my son, or better put, known each other?" Amid smiles, she sized her up.

"About six months now."

Her answers were as crisp as telegraphic messages. The best way to know how love is like is to love and be loved.

Captain Crow's mom wasn't done with her probing questions.

"And I suppose you've taken him to see your parents," she asked.

"Yes, ma'am, I have done that already."

"And what was their impression about him?"

"They said he is a nice gentleman, and they liked him right from the get-go."

"Hmm!" She sighed and smiled again.

"Well, you seem to be a nice person too. So let's see how things would turn out in the coming months and years. As you already know, courtship or relationship affords partners to know each other well or better.

"In the course of this period I call probation, you may not like everything about your partner regarding what they say, how they act, how and what they eat, why they choose to do certain things, etc.

"That may lead you to another level of the relationship ladder. I call this one adjustment zone. You open the adjustment window to allow for sobriety and what you have. Then, you make the judgment," Captains Crow's mom concluded.

Having gone through the screening process earlier, just like Ama, his newfangled friend, it was time for the real deal. And from there on, the two would swing arms together like Romeo and Juliet.

According to friends of the Crow, there were absolutely no foot-dragging from both parents when the couple made the decision to take the courtship to the altar.

"With no hurdle on their way," said a friend. "They agreed to tie the knot shortly afterward."

The setting was the magnificent—Cape Coast Castle, built over five hundred years ago where unfortunate millions of black souls were held captives as slaves in the dungeons.

Why Cape Coast?

The coastal city, once the capital of the Gold Coast until it was removed to Accra in 1877, was dear to Captain Crow's heart. He loved the beautiful scenery, and he loved the rich history of the city.

"I knew it wasn't going to be big, but great. I like antiques, and I truly wanted to make Ama feel like a star. That is why I chose Cape Coast. Besides," he told his friends, "the city known for its higher education standard and is synonymous with choral music and patriotic songs was my father's most favorite."

Once, as the prefect of the Kwegyir Aggrey Hall of Mfanstipim College, he commanded respect and always ensured that during interhalls and quiz competitions, his house came on top. Captain Crow knew how to win and win well, especially when he sets eyes on something his heart desires. He shared the same house with Bosommuru Kofi Annan, the former UN Boss.

Tactfully, he cajoled Ama, and warmly, he won her heart. Once mesmerized by the beauty of the gorgeous damsel at the Adehye tavern, Captain Crow—an accomplished lawyer, a shrewd investigator, and a civil rights activist—was the luckiest man.

The officiating clergy was Bishop Palmer Buckle of Saint Paul Catholic Church in Koforidua.

"To God be the glory! Most gracious and most generous father, we have gathered here today to put together your son Captain Crow and daughter Ama Samanhyia as husband and wife."

"Now, do you, Captain Crow, swear to take Ama Samanhyia as your beloved wife?"

"Yes, I do," replied Captain Crow.

"And do you, Ama, also swear to have Captain Crow as your beloved husband?'

"Yes, I do."

"With this declaration made, I now join the two of you as husband and wife. Therefore let no one put asunder what God has put together."

As cool as a cucumber, Bishop Buckle slipped in an old joke he claimed a pastor friend told some newlyweds: "What God has put together let no dog separate them."

"Many a time," he continued, "you get reports from spouses that their husband or wife is always with the pet in their bedrooms, living rooms, etc. We don't want to hear or see geneticists' names such as 'Manog' or 'Womog'."

That was a straight shot from the blues, and he got the whole room resurrected to a good laugh.

"Please don't give dog a chance in your marriage," he advised.

In attendance were special dignitaries. The Asantehene Otumfuo Opoku Ware II graced the event. The ceremony also attracted thousands of people from the city and the countryside. It was described by many as historic and the biggest ever in the metropolis.

Indeed, if beauty is said to be the key to success in life, Ama Samanhyia one of the Garden City's most elegant ladies had it all. She was a placid lady by all standards and well-heeled woman from the Oyoko family. Both her maternal and paternal relatives were wealthy.

Her newly-wed groom (Captain Crow) was a man with style and finesse, who'd Asante Aristocrat antecedent *'krakyesem'*. His classmates said he was a 'gentleman's gentleman.'

"Ama really had a good time in her heavenly days," said one of her pals.

"Clubbing was one of our major hobbies; we hopped from pub to pub. But we weren't bad girls as some folks in the community assumed. We just loved to have fun and that was about all. Some called us tomboys and all sorts of labels. Ama was the leader of the group," Yaa Afriyie revealed.

Nonetheless growing up the luscious lady didn't have life easy-going. Her outstanding beauty created an axis of attention as scores of men of all shapes and sizes flocked-in in an attempt to frolic the juicy damsel.

However, she proved them all wrong as she had sworn: "I'll never lose my virginity to anyone except the man who marries me."

Months after their epic wedding Ama Samanhyia revealed to a confidante and a family friend how she had kept her word until the right man came at the right time.

"There is nothing more satisfying than to have someone you really love ask your hand for a marriage. Let alone to be deflowered by him…"

"We really had good time when we honeymooned at the Coconut grove at Elmina. It was absolutely groovy and sexy. He makes sex so harmonious and so appetizing. Takes time to caress you, teases you and flips you up like pancake till you feel you can't take no more," she noted.

Indeed, the two love-fellows lived their lives like stars and they both loved themselves to pieces. Ama Samanhyia and Captain Crow were just perfect cutting-edge to the word romance: like fire and ice they made their marriage a public toast.

The moon wanted to be surrounded by her stars. Akua Akyeampoma (Captain Crow's mother) had asked her son whiles in the UK to return home and give her a grandchild. Well, that obligation didn't take much longer. Just a little over two years, the couple was blessed with a handsome star, Osagyefo.

And within a period of twelve years, the pair had ably manufactured six able-bodied stars: Otumfuo, Odeefuo, Kasapreko, Yaa Asantewaa, and Benazir. Little Benazir the youngest of all, was charming and adorable.

And there was yet another promise he'd made to his mother, when he was a young boy—bringing to justice the assassins of his father. But that ultimate task required scrupulous planning and rolling out the right objectives.

Meanwhile, there were claims and counter claims that the four alleged killers of the heir had been dwelling among the innocent citizens.

So, with his secret agency already in place, the stage was set for the historic manhunt in the annals of the great Ashanti kingdom.

Chapter 12

In fact, it was a must-see sting operation and not a tale to be relayed by an errand. Villages and towns within and outside this kingdom would be locked down by the secret operatives as they relentlessly pursued the runaway fugitives. And block by block they searched for the alleged assassins. The Intelligence Agency Big Eye had four dedicated staff on her payroll namely, Hawa Owoahene Ogede (a.k.a. Lady Dynamite), Marijata Beyeeman, Sundiatta Gbewaa, including Captain Crow. A few years later, the ubiquitous investigator formed an activist group which famously came to be called the Unflappable Seventeen.

Aside its core function of investigating and raking the muck in societies, the Big Eye team played overlapping roles, dabbling deep into civil rights activism.

Unlike the investigative group, the Unflappable Seventeen plied only into civil right activities. The seventeen-member body addressed themselves as comrades and relentlessly fought injustice, inequality, as well as discrimination within and outside Asanteman. It was a formidable force whose dynamic role helped influenced positive change in the Ashanti kingdom. For the records, here are the men and women, heroes and heroines who championed the activism course:

- Osahene Captain Crow,
- Sundiata Gbewaa,
- Marijata Beyeeman,
- Ghanatta Kwabena Sokoto,
- Hawa Owoahene Ogede,
- Osagyefo Diabene,
- Ofosagye Okumkom,
- Ogyampatrudu Kwabrafo,
- Kofi Ogidigidi,
- Bosommuru Ampontuah (the famous giant),
- Yentumi Gyeabour,
- Ahuabobirim Odeneho,
- Oyeeman Konfanko,
- Akua Patapaa Kru,
- Adwoa Bene Mabediabene,
- Kokotako Odiamono, and
- Cantankerous Kantanka Kakabo.

At the inaugural ceremony, Captain Crow told Asanteman that the Unflappable Seventeen had been formed to help free its oppressed and disadvantaged citizens.

"This group is here to stay," he told the gathering. "And we will do everything humanly possible to ensure that your inalienable rights aren't blatantly trampled upon."

Elsewhere in Graceland, the birth place of Captain Crow, expectation had built-up, and the gruesome murder of the heir remained a topical issue nearly three decades on. Some irate youth, who had been told of the ghoulish act, asked the maverick to help unravel, capture, and bring to book the killers of their royal.

Suffice to say that that mission to unravel the mystery death wasn't going to be easy.

And behind the Unflappable Seventeen was the secret agency, Big Eye, the prime mover. Though the investigators faced many obstacles, they're able to surmount them.

Evidently, it was time to get boots and tools on the ground, rake the muck, relive the cold case, and dust off the brown files and dockets. The well-resourced and logistically empowered squad would thoroughly rummage around the length and breadth of the country for the wolves clothed in sheep skin.

From the rainy city of Axim in the south, to the scorching sweaty town of Zabzugutatale in the north, across the Crocs' town of Paga, to the monkey sanctuary in the Bonoland, they ensured that no stone was left unturned.

Briefing the spying agency later, Captain Crow noted, "Crime detection is like hunting the hungry lion. It can hound you if you lose your guard."

"Intelligence gathering is a mosaic. We have to treat every piece of information we chance upon with utmost seriousness," he told them.

Big Eye put its searchlight on the Bureau of National Intelligence (BNI) and had his daring personnel infiltrated the inner circle of the nation's elite security agency. The inexorable and slick Hawa Ogede (Lady Dynamite), the agency's only lady, would make her interviewees or victims piss in their underpants during interrogations.

She had served five years in the US Marine Corps as an undercover agent, ten years with MI6 in the UK Intelligent Agency, and worked as a pilot for the German National Carrier Lufthansa Airlines for two years.

Already in tango with the Police Chief of Kumasi, uncompromisingly snooping into all the old, cold, dirt files at the CID headquarters. Lady Dynamite had the police chief's office bugged, and every conversation that took place there was captured.

Equally, the men brought to the table loads of experiences. They had under their sleeves good track record: Sundiatta and

Marijata were KGB-trained agents. Additionally, both had a stint with the French secret service DCRI. The duo had worked also for the Reuters, AP (Associated Press), and the almighty tabloid, the *Sun*, of London, as their foreign news correspondents.

Perhaps, one major thing that made the whole exercise enthralling was the fact that the spying agency occupied the fiftieth floor of the Pyramid Buildings that overlooked the tiny colonial police post opposite her.

Sitting at such strategic position, Captain Crow and his team could survey all the land. Literally, they knew who was frequenting the chief's office, and possibly every nook and cranny of the territory. They'd cast their net deeper and fished wider.

And from the great height, the protagonist and his team spread their wings as wide as the North American XB-70 Valkyrie and like a shaft of light parachuted deep into the dark belly of Mother Earth, where the assassins of his slain father had sought unholy refuge.

The historic manhunt code named Operation Walatu-Walasa spearheaded by Captain Crow had finally let loose their artful modus operandi—posing as marketing agents, Susu collectors, security officers/night watchmen, bar attendants, as well as palm wine tappers.

Like the canine, they sniffed around. They knew where and how to source for the right information: checking diaries and calendars, surfing through the Internet, and listening to radios for upcoming events, including reading newspapers.

At 5:00 p.m. on Friday springtime, the Association for Ghana Industries (AGI) was holding its annual stakeholders' meeting at Giraffe Hotel in Aboabo, a suburb of Kumasi. The AGI management had blacklisted a journalist with the *Pioneer* newspaper and any reporters from the tabloids.

"When you invite them, they don't report on the main or actual event. Instead they write stuff that never took place at the event grounds. They have their own agenda. And they snoop around like dogs," an official narrated.

That's right! Journalists are agenda-setters so never tell a journalist what he must do and not do.

But if in doubts of the reporter's credibility and honesty, do as you've done. And that I think settles the score. Tit for tat is a fair play.

Anyway, the keynote address was to be delivered by the Metropolitan Police Chief Kofi Babone Akamenko, who had long been on the radar screen of the Big Eye. There will also be other special dignitaries.

"This would be a good setting," said Captain Crow.

Preferably, the slick Lady Dynamite would be assigned to execute the job. Her good looks, youthful exuberance (at twenty-five), and knack for excellence played to her advantage.

She was representing a nonexistent newly inaugurated marketing company, Telinoff Ventures. On her business card she is Akushika Bibini, a marketing intern. Sometimes she carried the name Jezebel Enokwa.

Of course, posing as an intern was a big bait. More often than not, most CEOs attending such functions alone fall prey to these beautiful ladies. They get swept away by the charm and beauty of the starlets and end up deep into the lioness den.

But why are men so vulnerable or crazy when it comes to sex and power?

Perhaps it is ignorance or forgetfulness or stupidity or all the above. Nonetheless, as matured species, we've got to be mindful that not all apples are eatable.

The police chief in this episode was sitting at the edge of the cliff. The slick goddess was cunningly preying around. The offer was beefy, too juicy to let go. Time was ticking to the close.

Shortly after the program, Dynamite inched up to the podium to engineer rapport with the metropolitan boss. Mr. Akamenko couldn't refuse the gorgeous lady's request to chit chat with him.

He had been eyeballing her right from the get-go of the evening's event. And the undercover agent sitting close to the camera's stand already knew the predatory eye. In other words, she was well aware of the eye preying on her.

Remarkably, her beauty and charm had hypnotized the tough-talking officer. The police chief had given Dynamite his business card and set up a date with the slick.

Two weeks later, Dynamite met Mr. Akamenko at his office for the first time in a series of meetings that would follow weeks, months, and perhaps years afterward.

"Can you meet me at my office?"

"Okay, I will. What time, sir?"

"Hmmm, let's meet at 3:00 p.m. on Thursday next week. Is that fine with you?"

"Yes, I will be able to honor it. Okay. I've got to take leave of you now. Hopefully, I'll see you next week. I am a bit shade late. I've got to run to the office to see my boss before he leaves for the house."

"All right then. Have a good day."

"And you too, sir."

The lion had already swallowed the lead-laced bait. And it wouldn't take long for the highly toxic substance to begin to have effect on the prey. He would experience stomach-turning and eye-popping symptoms, and in the long run fall helplessly into the predatory arms of the detective as her victim.

❈

Dynamite had stumbled on yet another lead. And early on Monday morning, the following week, she was heading to Tema, the port city, which lies roughly twelve miles southeast of Accra, Ghana's capital to meet with a tipster.

The supposed tipster, Grace Omaboe, believed to be a retired civil servant who once worked at the CID headquarters in Kumasi. Actually, she was Mr. Akamenko's personal secretary. A shrewd escritoire who understood the language of the police very well. Grace had a whole dossier on the police chief, reaffirming his complicity regarding the heir's assassination.

She'd also revealed a long-term amorous relationship they had together, giving Dynamite more drive to tighten the hangman's noose on the tough-talking superior. The seasoned investigator brimmed with smiles while she elicited the damning information from the impeccable source.

"My last question to you, madam," said Dynamite. "How long did you work at the CID department?"

"Oh, many years," she replied.

Dynamite butted in, "Exactly how many years?"

"Thirty-five years," said the former principal secretary.

"Thank you so much, madam," Dynamite said. "It's been pleasure talking with you."

"The pleasure is mine," the woman replied. "Don't hesitate to call me if you need any more clarification," she added.

Dynamite's wide-eyed stare remained stuck on her host. She had observed something absorbing—the beauty and charm of the sixty-plus woman. Being modish herself, the detective couldn't let go. Perhaps one final question: "Sorry, I have one last question, Madam, if you don't mind. You look so beautiful and so youthful. What's the secret?" Dynamite asked.

"Oh, now you're looking for the platinum card, huh? The secret is good exercise, good food, and good lotion. As a young lady, if you want to maintain your beauty, remember to use the good ointment. It makes your skin smooth and sexually appealing. So, that's my secret," Grace answered with a contagious laughter that showcased her beautiful white teeth.

"Thank you so much, Madam."

"You're most welcome, sweetie."

Finally, Dynamite got up from a swivel chair, stretched forth her hand for a handshake and bade her host goodbye.

By the end of the pleasantries, the clouds had gathered momentum along with tempestuous weather. The day was sloughing itself from the embryonic stage. It was just four o'clock in the afternoon but darkness had already held sway the seemingly blue sky. The next three to four hours journey would be expended behind the wheels.

She was racing like a jet from the Tema Motorway through to the N1 Highway in Accra, in anticipation to get back to Kumasi by half past seven or eight in the evening. With her eyes firmly glued to the over 270 miles road, Lady Dynamite galloped through the low and the highlands as she continued to process and knit together the medley facts gathered from the marathon meeting with her host.

Firmly, she clutched to the carpet and would hardly have a look at the speedometer. She had missed Exit 133 awhile back, and might have to exit half a mile ahead. Still musing on her new find amid terrific speed, the sound of police siren blared, and the blue lights flickered voraciously about forty yards behind her.

Instinct told her something wasn't right. And her rearview mirror confirmed that. Quickly, she pulled over. While a young police officer surfaced from a camouflaged car.

"Excuse me, lady, do you know why I've stopped you?" the deputy asked her.

"I guess I was speeding," said Dynamite.

"Right, my censor picked you up, you're incredibly driving 90kph instead of the 70kph speed limit in this section of Highway 99."

"Wow! I didn't notice that."

"Have you been drinking today?"

"Not at all, sir," she replied.

"Well, I would have to put you on a breathalyzer test."

She came out clean. But the deputy wasn't sure why the elegant woman was driving at such ferocious speed. He perused through the vehicle and later asked her to open the trunk, ostensibly to check if she was carrying some narcotic drugs. Surely, there was nothing like that.

"Why were you speeding like that?" he asked Dynamite again.

"Sir, I received a message awhile ago that my mom had been rushed to Komfo Anokye Hospital. Her condition is life threatening. I am quite traumatized now," she explained.

"I see, but be very careful," the officer cautioned her.

She had narrowly escaped a ticket from the intrepid deputy.

In that terrific speed, she had made it safely back to Kumasi and off to the office. She stepped out from her posh Pathfinder and ran into the waiting elevator.

Meanwhile, Captain Crow was alone in the office at the time, getting ready to leave for an important meeting and had asked Dynamite to go home and rest till the next day.

By sundown Tuesday, all the investigators had converged at the Strategy Room, brainstorming for the first time in three days. They'd all been busy scouting and snooping around for scoops.

Captain Crow had walked in exhausted barely fifteen minutes earlier.

His face looked drawn; possibly, he needed some soda or coffee to soothe his nerves. He got himself a cup of coffee. With legs crossed in the reclining black leather chair around the conference table, he sipped his coffee.

"How did you escape from being ticketed you hinted last night, if you were pulled over by the police on this notorious highway?" he asked Lady Dynamite who'd come in moments later.

"You need to ask. He thought I was drunk and asked me to take breathalyzer test.

"Oh, you did all that?'

"Yes, this was a young police officer. He looked smart and sleek in his uniform."

"And what happened?"

"My mom had been admitted at the Komfo Anokye Teaching Hospital and I needed to be there as early as practicable. I lied to him. But, I guess the look on my face at the time might have stole his heart and let me off the hook."

"Glad you made it here half hour before scheduled time. Sundiata and Marijata aren't here yet. But I trust they would be here on time."

Talk of the devil, the two musketeers, Sundiatta and Marijata walked in and helped themselves with some soda and coffee.

"Hey buddies, how did it go?"

"Ugh! We hit the brick wall again," said Sundiata. "On our way to the office, we saw this guy over by the shoulders of the road leading to the Prempeh Assembly Hall. At a first glance, we thought he was dead. He had his body draped from head to toe.

I pulled over, got closer to him and tapped his foot gently with my shoe to check if he was alive. Surprisingly, he resurrected from his tarp. He looked very unkempt.

The disgusting odor that radiated from his tattered clothes nearly made me vomit.

We couldn't leave him looking at his condition. Instead we called the medic and had to wait till they showed up."

"That's a good Samaritan's work," said Captain Crow.

He opened the meeting with a short prayer, recapitulated the highlights of the last meeting and reminded them of the dire need to tighten the noose up on their culprits.

"Time is gracious," he said, "but some days you find time move slowly, and other times she doubles her pace as though she's catching up with the inescapable shadow. I have no idea, why the genial lady does that. Perhaps, there is mystery about everything in this world.

"For instance, there's mystery as to whether our great-great-great-grandpa Adam ate a real fruit, there is mystery about why all the seas, rivers, rivulets, streams, and creeks flow into the ocean, yet the mighty ocean never overflows its banks. Also, there is mystery about where man goes hereafter. And of course, there is mystery about the death of my father.

"Obviously, one cause leads to another, then to another and another, and the vicious cycle moves on. They say cause is an elusive concept. I believe that.

"So far, we have close to one hundred leads, and it portends that we might even get more as the days roll on. Thus, as we continue to brain storm, I would like to entreat to one another here gathered to give old leads as well as new leads all the deserving attention. By so doing, I believe we won't risk being outran and outsmarted by the crooks.

"I must also give thumbs up to the team. We've made great strides over the last couple of years since Operation Walatu-Walasa was launched.

"Anecdotally, we can cite Madam Fuseina Issaka, the proud widow I met at Kpunkurugu, near Tamale, about two decades ago as one of the success stories. Her husband had been killed by a known nincompoop, but for many years, she was denied justice.

"Today, that woman and her friends in that enclave as well as other victims' relatives are breathing a greater sigh of relief.

"The so-called almighty *kalabuleism* [cutthroat prices] at Makola, Tudu, and Asafo markets is gradually crumbling on his knees. And so is the iniquitous female genital mutilation [FGM] of our young sisters and daughters.

"The land-grabbing syndrome in our towns and villages seem to be equally fading away in a snail's pace though. Even heartwarming to note is the voting rights given to women in our society today, and the girl-child education which has received huge boost.

"Also today our classrooms are full of young girls who hitherto were made to stay in the kitchen and cook for the households. Glad we're reliving the wise-saying by emeritus Dr. Kwekyir Aggrey who once said: 'If you educate a man, you educate one person, but if you educate a woman, you educate the entire nation.'"

Above all, the poor can now own a parcel of land. The peasant farmer at Akromanto and Bogyeseanwo or the fisher folk at Kormanste and Abandze can also put food on the kitchen table. In like manner, the pito seller at Hamale, in the northern region, can put his/her child to the classroom. The color bar system is debarred, and the rule of the oligarchy is steadily being supplanted.

"I say kudos to you and the comrades in the Unflappable Seventeen.

"That notwithstanding, we have to be careful not to get ourselves embroiled in the Kumasi morass. Bearing in mind that the task ahead is arduously challenging, but we need to do everything within our power to smoke out these nuts.

"We're dealing not with ordinary folks but the powers that be. We're operating in a system that could well be described as putrid. A state that has found itself neck-deep in canker. Deep-rooted corruption, a community warped in malfeasance. Corruption is endemic in our society as it is prevalent in the great Anagoland, our beloved neighbors and cousins.

"The police today are as corrupt, if not worse, than the precolonial Bugabuga men. In fact, the difference between the two is just about the same or exactly the size of a carbon copy sheet. That said, the cases before us, particularly the heir's assassination, is like a chronic cancer that has eaten deep into the moral fiber.

"But here is my philosophy—calling the devil by his name makes him aware that you know who he is and what he does. And get this folks, you don't yell at the devil when you aren't combat-ready. Having identified him or our enemies gives us leverage. That automatically takes us to another level, setting us on the collision course with the detractors. Casualties would be incurred which may include loss of lives and property, loss of time and energy, loss of your freedom and my rights, etc. However, we have to remember that our ultimate goal is to bring these crooks to book, and anything shot of that defeats our purpose."

Chapter 13

As the trio locked horns with the wolves in the jungle, the battle lines between the shrewd investigator Captain Crow and the chief butler, Tweneboa Kodua, also had been drawn. The seasoned detective had embarked on a journey described as incongruous. This followed a tip-off from a credible source.

The midnight meeting he had with the informant had produced a name—Kodua was the killer of his father.

"Youngman, this is between you and me. Kodua is your father's killer, but if you doubt my claim, please go to neighboring Guinea-Conakry. There's a powerful sorcerer he can be of help," the tipper advised.

Again, the informant on Monday had traced the root of Kodua's power from the same sorcerer in Guinea-Conakry.

According to the grapevine, the Walatu-Walasa team could only break the jinx of the mystical man if Captain Crow consulted the shrine in Conakry.

The sub-Saharan country had been known over the years for its black powers, also known as *juju*, but it never occurred to the maverick that the then executioner at the palace would travel that far and source for dangerous mystical powers.

But that was even beside the point. Kodua was a sworn enemy to mercy, and he was known to be a fellow who would do everything to win power, even at the expense of his life.

Captain Crow was excited, at the same time shocked, at the news that some people would move mountains not to do good, but to cause mayhem and inflict pain on others.

He would, however, as matter of urgency, call his teammates and briefed them about the latest development.

"Comrades, I've got news for you," he said. His piercing eyes emitted eagerness and hunger—hunger after the big wolf. "This is really going to be a treasure hunt. Tweneboa Kodua has been mentioned again. And it portends all the roads now lead to Guinea-Conakry. God willing, I'll be leaving for that country tomorrow or the next day.

"My going there isn't so much predicated on seeing this sorcerer and his fancy stuff. Basically, it hinges on the fact that the *malam* could be a star witness for us someday when needed. Because you'll never know.

"And if I had to travel days or even weeks on horseback to meet with this strange man, I will do so. I promise.

✄

The soothsayer, Malam Tanko, a bald-headed man, stood about six feet tall. At age eighty, he appeared to have more than twenty years left to go. In his little red brick house, situated at Ndogo, a slum of Conakry, the octogenarian received more than a quarter of a million clients per day.

Like a physician, Malam Tanko's patients cut across all demographic spectrum, and their objectives spanned from the needing children, financial breakthrough, self-protection, fame seeking, etc.

Nestled in between malodorous Refuse Mountains, where like vultures, Ndogo's children pawed daily through garbage cans and incinerators for food or some scrap metal to sell. This was where the protean, Tweneboa Kodua, sought his mystical strength.

It took Captain Crow one week to reach Guinea. He spoke broken French, so it wasn't too much of hassle to catch a cab to the shrine of the spiritual guru.

And as the day wound down, around 5:00 p.m., after a three-day's wait at mosquito-infested tiny room in the slum, it was the maverick's turn to see the most sought-after diviner. But that luck would quickly fade away. A disheveled woman, probably in her early sixties, had popped up out of the blue with a "troubled shoot."

Her case deserved urgent attention and like being whisked to an emergency ward, the sorcerer would have to grant her immediate audience. The troubled woman was accompanied by two macho guys who held a young lady in their arms.

She kept crying and crying, as though her daughter, who appeared healthy, was going to die in a moment.

But none of the teeming crowd at the shrine knew what was amissed. They had no clue what the beautiful lady was going through. Apparently, beneath her cloth, she had a strange visitor, an unwanted guest who came with unwanted stuff. It would be safe to say she was sitting on pins and needles.

And looking more confused and bemused than her daughter, the sixty-plus woman howled for help, "Monsieur...allow me to see the diviner right now. My daughter is dying," she told Captain Crow.

"Pardon, monsieur," she repeated, weaving her way through the traffic of legs.

The continued scream had attracted a lot more people to the shrine and the maverick would have to wait for more than three hours before he could see the diviner.

Fusena Iroko, the young lady who lived at Ndogo, had about two feet long snake-like object sticking out in her genital.

They'd earlier tried a certain malam in the vicinity, but he was unable to exorcise the alleged demon. So they decided to see the Kankan Nyame Malam who many believed could tame the ogre.

When Malam Tanko came out to get a peek for himself, he cried out, "Trouble! I can't believe what I'm seeing. You must be going through a hell of trouble."

The crowd thickened by the minute. Men who couldn't stand the nudity of the young lady literally took cover.

Malam Tanko darted back into a small room next to the main shrine and in less than twenty minutes, performed a ritual ostensibly to purge the perceived demon that had sought haven in the panic-stricken lady.

First, he sprinkled what appeared to be holy water on Fusena and opined that she'd been hypnotized by a guy who slept with her over the night. After brief incantations by the diviner, water began to gush out from the lady's womanhood, the mystery object had disappeared, given her some semblance of relief following nearly twenty-four hours of nightmare.

About half hour later, when she felt okay, she told the malam, she met a man- who only gave his name as Yakubu at a drinking pub in Nando a suburb of Conakry, and upon brief chitchat, she agreed to go with him to a place called Ogyakrom at the west end of the city.

The area had been hit by power outage, and so they slept in the darkness after having first bout of the night's jamboree. But just about an hour they went to sleep, Fusena saw what seemed like some ghostly images in the room. She alerted Yakubu to have a look at the strange figures, but he wouldn't bother.

Then she felt a poke on her toe, generating uneasiness all night. Back and forth the snake-like object jockeyed in Fusena's underpass. It then twirled around her neck and intermittently on her thighs, she claimed.

"I promise you, Malam, never again will I go back into this business."

"What business?" Malam Tanko asked.

"Prostitution," she replied. "I've been through hellfire, and I've had enough of the ordeal. Today, I say goodbye," Fusena concluded after her revelation.

The sorcerer asked to know the whereabouts of the man who purportedly slept with her, but she couldn't tell. And so, the juju man had a word of caution for the twenty-five-year old lady, "Go and sin no more. Do not engage in this act of prostitution."

The clairvoyant had exorcised the demon that tormented the young woman. It was finally the turn of Captain Crow who had braced the blistering Sahara weather, amid heat wave to make it to the mystic man.

"Massa, this way," a young guy beckoned to him. He had been summoned into a small room of the unpainted brick building that hosted the seer.

"I'm sorry for the undue delay, we get situations like this often, people being hypnotized or bewitched," Malam Tanko told Captain Crow. "Where have you come from? I can tell you aren't from this country.

"Are you *Ashantey?*" he asked.

"Yes, I am," Captain Crow replied. "I am from Ghana."

"So tell me, what brings you here today?"

And without mincing words, Captain Crow summed it all up, stressing the dire need to find the killers of his dad, Barima Adom Yiadom.

"You're welcome, my son," he told the maverick.

"Let's get into business right away," the spiritualist said.

Thirty years ago the palace police, Tweneboa Kodua approached him with a request that he gave him black power that could help him vanish (*ayera*) as well as be able to withstand any weapon that might be formed against him. That power also ensured no enemy could defeat him as long as he obeyed the laws.

"I agreed to help him," he said, "on the grounds that he would strictly adhere to the rules of the game. I have my dos and don'ts.

I cautioned him not to use the powers given to terrorize innocent folks except enemies. And what do I hear now, the spirits tell me Kodua had over stepped his boundaries. He has trespassed. The upshot of it is punishable by death or bad omen will befall him.

"Come with me, strong man," he instructed Captain Crow.

The maverick tailed him into a small room which housed all his mystical accoutrements. He offered him a chair next to a big gourd and closed the tiny *odum* wood door behind them.

"Now, listen. Can you hear the voice?"

"I can hardly decode," Captain Crow said.

"Well, listen attentively now. Give it mouth, Great Kanka, please say it again."

"Timbo Koduo, the palace police, had killed more than one hundred people in the Asante kingdom. He hired two young men to kill Braima Ado Yiadum, a successor to the Golden Stool. The wicked plot was executed outside Komashie. I am very angry, because he didn't use the powers for its intended purpose. In view of this, I am going to strip him off all the powers arrogated to him. He is currently hiding at a suburb called Dekremso in Komashie. Nobody had been able to see him yet because of the Kanka Nyame powers. But it's all over today."

Of course, the ubiquitous investigator had to decode a few of the butchered names such as Timbo Koduo the antagonist and Dekremso (Dekyemso), Komashie (Kumasi) including his father's name.

"Here, look closer into that big bowl filled with water, and tell me who you see there," asked the mystery man.

"I see some image," Captain Crow replied.

"Whose image is it?"

"Hard to tell."

"You mean you can't see well? Okay, I'll zoom it closer for you now."

"Wow," Captain Crow exclaimed. "That's Tweneboa Kodua. I can't believe this. How is this possible?" He wondered.

"It is possible, young man. I hear even in the west, sometimes investigators or police fall on psychics or clairvoyants when they hit the brick wall. See, civilization, science, or whatever you may choose to call it, is good. But you don't throw a whole tradition away just for the sake of the new entrants. In other words, don't spite the supposedly bad priest who took care of you prior to the advent of modernity. Certainly, there were stars before the moon showed up with his gigabyte light." He laughed.

"I tell my clients very often that I derive my powers from the Supreme Being [the Europeans call him God] whom we serve through the lesser gods because we believe they're His messengers."

"How do your people call him?"

"The Akans call him Nyame, and the Ewes call him Mawu."

"That's interesting to know. So what's the deal now?" Captain Crow inquired.

"There is no deal, young man. I won't charge you a pesewa or cedi," the sorcerer told his bewildered client.

"But I'm going to leave you with this message as you go back to your home country, Ghana. The fall of Tweneboa Kodua is near. Darkness will smite him in a broad day light. His household will not know peace. Trouble will sweep him away like the salmons swept to the shore of the mighty ocean by the merciless tidal waves. His death would be bizarre and shameful.

"There would be no more hiding place, as you pursue him from this day. He can run but he can certainly not hide or vanish any longer. He will crawl like a cockroach seeking for hideout yet there won't be safe haven. Bottom line, the Kanka Nyame powers had gone and gone forever.

"Let me tell you something before we wrap up this. Your case is different. You're not seeking power or trying to harm somebody. You came to ascertain the truth or otherwise. That's why I didn't charge you. Juju comes with hard price. The doom is bigger than the boom and the glory. So I often ask my clients: Have you considered your decision to do this?"

"And what do they normally say?"

"The response is always, 'Yes, we've thought about it.'"

"Well, thank you so much, Malam."

"The pleasure is mine, young man."

"Here," Captain Crow handed him a bottle of schnapps. "This is just a token to show my profound appreciation for what you've done. I wish you God's blessings and his divine strength."

Two weeks later, Captain Crow returned home and as required briefed his contemporaries on the findings.

❋

During his absence, the team had been working around the clock. They understood that in tracking down criminals, you've got to stay up 24/7 in order to get the job done. The intelligent veteran couldn't have stated it better. "You get the stinging punch as soon as you lose your guard."

The detectives were all upbeat, scrupulously tightening the hangman's noose on their suspects.

It was Thursday afternoon, the month of June, a typical rainy season in Ghana. The apparently abandoned streets of Kumasi were totally wet after a heavy downpour. It had rained cats and dogs the night before. Nobody dared to come out. Even goats and sheep had gone to sleep. Stores and businesses had closed earlier than as usual.

"Residents in this city don't fear vehicles," said Sundiatta. "They rather dread rains."

After the breakneck speed meeting, the duo was on their way to the rugged mountains of Sowoboduam. They had worked up their strategies. It remains to be seen whether the detectives would live up to expectation; after several, perhaps many, of such operations came to naught.

With a few groceries packed into haversacks yanked over their shoulders, Marijata and Sundiata, set out the second time in twelve months returning to Agyewodin. They had shared relevant information already collected at their beats with teammates at the Strategy Room. This was to ensure that the squad was working in sync, leaving no loopholes.

They went back to the jungle, where mosquitoes, bed bugs, and even snakes had not been kind to them. "We've enjoyed our time here. It seemed it was never going to come," they both said appreciatively.

But what appeared like cozy vacation to them was soon gone. Undoubtedly, for the coming days, weeks, months, and probably years (depending on the outcome of their toil), they would have to work harder to nail the suspects to the coffin and track down credible witnesses.

So far, they'd managed to carry out their covert operation at the blind side of their hosts. The only device they refused to carry the last time was a camera. They're carrying it this time alongside other potent investigative tools.

On their maiden trip to Agyewodin, the tiny village stashed deep in the Evergreen Sowoboduam Mountains, the two had feigned as truck pushers at the Kejetia lorry station in Kumasi. They also hawked vegetables and dog chains. It was here that the spies struck an acquaintance with an elderly man called Agya Koo Nimo, a native of Agyewodin.

And about two months later, the two traveled to the wonderland.

That jaunt was initially dogged by uncertainty because they weren't sure if they could locate their yet to be host. Agyewodin wasn't a friendly village; its inhabitants can be hostile.

However, providence smiled on them. Agya Koo Nimo received them with great excitement. Both guys enjoyed their stay in this village so well as they savored life pleasures like sex, music, wine, and good food sometimes.

Nonetheless, the detectives never forgot that they were on a mission—the grand mission to nab the runaway fugitives.

Agya Koo Nimo was a prolific hunter. Aged seventy-six, a bachelor who had been divorced six years back to a woman of thirty-five long years in marriage over infidelity.

They had no issue; perhaps, that was good news for the lone ranger.

"Some people say I'm bad-tempered man," said Agya Koo. "How can I keep silent over stuff like that?"

"What does 'keep silent over stuff,' mean in euphemism?" Sundiata asked.

"I found out," Agya Koo revealed, "she had been sleeping with a neighbor for nearly ten years."

"Ouch!" screamed Sundiata.

"You know something, guys," Agya Koo continued, "the bug always bites you from inside, and not outside your clothes."

"How come you didn't know such a thing was going on?" Marijata asked him.

"You need to ask my son. Anyway, tell me about how you guys fared on your trip down here. Was it smooth?"

"We had a monster's ride today," remarked Sundiata.

"It had been raining almost the whole day and I thought we couldn't make it here, Agyewodin. The driver was rude. The passengers were rowdy, and the road was bumpy.

Oh lest I forget, we saw a huge bird with muscular legs and broad commanding wings the natives said it was an eagle….."

"Yeah that was an amazing scene," Marijata interjected!

I'd never seen an eagle in my life time; let alone sighted one flew that low and captured an animal. With terrific speed and accuracy the predator latched upon her victim and carried it with its powerful talons.

She took her game away up in the heavens with almost the same speed she descended and then landed on a huge tall Mahogany tree nearby, attracting handclapping from some of the passengers.

"*Onnko babiara aha na otie,*" a woman said in Twi; implying the huge bird had her nest (eyries) on that tall tree and lived there. Many confirmed her claim. They had seen the eagle on a number of occasions, preyed on animals particularly birds and tore them into pieces with her hooked beak.

Asked what enabled the eagle to hunch down her preys with that ease; they told me eagles naturally have extremely keen eyesight (up to 3.6 times human acuity for the martial eagles) which gives them advantage over their victims.

"But all said it was a learning journey. We wound our way through the mud-covered tiny road to the mountaintop to some point where all of us had to come down and give the mummy truck a good push. I really mean good!"

"You see how villagers like us suffer everyday," Agya Koo told his guests amid laughter.

"You're right, sir," said Marijata. "Everybody was tired, but we didn't give up till we got it off from the quagmire. My white T-shirt had turned creamy."

"How about mine," Sundiata punned.

"Yeah…I know it was worse than the eyes can see. I had my old frayed shoes stashed inside the haversack because I couldn't wear them any longer. The dirt was too much," Sundiatta continued. "Marijata seemed untroubled. I had no idea where he developed that attitude from that day. He was calm, sitting on the hard seven feet flat-board. Now and then he would tell a funny joke that would put everyone on stitches. The bone-shaky truck's windscreen that had a crack through it was tainted with the slush."

"Don't mind the body," he carried the philosophical name etched boldly at the crest of his frontage. "You get the sense that we could hardly make it to our destination. The wheels squeaked harder as we galloped through the seemingly impassable road. And little by little in the swampy, bumpy, rocky, wobbly way, we arrived unharmed.

"Ironically, the rooftop riders and the guys who hang on to the sides of the ramshackle lorry also survived the trip. They were however not spared with the frequent whips and nicks from the branches of the trees that had encroached half of the road.

"Not many people were seen at Agyewodin's petite street. It wasn't part of our expectations. We were even taken aback somehow when we randomly counted at least twenty people, looking at her size."

It was half past four. The sun hadn't set yet. Thick darkness would soon blanket the gorgeous gray sky. They might be lucky, though, to see snippets of lights from small insects; perhaps the owl's pungent lights.

Almost all the villages around the region hadn't been powered with electricity yet. God knows when. Their mission to this depressed village was single——go into palm-wine tapping. A trade they said was easy to come by. After all why buy a he-goat, if you don't have a pen to keep him? He would become nuisance to your neighbors. And you might earn the dishonorable name 'noisy neighbor.'

But it wasn't as simple as that.

How would they sell it to the village folks?

It might seem strange to them to see someone from the city (not an indigene) come to Agyewodin and worked as palm-wine tapper. The night came and they passed it at Agya Nimo's home. His mud house built in 1875, nearing a century at the time, sat on a small plateau close to the village's cemetery.

The holes in the roof of the windowless small chamber-and-hall house offered some rare ventilation. Also infected with the same disease, was the host's aged-old door that gave an unselfish peep outside. The squeaky door was merely supported by a rusty six-inch-curvatured nail because it had no locking key from inside.

Grudgingly, they rammed themselves together on his medium-size bed.

Wrought by sleepless nights, the detectives pinched each other but to their amazement, Agya Nimo they noted: "Often had sound sleeps, sometimes emitting pong gas.

Months later, Sundiata found himself a woman (a fishmonger) in the village called Adwoa Sika. The slow-but-sure guy graced himself with loads of information from his newly found girlfriend. Though their friendship didn't last long, he stumbled on a crucial lead that perhaps helped broke the ice. He decided afterward to work as a laborer for Paa Kofi Yentumi, a cocoa farmer.

His long acquaintance with the village's chief palm wine-tapper, Yaw Boye, who lived across the street helped the duo gravitated to the hotbed. Sundiatta had told Boye whilst working for Paa Yentumi several months back about his insatiable love for the palm wine-tapping trade.

"I like this job," he told Boye. "And I hope that you'll someday give me the chance to work with you." As it was meant to be like a fox, Sundiatta forced himself into the snake's pit albeit playing smart at the same time being clever. His boss (Boye) liked him because he never moped around on the job, and he never complained about how hard it was.

A few months later, his right hand man Marijata joined the fray. The two worked so hard in this odd job as though they'd done it before. And within months, the detectives had earned the ignoble name *obetwani* (palm-wine tapper). Their whole lives had changed. They lived like hobos and behaved as gypsies.

Sundiatta virtually lived on tarps and cramps as nobody in the village respected him. He crisscrossed the villages far and near Agyewodin sniffing and looking for scoops. The sneaky man trekked alone to the mountains of Sowoboduam, occasionally running into danger. Once bitten by a black cobra in the tropical forest, he was lucky to have survived the vicious attack from the poisonous snake. Incredibly, he killed the six-foot reptile.

One beautiful evening, Boye decided to officially introduce his new friends (laborers) to Kaku.

"You haven't met my two apprentices yet," said Boye. "Have you?"

"No, I haven't," Kaku replied.

"This is Sundiatta, and next to him is his brother Marijata. They're both from Damango in the northern region."

"Oh, Damango. I like that name. It sounds as mango. Nice to meet you, guys," he gave them nice handshakes. "Do you like it here?" Kaku asked.

"Yes, we do," they replied in unison.

"I guess it isn't like back home, huh?"

"Not really, we're honored to be here."

"Believe me, guys," Kaku injected. "There's no place like home. Even though this town (Agyewodin) is no stranger to hunger, I won't trade it for anywhere else."

"You're right. But we've enjoyed the love and the camaraderie of the good people in this village. Everybody shows love and gives smile, wherever we meet them," said Sundiatta

"Wow, I am amazed you're being chatty today. You of all people," said Boye to his friend.

"Well, they seem to be good fellows. But, remember once a while the hermit talks," he said brusquely.

Kaku was a carpenter. Unlike his pal, Boye, he wasn't the chatty type, an introvert and quick to anger. Though he wasn't as warm as Boye, they both shared common trait—apathy in any social issue.

So now, through their employer, the spy men had gotten to know his closest friend and partner in crime.

This impervious disposition of the hit men made it tougher for the Walatu-Walasa guys to break even initially. Nonetheless, the investigators kept their fingers on the tab socializing and keeping constant visits with good old Agya Nimo.

And having gained his utmost trust over the years, Agya Nimo would tell them the secrets and history of the village. Among them was the infamous murder of the heir to the Ashanti Golden Stool.

"I'd always wanted to tell you guys some story, a story that would arouse your interest. Perhaps the rest of the day. Did any of you hear or read the murder of the heir to the Ashanti Golden Stool about three decades ago? I know you were kids at the time.

But maybe someone might've told you the atrocious story or read it yourself," he told his guests.

"That incident shook the entire foundation of this empire. I was about forty three years at the time working at Asokwa as mechanic. I surely remember that. Around 6:00 p.m. that evening, Yaw Boye,a nephew of mine, and Kwaku Kaku, both from this village approached me with a stranger. They had introduced the man as a friend and businessman who was looking for young energetic guys to help him undertake some lucrative assignment."

"Being an inquisitive man, I asked the gentleman what kind of job was it. He replied, 'It's construction work.'

"'Well, I don't think I can do that kind of job.'

"'Why?'

"'I have back problem,' I told him.

"And that brought the curtain down on my conversation with him. However, I figured out, I wasn't the kind of guy he probably was looking for. You can see for yourself my nephew, Yaw Boye, is six feet six inches tall and beefy. So is his pal, Kwaku Kaku. I suppose Kwaku is even taller than Yaw. But they're both macho men.

About an hour later, I called my nephew, Yaw, into my little kiosk and asked him a few questions regarding the work."

"He was a young man, perhaps, twenty-four years at the time."

"'When is the construction starting?' I asked him.

"'Next week Monday.' Yaw replied.

"'How much is the wage?'

"'It is not a wage business. He will pay us a lump sum after the work is done.'

"'And where is the job?'

"'He said he will take us out of town.'

"'Where is out of town?' I asked him.

For well over half an hour, Agya Nimo grilled his nephew, firing lethal questions from all fronts and all angles. However,

Yaw's unsatisfactory responses would make his uncle resume the questioning.

"Where is the job? I mean, where on earth is this man taking you guys to go and work?"

"I don't know," Yaw told Agya Nimo again.

"Why didn't you ask him?"

At this point, I was firing the missiles from all fronts and all angles."

"'Hey, Yaw, you've got to remember this is Kumasi and not Agyewodin. Not all the people who pride themselves as business men are doing true business.' I told him.

"'Why don't you call him now and find out.'

"'Do you have his phone number?'

"'Yes, I do.'

"'Okay, let's go to the post office and use their pay-phone system. It's just a penny. It costs less to call there.'

"'Hello...hello, sir. This is Star. I want to know where we are going to do the work."

"'Did you say Agyewodin?'

"'Okay, that's fine.'

"'Thank you, sir.'

"'Is Star your new name, Yaw?' I questioned him. 'And what name did he give to Kwaku too?'

"'Kwaku is called Moon."

"'Asem beba dabi," I said. [Coming events cast their own shadows.] 'So you're going to Agyewodin on Monday afternoon? I wish your enterprise may thrive.'

"'No problem at all with money,' the self-styled businessman told the boys.

"They'd no clue what exactly they were supposed to do. But my guts instinct informed me it might be some creepy deal. Perhaps use them as drug-peddlers or couriers, or to smuggle cocoa to neighboring Ivory Coast, or to rob some wealthy man/woman or a bank, or hijack one's vehicle.

"All of the above seemed possible. However, I had less suspicion concerning the latter. For instance, if they hijacked someone's car/vehicle and a fight ensued what might happen? Possibly, something nasty can occur because the victim won't let go his classic property without putting up stubborn resistance. In that vein, the aggressor would apply brutish force to reap what he hasn't sown. The result would be horror. Isn't it?

"I had no plan of leaving for Agyewodin that week, but the above-mentioned imaginative scenarios, plus the fact that I feared these young men could probably run into deep trouble anytime soon compelled me to have a change of mind.

"I woke up early Monday morning and caught the village's first-bound mummy truck. And what I witnessed that fateful night is the rest of the infamous murder that rocked the whole Asanteman in the aftermath."

The hunter told Sundiata and Marijata that around midnight of July 24, a car that appeared like Peugeot Caravan pulled over at the precincts of the quiet village.

"There were four occupants, all wearing masks in the said car—two young men possibly in their midtwenties and two middle-aged men probably in their early fifties," he told the investigators.

Upon a close look from the cracks on his rickety door, he saw the four men pulled what appeared like a huge animal and dragged it a few yards into the thicket in front of his house.

"With one eye still fixed to a hole," he narrated. "I followed the light from their torch till I could no longer trace its existence."

"I hurriedly stepped out from my cluttered room and ducked myself at a fairly good distance from the spot they had parked their vehicle. No sooner had I taken cover in the shrubs than I spotted a light emerging from a furrowed footpath."

According to him, one of them returned and collected some items that were supposedly picked axes, shovel, and machetes. "He nearly spotted me," Agya Nimo intimated.

But he sensed the guy was also afraid. And as he walked back the same way he came; the hunter also followed him crawling literally on his belly, sustaining bruises all over his body.

"Nothing is going to stop me from my unorthodox detective work tonight till I find out exactly what's going on in my little village," he said encouragingly.

"Adjingo River, which served as the main drinking source of water for the surrounding villages, is less than half a mile from my house, and I thought they were out there for a grand scheme. I reached for my flashlight and followed a nearby footpath, treading stealthily and cautiously.

"I was pretty sure they headed down to the Adjingo River.

"My instinct was right. When I got there, they'd already changed their clothes and had only boxer's shorts on. The masks were gone as well. What next?

"They reached for the digging tools and straightaway stepped into the river. First, they dammed Adjingo upstream and then, started digging ferociously. When it got waist level, one of them remarked, "It's okay now."

"Facts checked. Having had closer view to what initially seemed like a huge animal, I was struck by fright. With hands and legs tightly tied together, the bohemians lowered the body of a giant into the belly of the stream and covered it first with cement papers, put some dirt on, then cement and dirt before they opened the dam to allow the river to retake its course."

"River Adjingo had been disturbed. He was hoarding contraband cargo, something he hadn't planned to store. The river had been polluted and all the inhabitants who lived downstream him would certainly be drinking contaminated water.

"How close were you to the scene, if you remember?" Marijata asked.

"Oh, I was very close but it was too dark for them to make somebody out. Besides, I think they believed that there wouldn't be anyone around those wee hours of the night.

"I had ducked low, so low in the bushes watching them closely. The whole exercise, lasted for about three hours, I recollect. They appeared tied, sat down to have some drinks, and I saw one of the middle aged-men handed the young guys wads of money. He made them swore later, that they would never, under any oath or duress, reveal the secret. With shovels thoroughly cleansed, pick-axes washed, and shorts rinsed, the killers left the scene hurriedly," he narrated.

Chapter 14

If the capture of Kodua was believed to be at its dying embers, his partners in crime tucked deep in the Rocky Mountains of Sowoboduam had already met their waterloo. Detectives Sundiatta and Marijata had relentlessly unleashed more pressure on the wolves and sworn to keep stoking the fire until they sink the smoking gun.

In the meantime, Captain Crow had launched an equally stinging operation at Dekyemso. At the onset, it'd appeared abortive as search for the residence of Tweneboa Kodua proved elusive. Plot No.TF/88 had a magnificent concrete and barb-wired building occupying it. However, residents at the peaceful neighborhood had no knowledge of its owner whatsoever. Ironically, her occupants, if they existed, were rarely seen or known.

"We see lights in the nights sometimes, but I won't be mistaken to state emphatically that not more than twice have I seen somebody come out from that flamboyant house," a neighbor told the investigators. "Sounds weird isn't it?"

Captain Crow had a generic idea. The ubiquitous went to Town and Country Planning Office headquartered at Adum, followed it up to Land Title and Registry Department where he gleaned through the bureaus' voluminous files.

Incredibly, records showed the said plot was undeveloped and had been registered under the name, Kwabena Bonyah, a Ghanaian based in Hamburg, Germany.

An auxiliary check on the named Mr. Bonya from the German Embassy's office at Ahayede Ghana also revealed that such person never existed.

"So who at all is Mr. Kwabena Bonya?" Captain Crow queried. The puzzle would lead him into another world of thoughts.

He fell on omnipotent Plan B—rented the fourth floor of the building that previously housed the staff of Yokohama & Jay-Jay Bros., Enterprise. She (the structure) had become vacant, and the new occupants would impregnate her with action and passion.

At its strategic position, sitting approximately two hundred yards away from the runaway chief fugitive's residence, the shrewd investigator installed state-of-the-art surveillance cameras that gave the team telescopic view over the entire surroundings.

And then the countdown, Big Eye had mounted a twenty-four-hour observatory exercise, and they continued their incessant onslaught up until the D-day.

❀

Unquestionably, the stupendous operation by Captain Crow and his phenomenal intelligence group had already wowed many across the nation. Five years in its existence, the fame of the man behind the Big Eye and her sister company, the Unflappable Seventeen, had sparrowed into the heavens.

Beyond that, the maverick's name had eclipsed the monarchs and the oligarchs, and his depth of bravery had flooded the entire monarchy and beyond. Day after day, the group perused cases brought to them from east to the west coasts, across south to the northern part of the country. From the city of lights, Apollonia, toacross with their intrepid spirit.

Individuals, group of persons, including company owners trooped to the offices of the Unflappable Seventeen (fronting for the secret service) to lodge complaints or sent-in letters. And painstakingly, the agency ensured that all cases brought before them received the deserved attention.

In Kumasi alone, nearly 5,000 cases declared cold were reopened and dispensed off swiftly. A thousand cases came from Tamale, the northern regional capital and its surrounding villages and towns. And across the nation, there remained 12,050 unsolved cases.

Upper east and west regions shared 2,000 cases respectively. Whereas, western, central, Brong Ahafo, and eastern regions had 500, 1,000, 1,050 and 1,000 correspondingly.

The remaining 4,000 cases came from the Greater Accra and Volta regions.

But the Big Eye team remained resolute in its avowed mission. The mission to pursue, capture and bring to book the nocturnal activists. It was time to regroup and reload. Once again, the squad had converged at the great height of the Pyramids, with the blind curtains and windows opened to allow in sunlight and fresh air. The sun never stopped to eavesdrop. Even when the rains set in, she came back later.

They had come to synthesize ideas, find new leads, delve deep into old leads, and ensured that all loopholes detected, if any were sealed.

After trekking the rough terrain at Agyewodin in Bonoland for close to five years, trying to smoke out two of the untamed wolves, Sundiatta and Marijata had returned to Kumasi to brief their colleagues about the latest developments.

The unstoppable lady Hawa Ogede who braced the southwest monsoon winds through Gamashie to Tema had also returned. She was upbeat with her findings.

Captain Crow poured more coffee into his auburn mug and asked Sundiata, sitting next to him, if he cared to have coffee as well.

"No. I am taking pito, the local drink made from millet and brewed in the northern pot in Tamale and its environs."

"Oh man, you've really reminded me the good old days. It was my first trip to Tamale, and even miles away, I could smell the northern contagious drink."

"Yep, you said it best, Captain. That's our baby [northerners]. I have stopped taken coffee now."

"Why?" asked Dynamite who had just emptied her cup.

"Just tired of taking that brown stuff," said Sundiata. "But more importantly, it is about time we domesticated."

"There you go... always blazing the trail," Dynamite butted in. "I'm considering hanging my gloves soon."

"Should I take your word?" Sundiata asked.

"You bet," Dynamite gave the assurance.

"All right guys, so what is cooking?" Captain Crow interjected.

"Ladies first," Marijata cut in.

"There you go. Ladies' man," Sundiata said it jokingly.

Of course, the lady with the broadest smile cuddled the prettiest face in the whole wide world would have the eyes. Dynamite had returned from Tema with a potential lead that could turn the scale on her side.

Three days before the journey, she had met a taxi driver named Jomo who magnanimously dropped a hint concerning an extra marital affair between the Metro Police Chief and his ex-secretary (who had then relocated to Tema).

Accompanied by Ghanatta Kwabena Sokoto, her boyfriend who went incognito to the spot, the shrewd detective as usual elicited groundbreaking information from the metro police boss.

But there would be more disclosure in her unanticipated meeting with the cabdriver, Jomo, and a young police officer he picked later that night while heading home toward the Asoka Interchange. Ghanatta sat at the front, and the two heavy-set guys joined Dynamite at the rear.

It's a detective's thing.

Somebody would fall into the trap. She'd pinned herself tight to the corner flipping through the *Pioneer* a local tabloid.

There had been an unreported lorry accident on the stretch between Ejisu and Kumasi, which had claimed seventeen lives. Three days later, an eyewitness called the newspaper's offices, and they picked the story up from there.

"So uncharacteristic of me," she said, "I had all this while not taken a look at the driver. This is something I always do whenever I take a taxi. Probably because Ghanatta was with me. It is very important, especially if you're by yourself with the driver. Try to engage him/her with some chit chat. It helps sometimes. Note, I didn't say all the time.

"He was a fairly middle-aged man, maybe forty-eight, fair in complexion, and quite articulate. I was surprised to learn that he speaks seven different languages fluently—Dagare, Ewe, Fante, Ga, Twi, French, and English.

"'Kofi Jomo is my name,' he told me.

"He wore a frightening goatee beard and disheveled whiskers. But I found him to be very friendly. Jomo hails from Tema. He resides in Community 10, but once in a while, he visits his girlfriend who lives here in Kumasi. Two decades and seven years, he has been doing this job. Amazingly, he knows all the nooks and crannies of the city, and the streets also know him.

"Along the way, the guys alighted at Kejetia. Then, in between Kejetia and Asafo, we picked another man [passenger]. It dawned on me right away that I had met him before at the police headquarters. But he couldn't recognize me."

"'Good evening to all,' he greeted.

"'Good evening,' we responded in unanimity.

"He was going for a night patrol.

"'How are you doing, boss?' Jomo, the cabdriver, knew him.

"'He's one of my regulars,' he said.

"He told me he was already tired for the night. Not only that, but he was sick and tired with his job.

"'I don't think I shall be staying in the service for a long time. Perhaps two years will be okay. I am getting job fatigue and facing all this occupational hazard,' he crossly said.

The officer couldn't recognize Lady Dynamite even though they'd met two years ago when the slick investigator enquired from him to give her direction to the metro police boss's office. Wearing beautiful twisters, killer eyelashes, and glamorous make-up, it was hard for him to make her out. The police constable would soon strike acquaintance with her.

Ghanatta (her boyfriend), sat coolly at the front as though he wasn't listening in. Woe betides this lanky guy if he tried to cause any harm to the apple of his eye. He would pounce on him like a hungry leopard.

"Nowadays, it is easier to make friends even in taxis than in neighborhoods. In fact, socialization is gradually drifting into the woods, while narcissism is coming home to roost. But lately, the almighty social media has taken cyber friendship to another level.

"Perhaps I could stumble on another lead. Sometimes, good things fall into right place when you least expect them. Detective work thrives on attentiveness, out of the ordinary, unusualness, curiosity, asking lead-on questions—can't list them all here.

Playing the devil's advocate is a journalist's or detective's trusted weapon.

"'Why do you want to quit your job so soon?' I asked him.

"'Well, I believe you know how the public views the police service. Our respect and integrity seem to be wavering, probably dead now,' he said amid laughter. "'And often times, when you tell someone that you're a police officer, you get this wry look as if you'd committed a heinous crime.

"'But somehow I think the public have cause to be angry and question our morale standing in society. They've seen officers in uniform take bribes from Trotro and taxi drivers for obvious traffic offenses and let them go scot-free. Even though I haven't been long in the service, I have seen a lot of rotten stuff. Some of which are as gross as the cesspool. You may perhaps be wondering, where is this guy coming from?

"'Fact is, not all police officers are corrupt as the general public perceives us. Nonetheless, there are a bunch of bad nuts among us who have tried hard to drag our reputation into the sludge,' the young officer submitted.

"While I listened to him lecture and ran his mouth, I thought he might have something worth pursuing in the near future, particularly in the infamous murder.

"'Sir, what would you say is the worse police menace or one thing that had dented the image of the law enforcement agency over the last decade or two?'

"'Oh, that's an excellent question. Even though I am young, I think if you had done a survey or Voss Pop on the streets of Kumasi today, you might have discovered that no case rivals that of the disappearance of the royal Barima which occurred nearly three decades ago. The Infamous Murder as the assassination of Barima Yiadom came to be called.'

"'Oh, yeah. Why?' I asked him again.

"The officer laughed mockingly.

"'When a whole docket of a slain royal vanishes into thin air, it tells you that the state has run into a ditch,' he noted.

"'Hmm…I never knew that was how things got to. So what are the police doing about it?'

"'Oh, my sister, I told you the whole case is dead now.'

"'But isn't it amazing that nearly thirty years on we're still talking about it?' Dynamite queried.

"'It is really amazing,' the officer replied. "'However, deaths like these, especially the royal who wielded so much influence and wealth in the kingdom, can't just go away. Surely it's been declared a cold case at the police end but not so amongst the populace and the loved ones.'

The officer had indicated to Lady Dynamite that he was coming off at Sofoline, a popular taxi rank. And from his perched corner, the slick lady observed, the Constable was stealing glances.

"He'd been eyeing me all this while," Dynamite revealed. "So, I knew what was to follow."

"'What's your name, lady, if you don't mind?' he asked me gently.

"'My name is Akua Agyeiwa.'

"'Hey, Agyeiwa, kodie ahoofe.' (You are beautiful,)

"'Thanks for the compliments, sir.' And we exchanged telephone numbers."

❉

"His father was once a police commissioner who worked with the then police chief. And the chief's youngest son, who is also a friend had his finger on something, he told me. I have the feeling that something shady is going on and he might have direct links with the suspects of the heir's assassination. But beyond that, I think what I got from the cab driver, Jomo, earlier would add more bite to the meat."

"Well, I hope this doesn't turn out to be one of the Apocryphas," intimated Captain Crow.

"Yeah, I hope not," Dynamite said.

Meanwhile, in some parts of Kumasi the faucet had gone bust; the most affected areas included the CID and BNI offices. The country's number one water provider, Ghana Water Company (gwC), had earlier issued a statement apologizing to its numerous customers for any inconveniency caused. It added that the company's experts would be sent to the affected areas to rectify the technical problem.

However, behind this glitch were Captain Crow and Lady Dynamite. The two had arranged with the technical team of the utility company to cut water supply to these areas, particularly, the offices of the police chief to enable them install the communication gadgets.

The police chief was due for an emergency meeting on Wednesday between 2:00–3:00 p.m., an insider told the Big Eye a period deemed appropriate to carry out the supposedly clandestine activity.

Dressed in GwC outfits Captain Crow and Lady Dynamite together with a staff from the water company stormed the chief's office, put the water back on, and more importantly, had his office bugged.

As fate would have it, his last meeting with Dynamite (who had posed as a marketing executive) didn't finish well, and so he'd asked her to meet him again at Boomerang Club. However, a few minutes later the police chief suggested they go to his office.

"I don't think we're safe here," he told Dynamite. "I need to protect you as an intern so that you won't get fired by your boss. I also need to protect my job and integrity as well. Is that okay with you?"

"Well, sounds good to me," Dynamite replied.

Apparently, the change of venue was much to her advantage. Unbeknown to the police boss that his entire office had been bugged and also his date was being chaperoned by two brawny detectives. At about 9:00 p.m. while they're about wrapping up their meeting, someone called him (Mr. Akamenko). It was none other than Tweneboa Kodua, the chief butler.

He had called to inform the police chief that the two suspects at Agyewodin were in deep trouble.

After the telephone call, Mr. Akamenko turned back to Dynamite, forced a smile, and apologized for the interruption. "That was one of my commanders," he told her.

His demeanor had suddenly changed. The message had not only ruined the night but ruffled the feathers of the police chief.

Elsewhere at Sowoboduam, the clock ticked toward the dying embers of the epic marathon, it had become increasingly clear that the hard works expended by Sundiatta and Marijata in the rugged mountainous region was yielding good fruits.

Agya Koo Nimo, their bonafide host had in the long run opened the Pandora box wide. The septuagenarian had become their closest friend.

And incredibly, the unpolished detective work of this man would gradually lead the duo to the end of their puzzle. What remained furtive though, was the fact that for all this years, their host absolutely had no clue whatsoever that his guests were detectives.

He treated the investigators as his children and was always at hand to assist them when needed be.

Interestingly, the gurus had literally pulled all the teeth in his mouth. There was certainly none left to help him bite anymore as he had been compelled to divulge all the information he'd kept secret for nearly thirty years.

But would the good Samaritan continue to help them find two of the fugitives, who he claimed still lived at Agyewodin?

They had to press harder. Be tactful and discreet in their day-to-day activities.

Though Yaw Boye was famously known for his palm wine tapping business in this small village, it was unbeknown to many that he was a killer and number one cannabis grower in this dense forest region.

His partner in crime, Kwaku Kaku, though a carpenter, had nothing to show for his profession. Known to many as notorious and mean, he spent his life scamming folks in Agyewodin. He often took their monies for promised jobs but never got them done.

The two musketeers had over the years proven evasive to the security officers but it certainly appeared they had reached the end of their wits.

�֍

When Agya Koo Nimo donned his most-liked football shirt, the detectives gifted him one evening, he was like a tiger handed with a red meat. He called Sundiatta and Marijata to share a gourd full of palm wine with them. Drank to a stupor the old man began to spill the beans.

"Trust me," he said. Head tilted over neck backward: "Nobody in this village is privy to this murderous attack. I'm talking about the slain of the heir apparent to the Ashanti Golden Stool. I have kept mute over it all these years, and sometimes, I ask myself whether I was doing society any good, thus keeping the names of these creepy folks in my head. And the killers seem to be going about thinking nobody knew/know what happened that night.

"That dark night…That night when the northern star and the galaxy of stars refused to lighten up the atmosphere. The heavens looked gloomy, and the moon appeared depressed. That night the rogues woke River Adjingo from his deep sleep, and Mother Earth was breathless. But one could still hear the sound of the crickets and the little insects. That was the night the mosquitoes got up from their ghettos and caused mayhem.

"Covertly, they'd executed their wicked plot thinking no man had seen them, but from a distance God was watching. Nothing under the sun can go uncovered, my sons. I am going to disclose to you today who they are."

And on the spur of moment Agya Nimo dropped the bombshell.

"My nephew, Yaw Boye, and Kwaku Kaku did that heinous crime.

"Perhaps, they thought their evil deeds would remain unexposed. From my own eyes in this village, I have seen ten or more detectives visit here but their activities came to zilch. For some reason, they never arrested anybody."

Cunningly, Sundiatta had managed to pick up other valuable exhibits from one of the suspects. They included a wellington boot and a cowboy hat of the slain royal, which he had on, on the day of his execution. The said items had been with Kaku for all these years.

According to folks here, he rarely wears them because he considers them as relic.

Kaku was indebted to Sundiatta. He had failed to do his work for him, fixing a table chair. When Sundiatta approached him (Kaku) one sunny day for his chair already paid for but still not done, it came down to this:

"You pay me today, or I seize all your work tools."

He decided on something.

"How about accepting these items?" Kaku suggested to him. "I have nothing, and I don't want to lose my tools, so you may keep these. As soon as I get money, I will pay you back and collect them."

"Fine. That's well with me," said Sundiatta.

The team had reached the endpoint of the operation. They had one credible witness in the name of Agya Koo Nimo. Adwoa Sika, the former girlfriend of Sundiatta had declined to take the witness stand after their whirlwind courtship fell on the rocks. That notwithstanding, she could be subpoenaed by the courts of the land should it become necessary.

The investigators also had in their custody two items believed to be the belongings of the heir. These can be used as exhibit during court proceedings. Above all, the startling tape-recorded voices lent more credence to the almost five year's painstaking operation. Against this backdrop, all was set for the final onslaught.

On Monday morning, June 15, a police contingent numbering twenty from Accra, stormed the Agyewodin village and her awe-stricken inhabitants. Every exit doors to and from the town were carefully sealed, made it even hard for tiny ants to maneuver escape. Agyewodin's heart thumbed aggressively. Her people haven't witnessed a scene like this before. It was an overwhelming experience!

Aided by detectives Sundiatta and Marijata, the police arrested the two scoundrels. Handcuffed amid taut security, the suspects led the police to the crime scene where they exhumed the mortal remains of Barima Adom Yiadom from the river bed. *C'est termine.* It is finished!

The camouflaged hound van was on its way back to Accra.

Lead detective, Akwasi Frimpong-Adeapena, who accompanied the recovery party described the act as 'barbaric' and 'inhumane.'

"Never in the history of this kingdom have we seen this cruelty act," he told journalists.

Elsewhere in Kumasi the unstoppable Dynamite and Captain Crow had led another police team to swoop the third suspect, Metropolitan Police Chief Kofi Babone Akamenko.

Alas, the momentous manhunt that snowballed for nearly five years had successfully led to the capture of Yaw Boye, Kwaku Kaku, and the police chief Kofi Akamenko. They were arraigned before the court.

All three had initially pleaded not guilty to the charge of intent to kill and killing the heir.

But as the high court judge, His Lordship Kofi Diawuo, began to set up the jury for the trial, defense lawyer, Anokye Fawomanyor, prayed the eminent court that his clients had rescinded their decision from not guilty to guilty.

He accordingly asked for clemency, urging the judge to tamper justice with mercy because of the plea bargain.

In the wake of this development, Mr. Diawuo had to summarily convict and commute a deservedly death sentence of the three to life imprisonment. The sentencing of the trio probably marked the end of nearly three decades of disappointment, misery, and laxity.

But, the grandmaster, Tweneboa Kodua, had gone into hiding several weeks prior to the arrest of his accomplices. He was just clutching onto a thin line; the Walatu-Walasa guys were closing in on him.

Like Osama bin Laden, he had been living in caves, valleys, and mountains from Okukuseku, Brahabebome, and Susubiribi to Fankyeneko villages.

Certainly, he had reached his wit's end. The telescopic eyes of the spy team had picked up the master chameleon from his hideout. It was an April Fools' Day, 1972, and many in the kingdom who heard the news about the death of Tweneboa Kodua expressed grave disbelief.

Some thought it was a prank, and others felt it was long overdue. Agyeman Badu, a *trotro* (commercial bus) driver, told passengers on his bus, "Not until I see the body of this terrible terror, I am not going to believe this story."

But before the sun went down, the entire empire had accepted what originally appeared as a hoax to be a veritable story. Kodua had long served with the *Abrafo* group which operated like a secret society. And he proudly commandeered it until he became the chief butler at the palace.

The notorious man reputedly known for his hocus-pocus disposition had at long last succumbed to pressure.

Ayera Mekodada, the Twi word or phrase for disappearance was Kodua's catch phrase. Indeed, like a mythical camouflaged creature, the executioner as myth had it, could peter out in thin air, and either mutated as a bird or a cockroach in a flicker of an eye whenever he sensed danger.

Invoking *Ayera,* or touching a wall did the whole trick. And even though he professed to be a Catholic, often seeing with huge silver crucifix dangling around his neck, he never lived as one.

The man with owl eyes large and forward-facing; perhaps it was this wide range of binocular vision that hypnotized many and turned their heads as pepperoni. All he had to do was to pinch his waist-wrapped talisman like a five-star general's epaulette fastened to his shoulder, and invoked the name of the legendary Kanka Nyame of neighboring Guinea-Conakry.

Whiles it was strongly believed among many that Kodua obtained his mystic powers from Kanka Nyame in Conakry, another myth held that he got his magic from the *kamajors* (Mende word for local hunter) in Sierra Leone.

He babbled strange words like "nsua ben" meaning which clan you belong to. The phrase should rather be "abusua ben" and not "nsua ben" as he was alleged to have asked victims during his nocturnal activities. Evidently, because they had no knowledge as to what that meant, they ended up being killed.

At the peak of his mystical prowess, the mention of his name alone sent shivers down the spine of many folks in Kumasi and its environs. In fact, the butler was an avowed foe of conventional clemency and had over three decades cast his teeth as chief executioner (*Adumhene*).

One humid evening, it is believed, during the Hamattan season, Kodua made a shocking revelation to his ten year-old boy. He told the little boy he had no remorse for the killings of the scores of folks who fell on his double-edged sword.

"I was trained to do that, and I did it scrupulously," he justified his inimical actions.

"I know it piques one's mind to question why I expended my time on this obnoxious act, but I have no explanation to offer except to put it bluntly as I told you.

"Not a gunshot, not a machete or sword, and absolutely no assault weapon whatsoever formed against me can send me to the grave," the pugnacious character boasted.

How quickly he forgot the admonition Malam Tanko gave him when he consulted the oracle for juju decades back. "You should strictly adhere to the rules of the game," the spiritual man told Kodua. "I have dos and don'ts. Therefore you shouldn't use the power given you to terrorize innocent folks except enemies. If you flout these simple rules the gods of the land will deal drastically with you. And you cannot blame the gods...."In fact," he stressed, "transgressors had in all cases been plagued by bad omen or struck by death." Unbelievably, on the eve of his demise, he (Kodua) had had a premonition that the end was nigh, but like an inescapable shadow, he couldn't disappear, neither was he able to avert the imminent doom. The obvious was as visible as the great Pyramids of Egypt.

His avaricious dark-painted blood gourd had been filled to the brim. And that moment he dreaded most had fast-paced him. The Big Eye investigators had stormed his backyard, and just by a nick of time, he would take cover at the belly of his residence.

"Come down with me," he told his son peeping through the burglar-proof glass window upstairs, as he ran helter-skelter.

"Dad, where are you running to?" his son asked him.

But he wouldn't respond.

In the meantime, the Indomitable, the Dynamite, the Snoopy Marijata, and the Foxy Sundiatta had made their way deep into the affluent suburb about three blocks across the west end of Manhyia where they had been taken recognizance operation at the vicinity. Surreptitiously, they zoomed in on the chief assassin's house at No. TF/88, cordoned the entire residence and lay siege. The wooded fortified marbled-house sitting on a four hundred acre land had a huge steel gate at its frontage.

The detectives rang the outer gate bell to announce their presence. Nobody would answer. But the creepy images inside the building could not sneak the prying lenses of the Big Eye team.

A young boy, believed to be in his early teens, had been spotted. However, not their importunate knocks on the door would cause any of the household members to come out to see who was at the forecourt of their property. A videographer and a driver were still in the Pathfinder cross-country vehicle outside the home, filming the unfolding episode.

The young boy had seen the men outside from the blind window upstairs and ran back into his father's bedroom to tell him. Having validated the truth from the boys' room, he thought of plan B.

"Shhhhhhhh!" Forefinger tightly on his lips, he quickly ran to the vault with his son to duck into a cluttered dark room.

"What?" his son asked him.

"They're investigators, looking for me."

"Why are they looking for you?"

"Keep quiet son, you're irritating me"

"But I need to know why they are looking for you," the boy insisted. You seem to be very grumpy and jittery today. Why do you care about someone pursuing you? I thought you said you're invisible and invincible. After all, you can disappear in a jiffy. Or you no longer trust your god, Kanka Nyame?"

Momentarily, his countenance had changed, flamed with anger. He looked at his son pensively and handed him a pistol.

"Shoot me," he grunted.

Suffice to say that in such crucial moments; even a private soldier is worth more than a brigadier particularly, when the latter loses his insignia for gross misconduct. For inasmuch as the lilies are synonymous with the valleys, so was the skullduggery Kodua to his talisman. He'd pinned his whole hope in this eerie object and would now realize that salvation doesn't come from objects made by the hands of men. And in a hard way, he learned that it was better to pursue than to be pursued.

However, Kodua would put up his last spirited fight. From the second floor of his house, he had unleashed barrage of gunshots on his pursuers. Though he missed his target, he succeeded in damaging the windscreen of the detectives' vehicle.

The mystic man reloaded his action pump-gun and launched another ferocious attack— this time wounding the cameraman. Even though the detectives had pistols, Captain Crow had asked them not to fight back. Instead they took cover.

Incredibly, Kodua had run out of time and bullets to continue the onslaught. And realizing that the die was cast, he asked his son to kill him.

"Shoot me, I mean shoot me now," he ordered his son again.

"No, no, Dad I can't do this".

He threw the pistol back at his father. Luckily, the revolver didn't discharge its loads; amid tears, the young boy ran upstairs. The butler dashed into one of the rooms at the basement which had light and looked himself closely in a mirror. And while there he engaged himself in an internal monologue.

"Do I deserve to die?" he asked the man in the mirror.

"Why not. I paid a ransom for an innocent soul to be killed," he shot back quickly.

"And not only that, I ensured none of his relations especially from his mother's line ever assumed this enviable throne. I hated Barima. I hated his name and fame. His name connoted bravery, grace, and multitude. I hated him because he was going to be the next king of this great empire. I ensured he never lived to see his dream fulfilled. I got it shattered and battered.

"Worst of it all, I failed to think outside the box. Instead, I resorted to backstabbing, backbiting, blackmailing, bootlicking, and mudslinging. But I pray the good Lord will forgive me for my hands are bloodied, my mind is botched, and my conscience is notched. My soul is troubled by the day. I need redemption, I suppose."

After that intense soliloquizing, which probably lasted three minutes, Kodua hurried back into the confined dark room which had no window and no light. That room in the crypt accommodated his idol, Kanka Nyame and other primitive artifacts—charms and amulet including human skulls that he inherited from his father Adum Mensa, who was another dreadful executioner. His father's maternal uncle was a renowned magician, a sorcerer, the locals said. His grandmother was a reputed witch and compulsive thief. And his paternal father was a hardcore wizard—a vampire!

He bowed before his god in curtsy to see if redemption would come. But that was a far cry from hope. Hope in oblivion, the villain would settle on one ominous choice. And like a snapshot, he drilled two deadly bronze pellets into his cocky coconut. He keeled over his paunch and prowled in his own puddle of blood.

They say those who plow iniquity and sow wickedness reap the same thing. Finally, the cheetah had outrun his peer—the tiger.

But could hatred alone have driven Kodua to kill Barima?

Of course no. The butler had sold his timber concession at Sowoboduam to the future Ashanti king. The heir had paid him fully, but greedy as he was, Kodua still wanted to his cake and eat it, too. And he indeed got to eat it!

❁

In the thrall, his son had called 191 for police assistance. They'd earlier fabricated a plot before his final demise. A lie, a crooked lie must be told. The only star witness in the crypt was the butler's own son, Yaw Addo.

"Captain Crow fired two 'stupid' shots," he would tell the police.

"Hello, sir, armed robbers are attacking us," he said. His right hand clasped to the landline phone, he continued, "they're at our residence trying to break in. Oh no, they just broke into the house. One of them shot my father."

"Did you say, they just broke into the house and shot and killed your father?"

"Yes, sir."

"How many times did the person shoot at him?"

"I heard two shots, sir."

"How's your father doing?"

"He is dead. Oh, he's dead!" he cried.

"Are the armed robbers still in the house, and where are you?"

"They're still here, but I've taken cover under one of the beds."

"All right stay calm. We'll be there pretty soon."

Outside the courtyard, Captain Crow and his team had also heard the gunshots, wondering what was going on there. The worst was their fear, so they called the Rapid Response Force

(RRF), also known as the Panther, a special police force trained to deal with precarious situations.

Within a twinkling of an eye fifteen armed policemen arrived. Guns drawn, they stomped the ground as though they're combating a gang of armed robbers.

"Hands up," the police ordered. Adding, "You guys will be summarily executed if you refuse to comply," they told Captain Crow and his investigators.

Another asked them to get on the ground faces down.

"Don't move," he yelled, while a burly sergeant held them down with his combat boot.

"You're armed robbers, so you are under arrest."

It's appallingly unforgivable when men in uniform do not understand any language except brutish force. In a kind of military drill style, Captain Crow and his team had been wrestled to the ground and accused of being armed robbers.

The police wouldn't even look at the IDs produced by the investigators. The officials remained adamant insisting, "We're on a special mission and under strict orders."

The quartet—Captain Crow, Sundiatta, Marijata and Lady Dynamite, including the videographer, didn't resist the arrest. They were immediately hauled into a waiting police van handcuffed and whisked to Adum Police Station; where they would be remanded.

Chapter 15

After two weeks remand in an unspeakable cell with one toilet facility used by fifteen inmates chocked-full in a single-windowless room, hell is perhaps the only place that could surpass Firetown cell. The heat, the sweat and the smell were nothing but unpleasant!

Its toilet bucket had been filed to the ridge and the spill-over was just sickening.

The disgusting load only got emptied once in a full blue moon; thereby breeding mosquitoes, cockroaches and mice in the vicinity. Maggots and thousands of flies were seeing each day buzzing around like airplanes.

Nearly a decade later two of the detectives plus the maverick's old compatriot would be brought back to Firetown's main maximum prison.

There was something spooky about Ogyakrom prison—its concrete-barbed wire tall wall overlooked a half-century old wooded cemetery, where it was said inmates who had the chance to escape later committed suicide.

Behind the graveyard was a mangrove swamp (which covered roughly ten miles of the earth surface) populated by reptiles and crocodiles and a little beyond that was a big river with a breadth of about three-and-a half miles.

Already sporting bedbugs' bites, looking untidy, frowzy hair probably with no bath for the two whole weeks Captain Crow and his colleagues dreamt for the worse if providence didn't show up early enough. They had been denied the right to an attorney for over a week but for the prison Chaplain who happened to visit the cells with a lawyer friend.

"He only visits the cells once in a leap year....We were just lucky," Captain Crow said; referring to the prison Chaplain.

Finally the opportune time came and the investigators were hauled before the infamous Bantama Magistrate Court. That day would be known as Black Friday. And the man who had long exhausted his time in seeking justice for many across the nation would himself be denied justice.

Earlier in the day, a prison officer named Wallace who stopped by that drab morning to check on the inmates had cunningly asked Captain Crow "What does justice mean to you and your comrades?"

This followed the maverick's assertion that their human and constitutional rights as citizens had been trampled upon.

'To me justice means the execution of fairness and equal rights. And by that whoever is executing justice must be conscious of the fact that their actions must be upright and sincere," Captain Crow told him.

He went on, "I'm aware of capital punishment. I'm aware of life imprisonment and I'm also aware of tortures and abuse that are often meted out to offenders in our prisons and cells. I'm a victim myself.

But justice goes beyond that mundane definition—killing, jailing, torturing, abusing etc. Captain Crow expatiated. It means punishment, it means compensation, and it means restitution and it means reconciliation. Sometimes we need to heal the old wounds and live together as one people, one nation with one destiny. Life is too short but we often don't realize that; because we have uploaded unto our small and big heads (SBH) power and greed."

Still looking into the eyeballs of the guard squarely Captain Crow closed his dialogue by drawing the officer's attention to the fact that though he and his comrades were innocent, they had their rights hacked and found themselves caged.

"Here we are Mr. Wallace," he pointed out, "we didn't commit murder, and we haven't committed any crime, but we are being afflicted with pain and torture.

"Is that justice?" he asked the officer.

✄

The scene at the Prempeh High Street on that overcast Monday morning, February 4, was just pensive and emotional as the Unflappable Seventeen led a million march to the grounds of the Old Courthouse overlooking the Bantama colonial housing units.

Their demand, among other things, was seeking justice for their idol and friends who had been arrested, maltreated, and wrongfully accused of a crime they didn't commit.

Though the idea seemed reasonable, it was a far cry.

Indeed, this magistrate court was notoriously known for jailing and ruining people's lives, convicting and handing down death sentences. Over the decades, it had convicted many folks for crimes they never committed. Regardless of their innocence, the authorities still put them behind the iron bars.

Given this condition, it followed that concern citizens like that morning's gathering had cause to fear. That fear, undoubtedly, drove them in droves to the streets and alleys of the Garden City.

The enraged crowd had demanded the court to give their friends a fair trial and just deal. And as the morning warmed up, the jeers, boos, and hoots reached tempo level. It appeared no one could deescalate the tension, which had fueled the surge of the mob by each minute—chanting slogans, singing war songs, waving red scuffs, and handkerchiefs. On top of that, banners brandished and placards screamed with bold captions:

> Give us Crow and let us go. Don't spoil our appetite.
> Stop the "Kangaroo Tactics."

Sooner than expected, the bullion van that carried the detectives showed up with their feet shackled and hands cuffed, hemmed-in and heavily guarded by six bespectacled security men. The mob went wild, the jeers peaked, and the guards would not stay there a minute. They whisked them into the packed courtroom. Faith and fate would interplay their game!

Trial Judge Kwadwo Obinim had taken his seat as he leafed through the docket (stack of documents) before him. In the meantime, the prosecuting team had lined up their men. And leading the defense council was lawyer Odartey Wellington, flanked by his able lieutenants Kwame Akufo, Yaw Bio, and Adwoa Bour.

It was time for hostilities to begin amid heckling and shouts of objection, "My Lord."

Lawyer Wellington who took the stand first told the court that on January 18, his clients led by Captain Crow as part of their routine work had discovered the hideout of the deceased Tweneboa Kodua.

Therefore, the indomitable, the Dynamite, the Snoopy Marijata and the Foxy Sundiata made their way deep into the residence of the late palace Chief Butler about three blocks across the West End of Manhyia. Whiles there his clients had been taken recognizance operation at the vicinity, he submitted.

Surreptitiously they zoomed in on the Chief assassin's house No. TF/88 cordoned the entire residence and laid siege. He said the wooded fortified marbled-house sitting on a 400-acre land had a huge steel gate at its frontage.

The detectives rang the outer gate bell to announce their presence. But nobody would answer. In the meantime my Lord, he told the court my clients spotted some creepy images inside the building with the aid of a surveillance camera.

My Lord, Mr. Wellington stressed those strange images could not sneak the prying lenses of the *BIG EYE* team. The camera had picked up a young boy believed to be in his early teens and the deceased.

With this new development my clients continued to buzz the deceased's door bell. However, none of their importunate knocks on the door would cause any of the household members to come out to see who was at the forecourt of their property.

At this time, my Lord, the videographer and the investigators' driver were still in the Pathfinder cross-country vehicle outside the home, filming the unfolding episode.

Your Lordship, whiles my clients remained outside the courtyard expecting any of the residents in the compound to answer the door, they came under attack. From inside the building, Kodua had launched an unanticipated attack on them. In the process, the videographer sustained injuries, though not life-threatening. The pathfinder the vehicle used in the operation had its windscreen shattered.

Frankly, my clients could have been dead if they hadn't acted swiftly to take cover in the ensuing attack.

My Lord, while Captain Crow and his team ducked low behind the deceased's concrete wall, they heard the supposed gunshots that killed Tweneboa Kodua.

And confused by the turn of events they wondered.

"What's going on there?" my client (Captain Crow) enquired. He said he feared for the worst. And he immediately called the Rapid Response Force (RRF) also known as the Panther- a special police force trained to deal with precarious situations.

In less than 20 minutes my clients recalled 15 armed-policemen arrived. Guns drawn they stomped the ground, yelling and swearing. The conduct of the police (RRF) or the law enforcement agents according to my clients, to say the least was barbaric and uncalled foe.

"Hands up," the police ordered them. Threatening they would all be dead if they move an inch.

"You guys will be summarily executed if you refuse to comply," they told Captain Crow and his investigators.

"My Lord, do suspects get precipitous execution when no courts in the land have found them guilty or culpable of committing the said crime?"

After a well-articulated submission to the hearing of the court, Mr. Wellington asked the plaintiff lawyer.

"Can a man's gun kill a victim when evidence had proven beyond all reasonable doubt that the ammunition in the said gun remains intact? I put it to you Mr. Kofi Gyato Diabene."

The prosecuting lawyer had time to speak, but he wouldn't answer the substantive question. Instead, he turned to the star witness of the defense council and asked if he knew about the killing of Tweneboa Kodua. His statement attracted objection from defense aisle, stressing that it wasn't time for cross examination.

There ensued hefty verbal blows with each side sustaining severe bruises and the trial judge would later bring proceedings to a close. "The next court sitting will be on February 11," he told the court. "That's a week from today."

If the tension in the courtroom at the preliminary stage presupposed what was to come the weeks ahead, the anxiety outside its courtyard surpassed it. The irate crowd went home without their icons and loved ones. But worse of it all, some of the protesters had their freedoms hijacked and thrown into jail.

On Monday, February 11, both the defense and prosecution teams had marshaled their resources—facts, witnesses, and other necessary exhibits that might be useful in the trial proceedings. The defense team would submit that evidence given by its counterpart cannot be used against its clients as the killers of the supposed strange figure Tweneboah Kodua.

Secondly, they would pray the court that the time line as given by the prosecuting team doesn't match with the time the chief butler was killed, stressing evidence submitted clearly show that the accused or suspects were outside the building when the gunshots that purportedly killed the mystic man was heard.

Thirdly, the defense counsel would submit that the video recording points to the fact that the suspects never got inside the Butler's home. In line with this existential and circumstantial evidence, they would argue that the accused were innocent and did not kill the chief butler.

That is to say they (the accused) can't be held reliable for the crime preferred against them. The defense council would again try to convince the fourteen-member empanelled jury that circumstantial evidence provided by the prosecuting team was bogus and flawed at birth.

"Your Lordship," said Mr. Wellington. "My clients are law-abiding citizens with good standing in our community and beyond. They're persons of international repute, good career, good homes, own companies, and above all have good track record not only in this city but the world at large."

In sharp contrast, lead prosecutor Kofi Gyato Diabene maintained that all facts surrounding the murder showed that defense's clients committed an atrocious crime and must therefore be subjected to capital punishment or face life sentence.

Mr. Diabene latched onto one more deadly blow, showing graphic pictures of Tweneboa Kodua. The emotive pictures had aroused sad feelings. Women in the court room began to show emotions. While others decided to walk out of the place because they couldn't watch the bloody wounds in the face of the villain.

"My Lord," lawyer Diabene cried out. "This is what these men have done. They have murdered a father, an uncle, and a bread winner of a family. And I crave your majesty's indulgence to hide them because they're a high risk to society.

"Captain Crow and his so-called investigators have committed a heinous crime," he reiterated. "They must therefore pay the price by either to face death penalty or life sentence."

Mr. Diabene's misguided statement attracted spiky rebuttal from the defense panel.

"Objection," said Mr. Wellington aflame with anger. "That's ridiculous to say and incite the jury to do your whims and caprices. To suggest that my clients should face capital punishment is just baloney. This is unspeakable, unheard of, and unjust. I think this honorable court should be given the latitude to adjudicate its own legal proceedings rather than someone telling her what to do. You should be ashamed with this uncharitable comment. Your emotive use of language, appealing to pity and compassion is calculated to manipulate the clear conscience of the judge."

But I strongly believe His Lordship and this honest court would not allow themselves to be swayed by these spiteful and unkind comments to give judgment in your favor."

And let me tell you something my learned friend, before I retire to my seat:

Your deliberate attempt to denigrate the high status of my clients is tantamount to slander and injurious to their character."

"Who do you think you are?"

The atmosphere at the courtroom had changed and one could feel and touch the pulsating presence of tension. As expected the team on the opposite aisle would shoot back spontaneously.

The lead prosecutor Mr. Diabene, who already had his finger on the trigger, however, wouldn't leave the courtroom without throwing his last jab before the curtains were brought down. Once again, both teams left amid bruises with no eye contacts, depicting the unfriendliness of the game.

❖

For weeks, perhaps months, Mr. Kofi Diabene had spent time and resources coaching his star witness, Yaw Addo, the son of the deceased man. And the well-choreographed act would somehow tilt the balance to their side, as he harped on pity, sorrow, and melancholy to win the hearts and minds of the gallery.

"Where were you when the thugs broke into your father's bedroom?" Mr. Diabene asked his client.

"I was sleeping, but it was a big *bang* that caused me to wake up."

"How many people did you see?'

"They were three…oh…four?"

"Did you mean four?"

Yes, there were four."

"What were they carrying or holding in their hands?"

"They were holding guns and crowbars."

"Do you believe they used the crowbars to break into the house?"

"I think so."

"What happened then?"

"They yelled out at him, cursed, and called him all sorts of names. He cried and begged them not to kill him, but they wouldn't budge, kicking and shoving him around like musical chairs."

"At what point did they attack your father?"

"It was when I stepped out from my room. I sensed danger. I wanted to remain in my room. But upon second thought, I felt I must come out, in the hope that they might stop their planned action."

"And what happened?"

"Without any provocation, one of them shot my father twice, and he keeled over."

"Would you be able to identify the one who shot him?"

"Yes…it is the man in the far right," he said, pointing at Captain Crow.

"All right, I'm done."

Meanwhile, outside the courtyard, there had been a crack down and eight members of the Unflappable Seventeen were rounded up by the police. Kofi Ogidigidi, Bosommuru Apontua, Oyeeman Konfanko, Akua kru Patapaa, Adwoa Bene, Ghanatta Kwabena Sokoto, Ogyampatrudu, and Cantankerous Kantanka Kakabo were now in police grips. The comrades would not be trialed but thrown into jail summarily.

The Big Eye squad's attorneys' efforts to get bail for them during detention even fell through the cracks—an indication that the worse was imminent.

After a two-week cliffhanger trial, a verdict was reached. The detectives had been charged with manslaughter which carried maximum sentence of forty-five years. Individually, the trial judge handed Captain Crow fifteen years, and ten years apiece for his supposed accomplices. Defense lawyers described the judgment as a "stolen verdict."

The armored van that waited at the precincts of the court hurriedly conveyed his new passengers to Apollonia, the state's most dreaded prison.

Inconspicuous was the massive protest that besieged the court during its pretrial. The crackdown was brutal as many had their limbs broken, while others had been put behind bars. They had been inhibited by the strong gun-toting police presence.

In his post-verdict press briefing, lead defense lawyer, Odartey Wellington, said his clients had not been given a fair trial.

"My clients are innocent, they are not thugs. They're not murderers. Their hands are clean. They've only been framed up and railroaded. I would fight tooth and nail to get to the bottom of the miscarriage justice."

Looking drawn out, necktie slackened to catch some breath after a lost battle, the seasoned lawyer believed there were still some knotty issues regarding the shooting of the palace police.

"This verdict raises a lot of questions," he told a group of paparazzi brandishing microphones.

"All evidential proof points to one unanswered question," stressed Mr. Wellington.

"How did Captain Crow's so-called two fired shots from behind ended up on the forehead of the deceased?"

"I clearly have no clue, and to have the state judge been swayed or perhaps bribed to give such ruling is absolutely ridiculous. But I'm certainly not giving up on my clients. I will continue to fight till justice prevails," he gave the assurance.

Paradoxically, the magazine in Captain Crow's gun was full, a check revealed he hadn't fired for the past seventy-two hours; nonetheless, he would still be found guilty for the killing of the butler.

Opinions on the sentence, however, varied among personnel in the fourth estate of the realm. The pro-government newspapers and spin-doctors hailed the jury's ruling. They welcomed the verdict as justice served. Captain Crow was caricatured in most of the government-sponsored tabloids.

The *Daily Punch* carried a banner headline, "Butler's Killers Jailed for Life."

"Crow the Liar Killer" was the *National Independent's* front page, while the *Investigator*, a bi-weekly, took the investigators' lawyer, Odartey Wellington, to the cleaners, "Killers' Lawyer Is A Liar."

Viewpoints by the Ghana Journalists Association (GJA) and many private radio stations as well as newspaper organizations were nothing but condemnation. They damned the outcome, calling it botched and atrocious.

Ten years on, defense lawyers continued their frantic search for justice; however, appeal after appeal yielded no positive results. There were even assassination attempts on Mr. Wellington. He had been warned not to pursue the case, but he pursued it anyway. His attackers had mistakenly murdered one of the prosecutor's lawyers. "We thought he was Mr. Wellington," one of the thugs revealed.

❁

Elsewhere, in Akuse and James Fort prisons, where some of the comrades had been doing hard time for merely exercising their civil rights duties, they had yet been dealt with a more callous blow. Day-in and day-out, as later chronicled by the Human Rights and Abuse Office, the inmates were subjected into torture and water boarding.

Unfortunately, Kofi Ogidigidi, Akua Patapaa Kru, Kofi Kofanko, and Cantankerous Kantanka Kakabo, all members of the Unflappable Seventeen couldn't withstand the wanton police brutalities.

It all happened one Saturday morning. A drunken prison officer had turned his loaded gun on the innocent folks, killing two members of the group instantly. And the up-coming week would witness carnage.

As usual, inmates had been called to gird on their physical training pants and make it to the drill park. But in a short while, things would go haywire. The dark clouds would eclipse the fervent heavens, real men would weep like babies, and blood would blanket the face of Mother Earth.

A ward sergeant by name of Terror had madly descended on Kofanko. The ugly man with ugly looks in ugly uniform searched the eyes of the lanky closely, as though he owed him a cigarette. Terror looked at the inmate up and down, sizing him up.

"Your pants aren't looking good," he told him.

"What about it?" Kofanko asked the officer.

"You must be a fool to wear these pants. You must be a bush man from a bush family and a bush town." Terror told Kofanko.

At that juncture inmate understood something wasn't right. There must be something wrong with the officer's psyche. "This man is either suffering from paranoia, or he is psychopathic or schizophrenic," he imagined.

Kofanko didn't utter a word. He waited for the instructor.

Terror looked at him again strangely, something unpleasant was unfolding, but no one had a wind as to what was to come. He grabbed Kofanko by his neck and just a blink of an eye strangled him in the broad view of the people gathered in the mid-morning. Kofanko had been killed.

A fortnight earlier, giant Bosomuru Apontuah was killed in similar fashion, and so were the other heroes. "They have one simple agenda—to kill and destroy us, but I trust the good Lord will hide some of us under rock. We will stay to fight and live to die." Captain Crow said.

Indeed, the mid-morning sun had been tampered, the maverick had never seen such carnage before in his life. He lost his father through tragic death but this grotesque act in his naked eye begged the question. Hardly did a day walk by that the group didn't witness something bizarre.

Nonetheless, he took solace from the fact that his colleagues at Big Eye and the three other survivors of the Unflappable Seventeen had been released. It remained to be seen though, if the civil rights icon would be able to endure the daily vicious attacks.

Just two years shy of finishing his term in prison, the appellate court of the land ruled that the maverick's conviction on manslaughter was flawed and had to be released.

Chapter 16

Though the good news of Captain Crow's release had scaled over the prison walls and made its presence felt throughout the Ashanti kingdom, it would be similar to an April fool's Day. Far and near supporters of the civil rights activist stomped the streets of the capital and celebrated the news as firecrackers soared the atmosphere all night long ahead of his final homecoming.

Mr. George Padmore, an Appellate Court Judge in Kumasi who gave the ruling maintained that his decision to release the convict was informed by the evidence the defense team submitted: "Based on the evidence brought before this court by the lead defense lawyer Mr. Wellington and based on my own long practice as seasoned judge, I hereby declare that the prisoner's conviction on manslaughter is flawed and he must be released accordingly."

"I'm also on record to have declared here today Tuesday, December 11 that the convict who had been put in prison wrongfully for over a decade in hard labor, ill-treatment and faced injustice must be compensated. He has suffered unduly for a crime he didn't commit. Therefore, this is to appease him for the time served and also to console and empathize with the loved ones as well as his family."

Finally, I would like to commend lead attorney Mr. Wellington for a good job done, having fought determinedly to defend your client and more importantly to ensure that justice is executed without fear or favor."

Meanwhile, the state Attorney General (AG) had refused to go public. He had also declined a Q&A interview with one of the nation's authoritative newspapers, "no comment," he told *The Firepower.*"

The AG's posture, according to the newspaper could pour cold water on the appellate judge's most-welcomed verdict in future, the paper speculated.

Elsewhere in the maverick's magnificent home, Confetti dropped from atop like flakes. While the drinks filled the crystal glasses to the rim like water. Two of Captain Crow's sons, Osagyefo and Otumfour had returned home from Great Britain. The two schooled at Harvard University, and they both had honors in law degrees. One cannot begrudge them, having successfully chalked such feats in the midst of all the turbulence the family had been through.

But their great father was still languishing in prison, firmly fettered to the four walls of the top-security castle in the murky belly of the antique dungeons of Apollonia.

Eerily, the authorities had, for the third time in six months, postponed his release.

His lawyer Mr. Wellington would continue to fight like never before. According to him the appellate court judge (Mr. Padmore) should have instructed the prison authorities to release Captain Crow on the day he gave the judgment.

"You know he had the judicial latitude to do so," he told the press. "And by not doing so, the state attorney general capitalized on the loophole and caused the discomfort. I don't know if he did it on purpose. But I do know one thing for certain... Mr. Padmore is a just man and I believe he did it in good faith.

His aptitude for fairness is unquestionable. He is not one of the judges that you can buy or manipulate, which is why everyone in the country respects him.

So, I strongly believe he forgot his soft-paw jab; that could have ended the whole legal tussle. It might've escaped him; we all make legal blips sometimes. See, it's like boxing he missed what I call the 'wicked chance' and his opponent used it against him."

And that lost chance has dealt another blow to my client. It saddens my heart that such an honorable man would continue to spend awful time in prison for a crime I know he never committed," Mr. Wellington bemoaned.

Meanwhile, at the Apollonia prison, Captain Crow remained broken-hearted.

He felt crestfallen because he missed the opportunity again to kibbutz with the family.

"Hey, guys go ahead and have the party as planned. I thought I could be home to celebrate it with you. But once again, they've postponed it, indefinitely this time. I can't wait to see you all. Kiss your mom for me, and tell her I will always love her. *Afehyiapa!*" He wrote. (Merry Christmas!)

It was Christmas Eve, many of them he had spent in jail. As usual, the powers that be had put sand into his *gari* (a staple for Ghanaians). Just like spilt milk, obviously, you can't fight over it.

The tabloid got it right on, it had feared the AG could cause havoc and he did exactly so not only to the Crow family but also the entire populace in Kumasi. Nonetheless, known for their 'never-say-die' spirit the Crows would not let someone or anybody sit on their joy.

Everything would go on as planned; Christmas apart from Easter was their biggest family re-union occasion.

"Ama Samanhyia (Mrs. Crow), what at all do these people want, today they say this, tomorrow it is that. Every blessed day they tell *'Kwaku Ananse'* (cock and bull) story," Ama Adade, a family friend wondered.

"Well, I have no idea, but I guess its sheer hatred against us. They just don't like us. They hate us and even hate our livestock," Mrs. Crow replied.

"It's been like this for the past six months—back and forth with no end in sight. Can't expect anything less than this when you're tried at Kangaroo's court," Mrs. Crow told Ama Adade.

"You're telling me?" Ama Adade interrupted.

"I'm told that court understands one language, thus throw them into the dungeon and let them perish."

"Yes, that's what they're known for...they're wicked and heartless. But I know as long as God lives my husband will live too. He always says this: "If God hasn't sanctioned your death no human being can take your life.""

"My sister you're dead right on that." Ama Dade said. "Let the enemy move the mountains and cross all the rivers on Earth: Until God gives the green light your pursuer surely labors in vain. After all, what haven't they done to Captain Crow," she rhetorically asked.

"We've seen him gun-butted, abused and misused, flogged daily and all the inhuman treatment. Yet, he is still alive and asleep with Jesus, because He who watches him is wide awake."

"Oh my good friend you couldn't put it better than that. Who can take our lives when we find ouselves in His Tabernacle? I tell you Ama, they will all fall one by one."

In the course of the all-consuming conversation, Mrs. Crow noticed that they were a little bit behind time. So the two friends doubled up to put together the Christmas boxes and the hampers for the Boxing Day.

Every year, the Crows sent nearly one hundred boxes and Christmas cards to family members, friends, and loved ones.

"Look," Ama Samanhyia (Mrs. Crow) motioned to her friend. "At ages twenty-four and twenty-five, they still jostle each other as kids. You guys remind me of my heydays."

"Ama, you still look young. Your children have already caught up with you," Ama Adade told her.

"Well, I am blessed at fifty-two, they call me sister. Back then, my classmates used to call me tomboy because I played football. I also played table tennis [ping-pong] and even draught [*dame*] which is known to be men's game. I didn't just play, I played and won medals. I was really good at it and got scholarship."

There was an afternoon. I watched these two adults over by the old Presbyterian Church house played draught. I believe you know that area well. The city is growing bigger and bigger now, some old structures pulled down and in their place massive edifice…"

"Oh yeah. I do remember," her friend interjected.

"To my disbelief, these grown-ups traded expletives and swore at each other as though they'd lost their minds or had a bone to pick. *Dame* is like that. Usually, the one who's the upper hand do the tough-talk, pulling hands, and at times, smashing the face of the potential loser.

In the case of football, I was as good as the guys. What I didn't like though about the beautiful game was its lack of team spirit at the time. It gained the notorious name, *Kokofu*, meaning you don't get a pass if you didn't have a sibling in the game.

But all in all, like the other sports, it was fun to watch and I loved it."

"See, the guys are still at it."

"Who is taller and stronger?" Ama Dade asked.

"I think Osagyefo is an inch shorter than Otumfuor. He and his Dad stand at six-foot-six."

"Please check who is at the door. I heard the bell ring a moment ago."

"Ponchoo! Ponchoo!" Came the loud noise from the hallway.

"Who's at the door?"

"Mr. Yaw Amoah Ponkor a.k.a. Poncho," Otumfuo replied.

"Legendary Poncho is here, the iconic broadcaster at Ghana Broadcasting Corporation [GBC]."

Earlier, Elizabeth Ohene, Abi Adakye, Ama Dwamena, and Lauretta Asare had all come to help their old buddy, Yaa Asantewaa put stuff together. They passed the night with the Crows ahead of what they christened the big day.

Eventually, what seemed like a long wait, the big jamboree arrived. And a good number of friends in the neighborhood and from afar stormed the Crows' villa to join them for the fête.

In attendance also were old friends and old boys from Amanfo, Volta, Katanga and Commonwealth Halls. The grounds began to breathe irritatingly.

By 5:00 p.m., the number had swollen, characteristically a boys-girls party!

The guys came with their bling-blings and *Otto Pfister* vogue baggy slacks while the gals showed up in glossy and charming bikini dresses. Observably, the cat was not home, so the mice could play.

Puffed-up like the horns of the Afadjato Mountain (of Volta Region in Ghana), their unbuckled headlights bound flirtatiously. And the showy navels (a.k.a. belly buttons) were more than a billboard advertisement. Interestingly, nobody seemed to bother about the free-fall property.

The maverick would not have tolerated such loopy dresses, not under his powerful eagle's eyes and more so in his quiet abode. But the indomitable had been hibernating in prison.

"Always dress good and respectfully," he told his children.

Ama Samanhyia (Mrs. Crow) was the moderate type.

However, she sometimes got hard on them too.

The face of their plush compound building overlooking the antique Bantama veterans' quarters had been festooned with colorful balloons. And the jubilant crowd feted themselves with food and drinks as the music from the loud speakers blasted inside the canopied shelters mounted at the forecourt of the giant house.

It was sheer joy. The enthusiasm and the fervor that typified the whole merriment couldn't have challenged any conventional wisdom. There were many drinks to quaff, much energy to burn, and a lot merryment to make. Testosterone was at work, sweats poured from the crown of their heads to the soles of their feet like Boti Falls as they displayed youthful exuberance.

What more?

They'd cracked the beers open, danced their shoes off, and popped up the champagnes. But the pain that followed nearly six hours later was unforgettable. All except Benazir, Captain Crow's youngest daughter who was in her third year in college stayed home with her mom and grandma, the rest went out later in the night to see the latest movie in town.

Then in the teensy hours of the night came the creepy sound from the large garage door. Four masked men brandishing guns and machetes had made it into the Crows' peaceful residence and threatened Mrs. Crow to immediately surrender all monies, jewelers, and other valuable items to them or she be killed.

The panic-stricken mother of six complied but that didn't pacify the whims of the crooks. They meant to do more harm and dent the Crows image.

"Are there any other persons in the house?" one of the armed robbers asked.

"No," she lied. "There isn't anybody here beside me. They're all gone."

"Gone to where?" the gun man inquired.

"Gone to see a movie."

"Are you sure?" the giant, about six feet four inches tall queried.

Meanwhile, Benazir had ducked under one of the beds. She had managed to place an SOS call. The distress call had been answered; however, lack of logistics—a menace facing third world countries in their crusade against gangsterism would give the lunatics free time to finish the pillage of the Crows and carte their stolen booties anyway.

Not only that they would also get their hands dirtied.

In between time, the giant embarked on a recognizance tour. Recce the military call it. Room by room he searched thoroughly.

Finally he got into the room (next to the guest room) where Benazir had been hiding. Like a sniffing dog the monster had sniffed her out as she was shaking violently from her hideout. And while this was unfolding in the eastern side of the house, the other three scoundrels were having a field day at the west end.

They had been busily subjecting Mrs. Crow into several crucial sexual bouts. Her mouth had been duct-taped, legs held firmly apart and hands tied to the gleaming brown queen-size bed in the master bedroom. She could barely resist the rough game from her sweaty-stinky attackers. The marble floored living room had beer spilled all over amid sickening smell.

Agony had visited the Crows home, fate was shaping a new life for the respected family, and in the ensuing bizarre episode, Captain Crow's mother who'd a family history of hypertension collapsed. Apparently, there was nobody to give her a CPR aid, she gave up the ghost even before doctors at GEE, [Komfo Anokye Hospital], as it is popularly known could revive her soul.

After their barbaric act, the spoilers immediately sped off.

When the rest of the children returned home all they could see was torture, pain, and grief (TPG). Three police patrol vehicles and an ambulance stood in front of their compound, while snuffling dogs sniffed around as detectives in search of clues.

Clues?

The crooks did not leave clues. They left behind humiliation and disaster.

Mrs. Crow lay unconsciously on the brunette woolen-carpeted floor (supine manner) gasping for breath in her plush bedroom. The officers from the fire department busily worked on her. At the brink of death was their lovable seventy-eight-year-old Grandma. Her pulse could rarely be read. Her piercing eyeballs diminished!

And the whereabouts of their darling little sister remained oblivious.

Kidnapped!

How would their father receive the news at the prison?

What would be his immediate reaction?

Can he deal with the loss of a beloved mother and the disappearance of an adorable daughter?

They searched for answers. And they grieved over the harm alongside the death.

Though the police later found foot as well as fingerprints of the attackers, the question remained: How soon can they put their act together to swoop the nuts?

Would they find Benazir—the youngest child of the Crows—alive?

Well, it didn't take long. At about three o'clock in the morning, a police night team patrolling the northern end of the city had spotted a white Pontiac maneuvering its way into the slum suburb of Sodom, a notorious haven for miscreants. Following a hot pursuit from the police, the occupants of the said car abandoned it and took to their heels.

However, one year later they (the criminals) would be apprehended and sent to jail; courtesy of the painstaking investigative work by the *Big Eye*. Trust the crows they will come for you when you think you are stubbornly covered.

There was a young female lying weak at the rear of the supposedly getaway Pontiac, police later told reporters. She had been blindfolded and appeared to be under the influence of drug. Evidently, her captors did so in order to cover up their identity and perhaps their hideouts. That young girl was Benazir.

Thankfully, the teenager had been rescued alive. The police rushed her to a nearby hospital for medical service where she regained her consciousness.

Elsewhere at KATH, doctors had diligently managed to put Mrs. Crow (Ama Samanhyia) back on good shape, and she could intelligently recall most of the atrocities the gangsters subjected them into. Captain Crow's mother Obaahemaa Akua Akyeampoma, now queen mother of Mogyabiyedom couldn't survive. She was put on life support at the Intensive Care Unit (ICU) but she died a few hours later.

✄

The news dealt a deadly blow to Captain Crow at the prison. Sergeant Baja, a warden at the custodial said this about the maverick, "He didn't eat anything for three days and cried his eyes out for the whole day when the news reached him."

"By any measure, I could tell that man loved his mother dearly, because he told me he was the only child of his Mom," officer Baja said. And inmates at the penitentiary later that evening would gather together to console their friend for the loss.

But all wasn't lost for the maverick. He still had something to cheer about.

While he (Captain Crow) and some of the Unflappable Seventeen remained in the horrible prison, his children worked tirelessly to keep the conglomerate business running. The Planetiers, they called them, pooled their energies, wisdom, strength, and resources together to keep their Dad's business operable.

For example the intelligence agency, *Big Eye*, was still operative and had become even more potent than before, swooping and scooping many in the metropolis, according to Kumasians.

Asked why they continued to stick to their fiery operation in the wake of all the atrocities meted out to them, Osagyefo the, oldest son of the Crows remarked, "It isn't about us. It is about the good people of this great kingdom whose rights have been thrown to the dogs for grabs. We are ever determined to continue the good works our Dad and the unselfish men and women began more than a decade ago. Because we know we shall win. "

Yaa Asantewaa (Captain Crow's older daughter) nicknamed Iron Lady had become the icon of the city as many corrupt officials, especially politicians, feared to come close into her zone. And *Big Eye*'s power and fame will grow by leaps and bounds.

As the time drew near for Captain Crow's freedom, for the first time in almost fifteen years, his family as well as friends and well wishers couldn't wait to see their adorable friend, activist, father, and a brother join them in festive mood. But that triumphant homecoming would coincide with Akwasidae—one of Asanteman's biggest festivals.

Chapter 17

The red and white porcupine flags, symbolizing the might of the Ashanti kingdom (Asante Kotoko kum Apem a Apem beba) fluttered high in the breezy dark clouds at the Baba Yara Stadium amid fears that the rains might descend.

The Garden City was in festive mood. Celebrations had hit fever pitch as the weeklong annual sweaty, sultry, gaiety Akwasidae festival reached its climax. People from all walks of life had swarmed the venue for the event.

Flanked by a high-powered array of paramount, as well as divisional chiefs across the empire, the Asantehene Otumfuo Osei Tutu II, in his beautiful regalia, sat majestically on the Golden Stool. He had earlier sworn the great oath of Asanteman (*Ntam kesee Miensa*) and been carried to and fro in a rich velvet *kente*-designed palanquin by six brawny bare-chested men, along with dancing and extending felicitations to his people.

In the inner circle of the huge dais stood the ceremonial macebearers who flaunted the high ornamented staff of metals before Otumfuo as a retinue of linguists also gathered themselves at the fringes.

Also mounted on the stage was the gigantic Fontonfrom drum (that measured six feet high and about 100 widths in diameter) single-minded by the master drummer, who propped himself upon a stool to dish out his nimble-fingered talents.

The trumpeters horned like peacocks, and the courtiers serenaded him.

Close at his majesty's feet were stone-faced squatted servants (*nkoa*), some of them prostrating, and behind him were sea of colorful umbrellas—big and small, bowl-shaped and curved in— that added visual value to the whole ceremony. On the far right side to the Asokwa end of the podium was a motionless lanky middle aged-man, whitewashed from head to toe.

He was Komfo Aku the chief fetish priest, clutched to his magic wand. His whole frame had been festooned with mystical trappings, charms, and amulets. Next to him was the fearsome Adumhene Kwaku Mensah (also known as Diawuo), he had the eyes of the hyena tattooed on his forehead. And his torso bedecked with charms as well. Diawuo also had a piece of traditional cloth called *danta*, which barely covered his manhood provoking many eyes at the stadium.

But in the midst of the dark clouds was this glorious light, veteran Captain Crow, the heartbeat of the historic city had been let out of the rusty chains that held him for more than a decade in Apollonia prison.

Nonetheless, the shackle marks on his feet stayed forever. They were as indelible as letters emblazoned on a grindstone and as crystal as spring water from the Rift Valleys of East Africa. Amazingly, he still brimmed with hope and confidence.

The authorities at the prison had delayed his release two weeks earlier to coincide with the big Akwasidae which was winding up, for the reason no one knew.

"The maestro is back," a tall-dark gentleman emceeing the program had broken the news to the crowd.

"Alas! The dark cloud is gone," he exclaimed.

And like a vacillation boat on high seas, the celebrants at the Baba Yara Park swung back to back, side to side, left to right, and vice versa. Their joy was over the moon, except that that infatuation would not last long. They had instantaneously switched gears, heading toward Jackson Park where tens of thousands had flocked to welcome veteran Captain Crow and the unsung heroes.

Undeniably, they're real heroes who had intrepidly transformed the political landscape of Asanteman and Ghana in general. As part of the gathering, three of the unflappable ex-convicts donned uniforms akin to prison gears to remind the proud citizens of Asanteman that their sweats and toils weren't in vain.

The event at the Jackson Park also saw the coronation of the maverick as king of Mogyabiyedom under the stool name Osahene Awiebo Kuntunkunuku I.

The impulse action would arouse the fury of the sovereignty, and the pandemonium that followed was as nasty as the notorious Thomas Nast. Within a matter of an hour, probably minutes, over three-hundred truncheon-wielding policemen would besiege Jackson Park to deal ruthlessly with the revelers.

Captain Crow had mounted the podium to say his thanks to his teeming supporters, friends, family members, and the good people of Mogyabiyedom, Graceland, Kumasi, and the entire citizens of Asanteman.

If one thought that his over ten-year term in prison was enough to scare the hell out of him, it was absolutely a shaggy-dog story. Unbelievably, he still plodded along; perhaps treading precariously on a long slow slippery slope. Indeed, he personified the sage. Winners never quit and quitters never win.

✂

On their way to the Jackson Park, an opinion leader, Sisulu Ghanaba, asked his friend Jomo Kenyatta once a jail-bird.

"Do you know Ali, Mohammed Ali? He used to be called Cassius Clay." "Who is Allah?" Jomo inquired.

"No, I didn't say Allah."

"Sorry, I have a hearing impairment. I can hardly hear from my right side, after series of notorious slaps from the guards at the prison."

Jomo told Ghanaba that he was yet to recover his mojo after that merciless beating at the prison.

"I have problem with words that end with I's and E's," he explained. "Sounds like A to me."

"What about him?"

"Oh, Ali is the first and only one Lineal World Heavyweight Champion. Well-known for his unorthodox fighting style which he described as 'float like a butterfly, sting like a bee' won him an enviable record in the fistic history. The word surrender was perhaps his archenemy even when the odds were against him. And like Ali, Captain Crow doesn't surrender. Maybe not until he meets his Joe Fraziers and the George Foremans.

He has been in prison for nearly fifteen years for fighting against injustice, inequality and discrimination in our society," Sisulu Ghanaba noted. "Yet, he comes back to fight harder than before just as Cassius came back and regained his stripped titles seven years later."

"Why did they strip him of his title?" Jomo probed.

"Well, he refused to go to war in Vietnam during the American-Vietnamese war in the 70s."

"Oh, I see!"

"Come on, let's hurry to the venue. They should be there by now."

Ghanaba with long props kept out-pacing his friend.

"You walk so fast Ghanaba," Jomo remarked.

"Were you in the military?"

"No. I got it from my Papa when I was a child." Ghanaba told Jomo. "We used to have most of our farms miles away from the village. And Papa would often urge us (four boys and eight girls) to double up when he noticed we were lagging behind."

"Gee I can't keep pace with you!"

"Hey buddy have you heard the rumor in town?" Jomo asked; still about 20 yards behind the bunny (Ghanaba).

"What is it?" He grudgingly paused to listen to Jomo; but still had his heels up ready to kick start.

"Just trying to catch up with you," he said amid laughs.

"Can you hear the deafening noise? It's going to be another momentous day. Trust me, Captain Crow will deliver his usual punchy speeches."

From the fortified castle that touched the heavens with her brown-pronged gable, the ubiquitous had stepped out. His face lightened up with a broad smile and walked grandly across the streets (which had built-up earlier with an awe-inspiring multitude) as though nothing had happened to him.

The crowd mobbed him. They wouldn't let their idol walk again. Amid drumming, dancing, and chanting of war songs, the jubilant mass held him shoulder high then into a palanquin as they soused him with a white powdery substance.

Street by street, block by block, and alley by alley, the elated crowd carried Captain Crow.

The chant went on as they tread along.

"Hail him, here comes the king. Hail him, here comes our king."

The euphoric procession, which made a detour through the byways, finally docked at the epicenter—The Jackson Park.

He inched up to the sea of microphones mounted on the podium pawed one gently to test his tantalizing voice that billowed below the thunderous applauds from the tumultuous crowd. He turned the ignition light on:

"Hello," he said under his breath.

"Good to go," Ogyampatrudu urged him.

"Choooo-boi!" he yelled

"Yei...," the crowd responded in a rapturous manner that shook the foundation of the earth beneath them. Every Tom, Dick, and Harry felt the temperature and the power at which he radiated.

"It isn't earth tremor. It is the Crow's fervor. That is his trademark," Comrade Ogyampatrudu assured the crowd around him.

"Cho...cho...cho-boi!" he bawled harder, punched the air with a clenched fist, and delivered what would be seen by many as the most moving, most powerful, and most prophetic speech ever in the annals of the Ashanti kingdom. "The strength I never paid for. It was hard for me to get traction in the wake of the snowy storm. There was no pocket of space on the face of Mother Earth that could grant me asylum. Callously, the downpressor man put me and the freedom fighters behind the rusty iron bars. And deep down the monstrous dungeons, we served hard times for a crime we never committed.

"With mouth duct-taped, wings clipped, and feet bound together, it seemed the inevitable end was nigh. The imminent end I dreaded most. Indeed, life flows by like a lazy creek, and death is nothing but an evasive abstract beast. He is merciless, he is unkind, and unyielding.

"As I pondered over his ruthless deeds, I began to write my own epitaph even before he knocked on my door. But let this message reach my beloved Graceland. I'm coming home my dear, 'cos I miss you. Let your smiling doors remain open 24/7 and, your vivacious lamp stay undimmed.

"But sooner than I thought, the whirlwind came, and I felt reinvigorated and re-energized. And he brought me an immeasurable strength. The strength I never paid for.

"Suddenly, the chains broke loose, the duct-tape disappeared, and my wings began to grow stronger and wider like that of the eagle's. And now I'm soaring, soaring to reach for the sky. Folks, fly with me if you're a daredevil."

The atmosphere was electric to say the least.

He continued, "May I humbly ask this lovely crowd to join me and the family in a minute of silence for our heroes and heroines including my mother, our grandmother," he urged the crowd. I also like to thank the metropolitan police and the good citizens of this great nation for your unwavering service in helping to rescue my beloved daughter, beautiful Benazir. Thank you, sirs!

"Even though some of our freedom fighters are not with us, they shared their blood for a good and just cause. In that vein, we aren't giving up our fight. In fact, their departed souls will be restless if we back down our avowed dream. We will continue to count on the infallible will of God, and we have no doubt on our minds that we shall one day make this part of our world a better place for living.

"The harder the troubles come, the bolder we will stand on our grounds to make history this day, so that posterity will have something to look up to. It's been an awful experience. However, we have one simple resolution. We aren't going to fight with kids' gloves. We aren't going to hang our gloves today or tomorrow. We will rather help chart a new course, build new social bridges, and refuel the justice and hope bus.

"The future is certainly unpredictable, but as long as I live, I will continue my avowed vision and mission to fight for equal right and justice for humankind and help free the oppressed from the oppressor in our societies.

"Be reminded folks that the carnage is not over and our struggle for justice has also not ended. It is however, reassuring to note that the good Lord, who resides above the heavens, listens to the prayer of the foolish man, he listens to the wise man, and he does so for the rich and the poor man.

"God listens to the prayer of the white man and the black man too. I know many of you here today are puzzled to see me alive. Isn't that amazing?

"It is certainly so. Nonetheless, there is something inside that is so strong, so powerful, and so awesome. Just by His amazing grace."

Meanwhile, as the crowd listened in the midst of cheers and round of applause, the police swarmed up the venue in anticipation to unleash the venom which the multitude had no wind of. Captain Crow was still speaking urging folks to stay united, stay committed, and be high-spirited.

And like a monster tidal wave, the police began to press forward. Even so, the crowd continued to dance to hi-life live band that intermittently dished out some traditional music. Suddenly, there came an unknown smoke.

The police had fired teargas into the jubilant crowd for no apparent reason. And the bizarre action would in a blinker spark more bizarre scenes.

Kofi Konfanko Darkwa (KKD), a broadcast journalist with Anibreaensogya, a local radio station, filed this live, uncut, uncensored, and unedited report from the Jackson Park.

"Oh my, Oh my," he screamed. "Good people of Asanteman, I must say the scene here is getting nastier, bleaker and murkier.

"The police have gone berserk. In pell-mell the crowd ran. Citizens of our dear kingdom have become punching bags, mere *Homo sapiens*, mere objects. Within the inner perimeter, around the center circle, over and across the Jackson Park, the celebrants are mercilessly at the receiving end of the madness of the heartless red-beret, boot-to-knee, and trigger-happy police personnel.

"Suffice to say that, all and sundry, including myself, is miserably nestled between ruthless crossfire. Ironically, in their feeble defense some of the people have resorted to pelting the police with stones, water bottles, and any objects they lay hands on, while the uniformed vampires are reciprocating with rubber/live bullets as well as water canon. This is complete mismatch. There have been many casualties resulting from the stampede. So far, I have counted at least one-hundred and thirty bodies.

The injured are uncountable—some with head injuries, bloodied noses and faces, fractured arms, swollen cheeks, split mouths, and broken limbs.

"Need I tell you Kumasians, blood is oozing from nostrils like Niagara Falls! "They have been jalapeñoed! I mean well-peppered, amid watery eyes and running noses. Oh, oh, oh! I have lost count of the dead now. What in the world is happening to our dear kingdom? Isn't this paradox that the people who are supposed to protect us and instill law and order have now taken the law into their own hands?

"What I am witnessing now looks like the destruction of biblical Sodom and Gomorrah, they have hand-cuffed Captain Crow and three others and bundled them into a waiting armored vehicle. To where I don't know, so don't ask me.

"Mr. Policeman, let there be peace. Let there be peace I pray, lest all of us will lose our dear souls here. It's just by sheer luck that I am still alive talking and walking in this hellish ground, but if I don't make it home today, tell my wife and the kids that I have some fresh goat meat stashed in the old fridge. They should feast themselves to the tender meat, and remember me always in prayers.

"From the Jackson Park, this has been your authoritative broadcast journalist Kofi Konfanko Darkwa, a.k.a. KKD."

In the aftermath, unconfirmed radio and newspaper reports put the death toll in the region of 1,200. KATH morgue had no room to accommodate the heaps of bodies that strewn its icy cement floor, most of them young men between the ages eighteen to twenty-five. The spectacle was so sordid and too grotesque for the naked eye—swollen bloodied-heads, disfigured faces, and broken limbs were all the eyes could catch.

Much to the exasperation of the bereaved families, the police denied they ever used brutal force on the innocent folks. They also refuted the number of casualties saying, the figures were doctored and inaccurate.

Police Public Affairs Directorate later issued a statement in part read: "Our officers and men acted in self defense, adding they will apply force when necessary."

But their nefarious activity wouldn't end there; it would be stretched to its elastic limit. The bootlickers embarked on what private intelligence agencies described as a witch hunting exercise. And anybody viewed as sympathizer or supported the Crow's revolutionary movement paid the hard price. Victims were subjected to ruthless torture.

Remember the emcee at the Baba Yara Stadium? He just disappeared into thin air. Though he never possessed the spirit of invisibility, the invisible world subsumed him. The police remained silent over his disappearance.

Ever-present Konfanko escaped by the skin of his teeth but not without injuries. He had a broken arm and a wounded head. In fact, he escaped from the scene shirtless and barefooted.

To this day, the incident at the Jackson Park remains the great oath for Kumasians.

�֍

In the midst of the chaos, the police arrested Captain Crow, Katakyie Afrifa, his long time friend Sundiatta, Marijata, and Dynamite. The three men and the lady were detained for three months, but not until comrade Katakyie Afrifa had brutally been murdered. However, Captain Crow was charged with mutiny and an attempt to dethrone His Majesty Otumfuo, the Asantehene.

Having been charged as a dissident and found guilty, he would spend another decade of his life behind the iron bars. This time he was court-marshaled.

"Send him back to prison," retorted one of the panel members.

Nevertheless, the maverick appeared unperturbed as the guards hauled him and his friends back to the Apollonia prisons shortly afterward.

"This is a travesty of justice," his lawyer described it.

The other two comrades Sundiatta and Marijata were caged in at the Ussher Fort penal complex, whereas Lady Dynamite spent her time at the female prisons at the Nsawam Medium Security.

Visitations at the Ussher Fort prison were quite better than Apollonia as the comrades alluded to. What they didn't like though was what they called the prison's ritual fly system, where inmates were erratically flown from one locality to another. This was done to disguise their location.

There were few times friends and family members found themselves being at the wrong place because they had moved them to an unknown area.

And there was yet another dilemma, apart from the already noted difficulty, visitors were occasionally not allowed to see their relatives.

"But despite of all that," noted Captain Crow. "We were able to cope until suddenly, three weeks before the release of my colleagues, fate unleashed a deadly blow to Comrade Katakyie Afrifa. It was around midday. The strong man had visited the penitentiary's chaplain to lodge a complaint concerning the inhuman treatment meted out to them by some of the guards.

Unfortunately, he met his untimely death on his way back to the dorm. A monster had ambushed him. Notorious Asobayire, a long time convict who had the proclivity to kill, got the brave man killed. The hard criminal was known to have murdered at least ten people in the city."

"There was no altercation whatsoever, Asobayire was just a sworn foe of mercy," Captain Crow told friends. Even though there had been speculation, one of the guards who hated Katakyie might have paid Asobayire to kill him. The authority at the prison did nothing on the matter. Contract killing exists in prison it is a well known fact.

"Though Asobayire was a buffoon and had penchant to kill, many believed it was an inside job. And he did take the life of a dear friend and a colleague."

Two weeks after that sudden death, another compatriots—Lady Dynamite and Ghanatta Sokoto—would meet their tragic deaths on a trip to the Middle East.

"You haven't heard the news, have you?" Captain Crow asked Joe Ndebugri a Bolga native.

"What news?" Ndebugri enquired.

"Unstoppable Lady Dynamite and her husband, Ghanatta Kwabena Sokoto, have died in a plane crash. There were no survivors the report said."

"This is shocking!" exclaimed Ndebugri.

"At what time and which radio station did you hear this?"

"It was the five o'clock evening news on GBC radio," Captain Crow replied.

"I couldn't, for a second, believe my ears. I remember we'd finished dinner and playing scrabbles. It was like a tornado."

"What at all is going on?" He wondered.

"Everything seemed to be turning upside down. Can't figure out what tomorrow may bring. Things appear to be good today, then disaster strikes within twenty-four hours later."

I never thought even Ndebugri, as I loved to call him, was also planning to take up his life. Surprisingly, the tubby figure had twice considered committing suicide, but I advised him not to do so."

"'Captain, I think it is better to take my own life rather than let these creepy worthless guys who sport no human face to crucify me. They wear hate on their sleeves and discharge venom on innocent folks as and when they choose,' he told me. 'Which is better to go on your own or to be sent?' He posed the rhetorical question.

"'Perhaps, the former. It might seem obnoxious and a little psychopathic idea to end one's life, however to allow a vapid vampire to send you to the grave would be outrageous. I see your point, Nde. But don't be quick to throw in the towel. You will never know what the future might bring. Just hold on to that thin line called hope. You will be vindicated by hope and posterity wouldn't see you as coward. Cowards they say, die many times even before their normal death. Good night and good luck, my dear friend. God willing, I will see you tomorrow.'

Chapter 18

Amid the patchy hitches and glitches, the freedom jet plane finally touched down. The stalwart quarterback player couldn't hold him down because of the gravity of weight he carried.

Apparently, it was a touchdown the euphoric audience at Prempeh Assembly Hall had long anticipated. Alas, a goal had been scored, victory had been chalked, and the maverick had returned home.

He wore a drawn face and looked thin. He wore no hair. It was needless to state that the king of a kind had trekked the roughest path on Earth and tasted the crocodile's bile at the Ussher Fort and Apollonia that held him captive.

The six-feet-six-inches tall, powerfully built man could barely fit in his *Gyata* embroidery *Fugu* or *Batakari*-made dress. Nonetheless, the iconic figure still exuded the energy and power he had been known for over the years.

Coincidentally, his newly found comrade, Ndebugri, had also been set free. Nde (prefix for Ndebugiri) a trade unionist and former bank manager, would perhaps spend the next twenty-four hours on the rugged road to Bolga, the upper east regional capital. Deservedly, he would also be treated to a feast and the local *Bugum* dance.

By midday Friday, all the streets leading to Prempeh Assembly Hall (the venue for the homecoming event), had been choked with human as well as vehicular traffic.

Farah Avenue, one of the principal streets, had contracted the virus too. The adjacent route, Adum Street, heading to Manhyia had hosted tens of vehicles, and hundreds had also lined the streets near the huge Hall.

Incredibly, the forecourt of the magnificent building had attracted perhaps the same teeming number of cars spotted on the streets and alleys.

But there stood at the courtyard two signposts on the parking lots that had been earmarked for Captain Crow and his entourage.

"Reserved." Scrawled boldly on the board.

Suddenly, a taxi driver pulled over in front of the Great Hall.

"Hey, Massa na wetin bi dis?"

Musa Toure, a cabbie asked a bystander.

Musa, a native from neighboring Burkina Faso was just two months old in the Garden City. He was one of the many who had come to Kumasi in search of greener pastures.

His broken English (*pidgin*) immediately gave him out. The bystander understood him.

"It means you can't park here," he explained.

"What?" he snapped.

He had circled the whole vicinity for more than half hour, trying to find a space. Frustrated by the uncharacteristic scene, he chose to park his car anyway. He damned the consequence.

"Well, I don't blame you, young man," the bystander noted. "After all, English isn't your spoken language. I hope the security guards would understand you when they catch up with you. Otherwise, you're inviting serious trouble."

The bespectacled taxi driver had already occupied one of the two reserved parking lots. He sat his exhausted body on the cab's bonnet, two hands fully engaged. His right hand squeezed ficelle or baguette, a French bread that measured about two inches in diameter. Baguette, though popular in francophone countries, doesn't boast that craze in English-speaking nations in Africa. The left hand also clutched onto Schweppes drink. He kept his mouth busy at least for the next half hour.

Meanwhile, a swoop of dark cloud hanged the gray-looking sky like mushroom smoke. And even though the sun was at its circuits, one could hardly sight her progress. Evidently, it was setting but a star had taken her place, leaving no void. Freed Captain Crow and family were on their way to the venue.

Osagyefo, the oldest of the children, was leading the family limousine with a Pathfinder which had two other occupants. Painstakingly, they made it to the Great Hall. Then out of the blues came a heavily built guy still communicating on his walkie-talkie.

"Hey, who asked you to park here?" The macho guy charged.

"Didn't you see the reserved sign?"

"No, I no see sa."

"You must be blind not to have seen this bold word scribbled on the board."

"Sorry. I no no Inglis."

"Nonsense," he snapped at the driver. What do you mean, you no no Inglis. But you're speaking English,"

"Massa na troot I dey talk you. I tin sey ibi for nobodi. Plis fogis me."

Already down on his knees, one hand on another's palm, Musa remained apologetic. He knew for certain that he would be no match against the six-foot-four dude from the hood with six-pack stomach.

"I should see you disappear by the mandatory count of three. One...two...and..."

"I for stay shere for one, two, and three hawa, thank you sa."

"This guy is a real clown."

He grabbed Musa by the hand and shoved him into his cab. Another order followed immediately.

"I mean start your car and leave right now. I mean now," the macho guy insisted.

He was lucky though that the burly guy didn't gift him a blow. It would have sent him flat on the turf or perhaps dead. As Musa ignited his car, the limousine pulled beside them and Captain Crow emerged.

"What's amiss, Osono?"

"He has taken your spot," he replied him.

"Come on, leave him alone and find the vehicle a place somewhere. I know it would be tough to find one at this time but allow him He has come to share the joy with us."

"Lucky you, you idiot," the muscular man retorted as he led the limousine driver to find a place.

Still caught up in the euphoria and the incredible release of their king, many citizens of Mogyabeyedom and Asanteman in general couldn't hide their joy. Talks about their idol also seemed to have eclipsed everything under the sun.

"Champions really die hard," an old soldier clad in white calico said. "And even when they die, it is believed they reincarnate. Captain Crow shuttled between the Apollonia and the Ussher forts iron gates like a jumbo jet, globetrotting.

"He had almost exhausted three decades behind the cagey bars, amid torture, water boarding and untold suffering," retired Major Kwame Pinto said.

"I am amazed to see this man still walking on the streets of the Garden City. Few, including myself, thought he would be dead, but here, we're so strange isn't it?" the old soldier intimated.

"I think he had to possess some sort of supernatural powers to be able to survive all this. No wonder some folks call him Asebu Amenfi," Major Pinto noted.

Many had defied the early afternoon downpour that seemed to mar the whole program to meet face to face with their icon whose sordid narrative they wouldn't want to miss.

"We've come from far and near to listen to Captain and get firsthand account about what happened to him and his compatriots," a young man told Crow's wife.

By 6:30 p.m., what was supposed to be a low-profile meeting or a mini-party at the august hall, it had recorded a staggering crowd. Young and old, rich and poor, men and women, retirees and pensioners, the oligarchs and aristocrats had besieged the roomy hall near Manhyia.

Though there wasn't pomp and pageantry, as it was the case in the previous event, this one didn't lack the steam and vibe either.

Ace gospel musician Omane Acheampong's infectious "Akyea na Amuye" boomed through the spacious auditorium, while the *vuvuzellas* blared on the sidelines.

The forecourt of the imposing building was decorated with red and white (signifying the blood shared and victory) cotton curtain tied by cords of fine mauve linen to shiny silver rings on marble columns. Pews at the auditorium had been draped with beautifully embroidery kente cloths, and the wall behind the podium sported a V-shaped white symbol with glittering lights.

But even as peaceful and low profile as it was, the Crow's event still attracted a great number of the black-helmeted metropolitan police (a.k.a the special brigade). As luck would have it, throughout the function the brigade did not act up. They enjoyed the lovely songs and danced their rugged boots off, lending more credence to the fact that music soothes the sadist beast.

Protocol demanded that Captain Crow's wife or the family be given the opportunity to address the gathering, and so his beloved and longtime better-half Ama Samanhyia took the podium. She held two separate documents, one a letter from the eccentric, and the other a chilling report of what happened to the family during the husband's incarceration.

The crowd gave her a standing ovation before she grabbed the microphone. Her wobbling feet and shaking hands spoke volume. And like her husband, Ama, knew how to talk and whip up public interest. She seized her audience attention by showing emotions—intermittently, she sobbed and used a white handkerchief to wipe the streaming tears.

"These are tears of joy for our husbands, uncles, and brothers who have joined us here today. These are tears for the martyrs," she told the gathering.

"It grieves my soul every now and then to think of these men who put their lives to fight for the just course for the people of this land. Unfortunately, they didn't live to see this day. But I trust the good Lord is with them and will give them a resting place in Heaven.

"I couldn't believe that this day would come so fast. Fast, the years appeared to have come, but not all the comrades arrested over the decade made it back home. Ladies and gentlemen, please permit me to share with you a letter my dear husband wrote to me whilst serving jail term in Apollonia.

"'Dear my love Ama,

"'I write with sore pain as tears run down my newly acquired bony cheeks. They aren't as firm now as they used to be. Yesterday, before twilight, one of our freedom fighters couldn't survive the police brutality. He succumbed.

"'Comrade Bosommuru Ampontua who stands at nine feet and two inches tall, gave up the ghost during the ritual drilling at the prison. The truncheon that hit his forehead on the right upper side of the eyebrow sent the giant to the tuff.

"'Like the mighty oak tree, he fell to the ground and dropped in the pool of blood.

"'His heart thumped like a dysfunctioned clock, and minutes later it stopped. He couldn't say a word.

"'I am sad, but I have the earnest conviction that we shall prevail. Keep praying for me and the rest of my buddies here, honey. God willing, I shall soon be home.

"'Your husband,

Captain'

She continued, "This gathering is not for me. This gathering is for you, citizens of Asanteman, who joined us steadfastly in prayers for our loved ones. Today, as we celebrate the homecoming of our husbands, mothers, brothers, and uncles, I solemnly urge you all to continue to keep the fire burning and never give up the battle for freedom. Amanda Awetu! Thank you all and God bless you."

Mrs. Crow handed the mike to her husband, and the maverick zoomed straight to address the audience.

"Citizens of Asanteman, lend me your ears." he said. "I'm humbled to be witnessing this august gathering. I greet you all in the name of our Father in heaven whose infallible will I will always count on. It is by His great grace that I stand here today. I therefore, on behalf of the Unflappable Seventeen, my family, and loved ones say a big thank you for your prayers.

"Today is a victory day, at the same time a sad one. I am pretty sure the news of the tragic death of our beloved Lady Dynamite and her husband Ghanatta are still fresh on our minds. The inseparable couple was involved in a plane crash six months ago.

"They both died in that bizarre accident on their way to Dubai in the United Arab Emirates for vacation. Nobody on that airplane survived [all 270 passengers perished], according to reports. Our hearts go out to the bereaved family and we would like to assure them that we would stand with them."

After a minute silence had been observed for the fallen heroes and heroines, Captain Crow continued, "The journey had been rough and tough. We were tortured, abused, and subjected to other dehumanizing acts by the prison guards. We tried. We fought hard to survive the harsh terrain.

"Unfortunately, some comrades couldn't make it to the end. They fell!

"But I have no doubt in my mind, as Ama earlier pointed out, that Comrades Osagyefo, Ampontua, Akua Kru, and Ofosagye are resting in the good bosom of our God.

"I like to assure you that we shall not rest on our oars. We will continue to carry the fight to any level possible.

"It won't be easy, let not anybody be fooled. There will be challenges and hard times ahead. However, we have confidence in whatever we plan to do.

"Next month, my colleagues and I will be leaving for the United States of America. We have been invited by the government in that country for a very pertinent deliberation. Be rest assured that we're coming back home immediately after business.

"I thank you all for coming to share the evening with us, and may the good Lord continue to bless you! Aseda ye mode!"

Chapter 19

On August 18, summer time, veteran Captain Crow crossed the Gulf of Guinea (the Atlantic) in the sub-Saharan Africa to the United States of America.

Accompanied by his able lieutenants (all dressed in native Ghanaian attire), they set forth in the land of the freed and home for the brave. Africans in diaspora, blacks in America, yellow and white men from Europe, and the Asia Minor, as well as the Far East, all descended to America's administrative capital, Washington DC to witness the civil rights icon.

The more than six-month trip was at the behest of His Excellency, the President of the US Richard Nixon himself, a great admirer of the African King. At the time, he had not been hit by the Watergate scandal yet. But it lurked like a hungry leopard around the White House. As dodgy as a tsunami, it would sweep the prodigious leader from his comfort zone.

Over the years, the maverick's hunger after a utopia world never seemed to wane.

He had long been intrigued by the prospects in the new world, and her touted flamboyant dream. This was his first state visit but second in two years.

The Crows had gone wild in their native land, Ghana. Their victorious capture of the killers of the heir apparent to the Ashanti Golden Stool held many spell-bound and transported them into the enthralled world of joy, hilarity, and reprieve.

They trudged the shadows of death and touched the untouchables, raked the muck, and left no stone unturned during their Walatu-Walasa operation.

Indeed, from the great heights of the Afadjatos and the Kilimanjaros, to the solitary depths of the Volta and the Limpopo Rivers, through to the great Nile River Basin, they killed the crocodiles and fed on their bile.

On top of that mega success, the indomitable leader and his group bridged the yawning gap between the rich and poor, abolished the horrible female genital mutilation, curtailed the land grabbing syndrome, and clamped down nepotism and cronyism, just to mention but a few.

Despite of this, Captain Crow believed there was still more to learn from the outside world, particularly from the US. It was this insatiable desire coupled with his demand-driven spirit that made him travel across the globe.

"I have heard and read a lot about this great nation, the US. I have toured Europe, journeyed to the Far East, across the Caribbean, and trekked the whole nations of mother Africa. I am yet to see the nation that accommodates the White House," he said.

This tour dovetailed their earlier visit to London in March the same year after Her Majesty, the Queen of England, knighted the iconic activist.

At the airport, to meet the high powered-delegation (amid a 21-gun salute) from Ghana were the secretaries of state, defense, roads and highways, commerce, energy, agriculture, and the vice president. And as expected, the paparazzi turned out in their numbers.

There were hordes of television cameras, lots of tape recorders, and a sea of microphones. First to catch the eye of the eccentric figure (not in derogatory term), was a journalist from the *New York Times* (NYT).

"Sir, how would you describe this visit?" he asked.

"Historic. Very historic," Captain Crow replied.

"Does your movement intend to seek political office in the coming years?"

"I don't want the group to be called a movement. The term movement carries negative connotations and evokes phalanxes of ruthless senseless rule makers in our part of the world where some disgruntled folks have over the years hidden behind the term to brutalize not only its people but also impoverish them.

"Decades back we had the NLM's, the JM's, the PLM's, the PMP's and all the likes. Look, here we have a simple mission—to fight for our inalienable rights and liberate our people from the economic doldrums.

"After all, what is good for the gander is also good for the goose. But the answer to the substantive question is a capital no. We are very proud of what we are doing now."

"So in that sense is that a movement?"

"I haven't said it's a movement. But if you so choose, we don't mind. We are a group. See, if you call yourself tiger and you can't hunt a prey, you're just as equal as a weakling church mouse."

"Where would be the groups' next visit?"

"For the records, we have toured some European countries, the Great Britain, the Soviet Union (USSR), France, the Netherlands, and Germany. We have also been to India, Burma, China, Pakistan, Afghanistan, Kyrgyzstan and Uzbekistan.

"There is so much to do back home. The whole African continent is on life support at the intensive care unit [ICU] having been pillaged and partitioned by former colonial masters. The obvious is, we risk extinction if our leaders continue to line their pockets with state treasures.

"Not only that, the continent faces the imminent danger of being used as a dumping ground for toxic and scraps from the west and the Far East if her people don't wake up from their long slumber and take their destinies into their own hands. The bottom line is, we will become slaves in our lands and suffer miserably for our ineptitudes.

"It's a long battle you can foretell, a huge task. But it doesn't seem impossible for us to fight. The secret to any success story is the beginning. Put the axe and the shovel to the ground, and the next thing you see is a giant edifice. When we kick start today, we can reach somewhere tomorrow, and our children will continue from there. The forbears have done their part. It is our turn to build upon that sweat and toil."

"Sir, how many of your members have you lost since you embarked on this warpath, and are you intimidated by the powers that be?"

"Sadly, we've lost seven great men and a heroic lady. Men of valor, real heroes who refused to lick boots and succumb to undue pressures. They never acted like poodles during the struggles. What was your second question?"

"Does the group feel intimidated by these deaths?"

"Not at all, my brother, we're more than emboldened and energized to stay on course. Old folks say: 'he who fights and runs away lives to fight another day.' Certainly, your attacker will always be haunting you because he knows you're nothing but a coward or a minnow.

"I've already made it clear to you that we will fight hard to liberate the whole African continent from colonialism and imperialist rule. That's our goal. That's our ultimate objective. Okay, I will take one more question. Er...the lady in red at the rear."

"Are you coming back to the States soon?"

"Absolutely. This is a beautiful country with beautiful people. We hope to have a fruitful deliberation with your president and enter into bilateral cooperation. Thank you."

❇

Later in the evening, the group had a state banquet with the president and his cabinet members, solidifying the existing bond between the two nations. There was a gymnastic performance climaxed by a boogie-woogie dance by the host, President Nixon and his august guest, Captain Crow.

The dance attracted a rapturous applause from the gathering.

President Nixon praised the group for their tremendous contribution in building Ghana and fighting injustice amongst its people. He assured them that the United States would lend the group both technical and financial support in their quest to building that part of the world.

"Our doors remain open to you and your people," he underscored. "Therefore, do not hesitate to count on us whenever you are in dire need."

Captain Crow on behalf of the entourage thanked the president, the vice president, and the good people of the United States for their kind gesture.

On wait at the courtyard of the banquet hall was a classic blue black Cadillac fully draped in traditional Ghana kente cloth with two mini flags of the two nations fluttering on the sides of the car.

A smartly dressed security agent opened the door for Captain Crow, while three other flashy ones pulled behind to transport the remaining five activists. They were immediately chauffeured into a five-star hotel over by the Hutchinson River.

About ten of its kind had earlier bussed other dignitaries and state officials who attended the feast. "It was a night to remember," one of the activists told a journalist.

Indeed, Washington DC was good city to sample.

❋

The group went to the Pennsylvania Avenue Park, the Statue of Liberty, and the JFK airport. They would later tour a number of sites that pique one's interest. These included New York suburban areas—Brooklyn, Harlem, Manhattan, and Bronx. This was followed by a series of town hall meetings, symposia, and workshops.

On the last day of their visits to these NY counties, a communiqué was issued at the Carnegie Hall after a day's symposium which urged the minority in the United States particularly blacks to stand firm in their struggles for total black emancipation and civil rights activism.

Below is an excerpt of the speech he delivered at Manhattan town hall on August 20:

> A new dawn is here. A new wind is blowing across the globe, and I am urging all peoples of the world over to welcome this change. Seeing brothers and sisters in any part of the world—either in Brazil, Australia, and the Caribbean, makes me feel nostalgic, and it is my fervent hope that the black race will someday see the glorious light. That light deeply stashed in the Akwatia valleys like a rough diamond will come out and shine. And then we shall all celebrate the victory together.
>
> Once again I must say, we feel great and honored to be here to share, and deepen the existing relationship, as well as deliberate upon the way forward. It's been a long wait. Anytime we plan to come something cropped up, and we had to postpone the trip. It's really been a worthwhile trip, and we would like to express our profound gratitude to this beautiful state and its wonderful people.

Next venue on the itinerary was Atlanta, Georgia. The group paid a courtesy call on the slain civil rights leader Martin Luther

King's wife Mrs. Coretta King and had interaction with her. They also visited the MLK museum and toured other state monuments.

"We are going to the Washington state to meet with my adopted mom and friends in the northwest region. It's been awhile, and I am pretty sure they will be glad to see me after couple of years or so," said Captain Crow.

There was absolutely much for the eye to savor in the Evergreen State. In Seattle, they visited the skeleton museum, the Space Needle, Pike Park, and then to Olympia to see the state capitol.

"I have always loved this state. Look at the greenery and the beautiful landscape. It reminds me all the time the greenbelt we have back home. Rights they say, go with responsibility. Individuals, stakeholders, government, and all institutions must take part in the development of the community. This is how people in communities should live and act.

"Looking up to government alone for everything doesn't work especially in our world today. Just give the little you can to help society that way it will never be as it is/was. Isn't this beautiful?" he asked.

"It is," replied Sundiatta.

"Aren't we visiting the Washington National Museum any longer?" Osagyefo, one of his sons accompanying the group inquired.

"We will, son. How can I forget about the National Museum? It is one of the most interesting places. Thanks for reminding me, though. I know what's going through your mind now."

Otumfuo was taking photographs. It was his hobby. In his albums are pictures of the Big Ben, the Buckingham Palace, the number 10 Downing Street, the Twin Towers in New York, the Statue of Liberty, etc. He took all the photographs the last time he and his brother visited the US while they were schooling in London.

"Look yonder, Dad," pointing to an incredible architectural work. "I think we should have these kinds of flyovers back home. Amazing, isn't it?"

"It is," replied Captain Crow.

Chapter 20

"Good old Rome wasn't built in a day," Captain Crow told Otumfuo. "It took the Romans years. Through hard work, sacrifice, communal spirit, team building, etc. This can be replicated in our motherland. We can make Ghana a heaven on Earth in our part of the continent, and many tourists would come to visit us.

"I've no doubt in my mind about what you guys can do today and in the future to help our great nation. Besides, I'm so proud of you, gentlemen, for returning home after your education abroad. I am so glad that you didn't disappoint me. Personally, I have problem with those who don't want to return home after studies abroad and even when they're blessed with wealth and knowledge don't want to share.

"They choose to stay outside forever, and then have the impudence to accuse those back home of being corrupt. The truth is, how would your country develop if you have nothing to do with her regarding its growth and prosperity?

"I am reminded of a certain guy I met in Tacoma a few years back, a Togolese immigrant. Togo is a tiny West African country which shares border with Ghana to the east. That young man is perhaps the most idiotic person I have ever met in the whole wide world. He talks so meanly about his own people, insults, and denigrates them. And like the other francophone I met while serving jail term at Apollonia a decade ago claims he's also from France. The irony, however, is he has so soon forgotten his own roots and where he comes from. He is like the western dog who tells the dog from the third world, "'My name is Tony,' and then turns around to his compatriot and asked him, "'what's your name too?"

"'I am dog,' third world dog replies.

"'Your name is dog? You are nothing but a beast. I am special, that's why they call me Tony.'

"'Well, you're a beast too, in case you didn't know. You will remain a beast as long as you tread on these four legs. Is that the image you see when you look yourself in the mirror, or it's your own figment of imagination? Either way, let me tell you bluntly, just be content of who you are my friend, Tony. Did you know being called special is nothing but to fool you?'

"'Undeniably, sometimes I see you at the car front, other times at the party, naturally feeling swollen-headed, but remember, all don't change your status as a beast. God made us animals. We belong to the animal kingdom. The human race is for mankind. We cannot be like them,' third world dog schooled him.

"See, that's why I always talk about our first president Dr. Kwame Nkrumah," Captain Crow pointed out. "Can you fathom gentlemen, how our country and the whole Africa would have been like, had Dr. Nkrumah not returned home?"

"Dad I guess, it would have been disaster! Or maybe cataclysmic," Otumfuo said. "Seriously, I have such a great respect for Dr. Nkrumah. I think but for him Ghana and for that matter Africa in general would have found herself today in a very messy situation.

"Indeed Africa would have surely been in that shambolic road," Osagyefo interjected. Even with all the good things we learned Nkrumah did i.e. championing total liberation across the continent she's still not out of the woods."

"Nkrumah to me, by far was the father of all the nations across Africa," he added. "I find his great idea of Pan-Africanism in the fifties as still the way to go… if we're to grow as a continent. I agree he had his shortcomings as a leader but arguably he stood tall among all his peers at the time."

"Well, is it right to learn from other economies?" Captain Crow posed the question.

"Yeah I think so," Marijata replied. "There are a lot to learn from our advanced friends, the affluent economies no doubt about that. Also I think the world over nations and governments continue to learn from one another. Be it small or big, developing or developed, of middle- or low-income, they've all learnt to inculcate the culture of interdependency."

"I'm for that too," Captain Crow butted in. "After all, which nation in the world did it better than the US. In the eighteenth and nineteenth centuries the US sent many of its intellectual abroad particularly to France to study art/literature and science, engineering, nursing, economics etc."

'Did you know guys that Thomas Jefferson America's third president studied in France and thereafter returned home to impart the knowledge acquired to his people?"

"I didn't know that," Osagyefo said.

"Neither me," his brother admitted.

"Yes, he did. And look at America today. She's militarily powerful, economically great and scientifically developed.

Again, despite the fact that she's the youngest among six children, the US has become the number one global force.

But isn't it sad that after decades of decolonization and imperialism our great continent is still suffering economically?"

"Captain I think the cause of Africa's woes is multi-layered," said Sundiata. "I would like to first put the blame squarely on the door steps of the so-called former colonial powers and some powerful governments of today who continue to hide behind the curtains and sponsor some disgruntled folks to stage coups or topple democratically –elected governments.

Second, I think so long as these powers determine the price of our produce and commodities such as cocoa, cashew, coffee, timber and gold as well as tell us how to write our budgets, Africa would remain in this economic doldrums."

"How about Africa's continued dependency on the Breton Woods Institutions," Osagyefo asked.

"You mean the IMF and World Bank…?"

"That's right!"

"Well, that's another layer of the problem." Sundiata noted. 'See, the good old aid packages aren't helping our people now. I strongly believe it's rather hurting the developing nations and perhaps deepening their woes."

"Hold your horses comrades," Captain Crow interrupted. "I know this might sound paradox to you. "But did you know that after decades of postcolonial era, former colonies of the Brits, French, Portuguese, Belgians, the Dutch and the Germans continue to be remote-controlled?"

"I suppose we're all aware of that," Marijata remarked.

"Alright if we accept so, then I think one cannot shove all the blame onto the imperialists: And which is why I disagree with Sundiata." Captain Crow noted.

"No, Captain I stand to be corrected." Sundiata interrupted. "I didn't mean the imperialists are solely blamable for Africans' woes. My point was that I wouldn't be hesitant to put the blame first on their doorsteps."

"So you mean you're on the same page with me?" Captain Crow enquired.

"Absolutely yes on that," Sundiata replied. "I couldn't agree with you more.

"Well as I pointed out earlier I think African leaders must also be held responsible for our anguish. Most of them if not all, have over the years betrayed and deceived us. They tend to line their pockets with the state funds instead of providing needed infrastructure to improve the standard of living of the critical mass.

In a few instances where a government did a little in terms of housing, roads, schools, bridges, hospitals for the people another government steps in and abandons the whole projects.

"Governments pay freebies and bribes to sponsored groups to earn projects. I hate to say that this kind of winner takes it all syndromes will never stop in our fledgling democracies in as much as the west continue to dabble in the affairs of our governance system. Nevertheless, not all is lost yet, and I pray we will find the solid grounds someday sooner than later. We have been wallowing in the mire for so long. I think new breed of African leaders with new political, ideological thinking and purpose-driven minds would perhaps be the answer. At least we've had a good start and put good structures and institutions in place now."

Chapter 21

While in the states, Captain Crow witnesses several revealing episodes. Some of which he unselfishly shares here with his people.

He simply identifies himself as Sam but Captain Crow preferred to call him Uncle Sam), burly-built, hairless, and inconspicuous. Uncle Sam visits the Tacoma Washington Wright Park during winter, summer, fall, spring, and autumn. "I am an all weather patron," he notes with laughing eyes.

He has come with his pregnant wife and their two-year-old daughter. They have come to feed the birds at the pool. Madam Monolissa Sam, cute and looking drawn has a small cart full of bread. She drags the handcart closer to the poolside and tosses a loaf deep into the waters and right away, the birds seize upon it, then a toss from her husband. Another toss from Monolissa would soon invite a swarm of birds. Each one of them struggles to get a bite. And rapidly, more of the animals will join the fray. The air space has been jammed. From the Far East, West, South, and from the North Pole, the migratory and nonmigratory birds have flown in like immigrants to the Wright Park in search of greener pastures.

Sooner the toss game by the couple would catch the eagle's eye. Veteran Captain Crow sitting a few yards away from the food connection site has noticed something unpleasant, something that smacks unjust and discriminatory.

To the maverick's surprise, while some of the birds feast merrily in the pond, others stand at the fringes with nothing to eat.

Why?

They couldn't get into the water because naturally they are not created to swim (they aren't amphibious). And this physical limitation would cost them gravely in as long as they continue to live in Uncle Sam's farmland.

As Captain Crow struggles emotionally and psychologically to twig his mind around the whole saga, he decides to meet with Uncle Sam and ask him why he has ignored those who could obviously not swim.

"Sir, why don't you feed the birds on the banks of the pool too?"

Surprisingly, the answer he receives from Uncle Sam is equally distasteful and unpleasant. His wife grudgingly tosses a slice of bread to the right side of the pond where a group of crows stand ready for their turn. That piece cannot assuage their hunger.

And looking frustrated, Captain Crow retires to his seat processing the entire episode. His uncharacteristic pent-up mood would betray him and attract queries from the other comrades. At the Right Park the maverick meets a retired Caribbean army officer named Paul Cook, who would later join the group in their fight against social injustice.

Mr. Cook nicknamed firebrand Paul has also expressed his displeasure at the scene.

"What's going on, Captain?" Paul asked. "You don't look cheerful."

Ultimately, his conscience has locked horns with reality, still trying to understand nature and man, life and death, and whether justice means justice and not something else.

Suddenly, the maverick breaks his silence. He opens a dialogue with his colleagues.

He begins, however, with a poser.

"Is it true that birds flock to where they can find comfort, food, and water?"

Marijata asked him, "Why this question, Captain?"

"Well, there seem to be an iota of truth in the old adage, but I have some misgivings."

"What are they?"

"I am not sure if you have observed the scene opposite us."

He points to the direction upfront.

"This is about the third time that I've witnessed this," he points out. "Some minority birds, so to speak, had to go home without food when there is so much to feed on here."

"What are you talking about comrade?"

Captain Crow positions himself well to face his friend squarely, apparently to hammer home his viewpoint.

"Have you perchance taken a closer look at the other side of the park? I'm talking about Uncle Sam's 'farmland,' where one could aptly describe as a 'paradise.'"

"Where exactly is this farmland? You're talking so philosophical. Do you mean the one by the twin pond?"

"That's right! Just look straight ahead."

"What about them?" questions Marijata.

"Just a moment. I will tell you.

"The two ponds [fraternal twins] used by Uncle Sam and his family has algae taken over them. However, they spawn contrasting features. The one to the north end often used by the conservative farmer has all the goodies as such it pulls crowd to her banks. But it draws ire too.

"The other at the opposite end appears malnourished and lean [*korshiokor* in Ghanaian phraseology]. She hardly attracts attention or patrons but for the trilogy that stands at her shores.

"Unthinkably, whenever she does, the result is ill-treatment. The reason: she has no depth at summertime. She looks so shallow, though she gets deeper during fall and springtime. Her attractive red fishes are so exposed to predators. Young inquisitive kids [mostly her patrons] have become her archenemies as they hurl stones at its red little fishes exposed by the vagaries of the weather.

"The red fishes can be seen perking feed and small insects. Mournfully, she meanders herself under a half-century-old elevated footbridge and empties into the contaminated, well-fed neighbor.

"This is what I saw the last time I visited here. And I should think this particular pond only takes solace from the hordes of trees like the plume/sawara cypress, the horse chestnuts, the English field maple, and the Carolina poplars that offer green canopy to her—a shade many patrons also enjoy during summer sizzling weather," said Captain Crow.

"Now, back to the substantive subject..." He draws his men closer to the pond.

"Isn't it amazing to watch how this farm has become a destination for many migratory and other birds—the seagulls, the geese, the ducks, the crows, etc? And yet some of them return home hungry in a number of occasions. Even nonfeather animals, like the squirrels, also transit here. There is absolutely plenty to eat and enough to drink.

"Unfortunately, not all of them are lucky. Perhaps, in many cases, some of the animals seeking pastures go home without food. Apparently, Uncle Sam has a way of feeding these birds. He throws the food into the water.

"Often, the aggressive seagulls are the most fortunate ones. From the waters, they jumped into midair to catch the flying loaf, which is on its way into the pond. And like a quarterback American football player, guzzles a whole slice of bread under her yawning throat.

"They clatter, they flutter, and their quaky sounds also produce another intriguing effect into the ears of onlookers. But in the midst of this merrymaking spectacle, some of the birds have become mere spectators.

"Turn your eyes to the left side of the pond, what do you see, a group of crows standing so morose. They are hungry, they are angry.

"Why is this so?" this time Sundiata questions.

"This is because the trend hasn't changed. Uncle Sam continues to throw the food in the pool day in and day out—a pattern that doesn't favor the non-amphibious birds while others feast themselves merrily.

"I wonder how these birds are faring now. And I wonder again how they might have reacted if they're humans," says Marijata.

"Comrades, these creatures are already aggrieved," Captain Crow submitted. "They don't need to be humans to demonstrate their dissatisfaction at the on-goings here. Fact is, they too must eat to live. Their survivability is dependent on food and water, which I believe are the essential needs for humans as well.

"This thing has been going on for awhile now, at least since the last time I visited here. Pathetically, these birds normally look on helplessly and go back hopelessly.

"But eventually, this routine or pastime [if you like] of Uncle Sam would ignite wild protest among the less fortunate ones, particularly the crows. They would petition the powers that be. It would be chaotic, but all the same, they would survive regardless.

"I think there is a great lesson to learn from the crows' episode. This story is so philosophical. It amply reveals the other side of the world—the animal kingdom. It more or less relate to the life of minority in this country, but most especially blacks.'

"Yes, you said it best," remarked Marijata.

"Indeed, the crows' story again relates so much with the lives of blacks. First of all, the birds are black. Second, the black-feathered birds are regarded as black sheep among their peers. And worse still even considered as demonic animals."

"Oh, I see. That is so revealing."

"But, I repeat, but," said Captain Crow, "their sense of intelligence has been equated to that of the giant ape."

"Similarly, blacks, as a people, have from time immemorial faced this uphill problem of injustice, inequality, and discrimination. A curse or misfortune, their skin color has become a stigma, and subtly used as a yardstick to determine their job status and other social engagements.

And as I have observed over the period, Uncle Sam's behavior wasn't exceptional. What we get however, is discrimination in the human race, discrimination in the animal kingdom. So, in a way we are bedfellows."

"Not long, this defiant and polarized posture adopted by Uncle Sam at the Wright Park as a means of solving the problem brought before him by the disadvantaged crows would spark more tension and discomfort. This is because of his (Sam's) stubborn refusal to yield to the demands of the people, in that sense, the crows."

Underneath this unhappy development, a fiery debate is just about to erupt. Dubbed the 'clash of the titans'—newly entrant Paul, a Trinidadian would take the spotlight at the Right Park to face off conservative farmer Uncle Sam. Issue pending—patrons must stop feeding the wild animals at the park. This decision has angered Uncle Sam and his cohorts but Paul and the crows support the idea. They're all for it!

Ahead of the debate comes a protest. The crows stand morose. They would soon begin to chant war songs and clamor for equal right and justice. Captain Crow and his group are all present to listen to the minority birds.

The chief crow opens his speech with a chant from the crows:

Feed the crows and let 'em grow
Don't throw the food only in the pond
'Cos we can't flow, no we can't roll
Need I tell you, keep it low on our throes?
We came here not with cloaks, yet we are treated
like rogues
Remember we can take it slow in the snow
Oh please throw 'em to the crows
And let 'em glow

Immediately after the crows' protest the Wright Park which has long been known for its legendary pastime braces itself for the much anticipated debate. The two men Uncle Sam and Paul Cook are already seated. And hundreds; perhaps thousands have thronged the area to witness the frenzy scene.

The moderator takes his seat and urges all present to observe decorum.

"No shouts from the foreground," he tells the crowd. "Ladies and Gentlemen I now present to you retired Captain Paul Cook," the moderator announces.

"Thank you Mr. Alan," Paul says referring to the moderator. "And Good afternoon to you'll my proud audience."

Paul clears his throat amid spontaneous reaction from the milling crowd:

"Say it all Paul," someone yells from the crowd . "Say it all for we're fed up."

"Calm down, calm down, folks. Arise my people, arise citizens of the New World [*Omanfoforo*]. You know a closed mouth never gets fed. I, therefore, beseech you to rise up and gird thee your loins for our journey for freedom, equal rights, and justice has just begun. A journey with many detours bumps and rumps, but I am hopeful we shall prevail in our travail.

"I want to assure you that we're not in this struggle alone. God is on our side!

"You can also see for yourselves that some white folks are in our midst including other minority—Jews, Latino, brothers and sisters from Asia, and of course my good friends—Brian, Daniel, and Lameck. From the flanks to my far right, I can see young Levi, Julian, Malachi, and their father Alex.

They've all come to lend their unwavering support and solidarity for this just course, which we're fighting today and we will continue to fight tomorrow. I also know that personnel from the secret services–the CIA, FBI, MI6, (now FSB), and the DCRI are here as well.

"But that won't stop us from fighting for our rights. We're not rioting, we're only staging a peaceful protest. Unless they change the definition of riot to mean any peaceful gathering. And of course, that is what we're doing now. Nothing short of that, we're peace-loving folks, and we promise to use nonviolence to put across our grievances.

"Amanda Awetu! Amanda Awetu!

"Let it be known to Uncle Sam that this is not a hunger strike. I repeat this is not a hunger strike. This is a positive defiance action, an action aimed at leveling the playing field.

"The wait is over, the fear is gone, and the time to act is now. We're hungry, sir. We're starving, and we fret we might even die before we get served.

"Is this not the land of the free and home for the brave? Where are equal rights and justice? I mean, where did they go? How long must we wait? When will our time come? What must we do to get our fair share of the national cake?

What did we do wrong to be treated this way? Enough is enough!

"We're murder of crows—ravens, corvus, jays, magpies, choughs, and nutcrackers. Young and old, meek and weak, we braced the early misty dawn, queued hours in the summer scorching sun in anticipation of getting our share of the national goodies. But it turns out to be an illusionary trip."

Uncle Sam butts in, "Are you done, Paul?"

"Not yet, sir. All we're asking for is please change the rules of the game. We want a level playing field. We're appealing to you, to right the wrongs. Decades have gone by, and promises of equality and justice have equally passed us by. Even the slow tortoise with all its sluggish mentality had finished going round the continent of the whole North America. And here, we're still marking time in the burning sun.

"Yet amid all this socio-political disparities in our community we've resolved to ever uphold our profound sense of modesty and genteel character.

"Nonetheless, there is a new dawn. There's a new light. The dark clouds have at last settled, and this family will now and forever live in that light. We will no longer grope in darkness. Never shall we sink ourselves in that gloomy situation. And never shall we have any marriage with the clouds.

"Let me emphasize here that we won't back down our positive defiance attitude. You'd see us at the traffic lights, on rooftops, on the streets and trees and the national parks. Yes, we won't give up. We won't surrender.

"We will continue to hammer home our reasonable demands [civil rights], and we are confident in ourselves that our avowed pursuit of the dream of this society will be achieved."

"Yeah, yeah!" the gathering cheered him on.

"Are we hated because of our skin color or just despised because of our raucous voices? I need an answer for this, Uncle Sam."

"I'm sorry, I am not going to respond to trivial questions," Uncle Sam replies.

"Well, sir, be informed that the prevailing condition is not helping folks like us, it is rather hurting and killing us softly at a fast rate.

"The irony is that the situation makes us seem like slackers and mere parasites.

"But you know we aren't lazybones. You know we're smart and energetic species, strong, and dynamic. Our sense of intelligence has been equated to that of the giant ape. Yet, we're often marginalized—"

"Enough, enough, Paul," Uncle Sam interrupted. "I know where you're coming from. A hungry man is obviously an angry man. And I think you and your group need some anger management therapy or class. Otherwise, you can basket and bath."

"No, sir, we're stating what's obvious. We've been sitting down here for far too long. Too much water has passed under the bridge. And too little, perhaps nothing, has been done in the past decades to ameliorate the economic shocks we've been going through. It's about time the rules were changed," Paul reiterated.

"Well, I don't mean to hurt your feelings but if you care to know, this is my country and this community belongs to me. Basically, these are my laws and I take no compunction for doing what I do. I choose to do what I want to do and give to whom I deem fit. Where were you when we built the ships and sailed across the Atlantics and the Antarctic? Where were you when we braced the turbulent storm across the Indian Ocean?

"Tell me, Paul, where were you when we sent man to the moon? See, you know how to fight but you don't know how to win. Don't I have the right to give to whom I want, tell me?"

Paul barges in again. "But, sir, ah…"

"No interruption. I'm still airborne. I haven't landed yet. You've made your case. It's now my turn to set the records straight."

"Set the records straight?" Paul asked rhetorically.

"You heard me right!" Uncle Sam continued, "See, you don't get it. You have no idea what is happening to this country. I'm profoundly worried and overwhelmed by the invasion of immigrants from Latin America [particularly Mexico], Africa, Asia, and the Middle East.

"This phenomenon has increasingly caused unemployment among my people in the entire community. Today, many of our young men and women have no jobs because of the intense competition in job search. No sense of pride and we're consequently losing our wives because we're unable to put food on our kitchen tables.

"Haven't you witnessed the spate of crime in our neighborhoods recently? It's all because of the influx of these folks. They don't have documents to live here, let alone work. Yet there are a good number of them who're enjoying the dwindling national cake. Where is the milk and honey? Where is the dream of the New World?

"My deepest fear is that if we don't stem this flood now by year 2050, the whole white population would be decimated. And I shudder to say we might as well lose our dignified identity.

"Today you hear terrorists here, terrorists there. Insurgents are increasingly growing in the Middle East, growing in Africa, and now we have homegrown terrorists. "

"What, in our own soil? "

"That's my deepest fear...If you don't get it now, you better."

"Deceitful," Paul said. "This is outrageous, Uncle Sam, for you to have employed this fallacious form of argument purely to mislead and hoodwink the masses. I am stunned by your comment, cataloguing all these menace and squarely blame it on the minority, or people of color. As though there were no crime and violence prior to our arrival in this great country. You know what, I am not going to descend into the gutters with you. Surprisingly, you're no longer setting the so-called records straight as you claimed. Instead, you're whipping up xenophobia sentiments. And for the past weeks or so, we've seen politically motivated violence on the streets resulting deaths and fatalities. This kind of posture, I'm afraid would do the good peoples of this diverse country no good and I entreat you to stop it."

"Well, tell me what will be good for this country?" Uncle Sam questioned, "Where in the face of this planet would you have had this platform or blab like the way you are doing? Is it in Communist China or any of the emerging democracies in the West Indies, Asia, or Africa? I certainly don't think it is Rhodesia or Ghadffi's Libya?"

"Sir, you're just beating about the bush." Paul replied. "You said you're going to set the records straight but up to now, you've still not touched on the core issues which brought us here today. The point is, we've heard these rhetoric and gimmicks time and time again. They didn't help my parents' generation, they're not helping my generation, and they're certainly not going to help the younger generation either."

"I don't understand what you're angst about, Paul?"

"Sir, I don't think you need a power point system to understand our agitations and the plight we're facing here." Paul told Uncle Sam." If your ears can't hear, your eyes can see, I believe. We're all clad in black. Black arm bands, black stockings, and black bandanas—signifying that we're already mourning our sorrows, though still alive. But it informs us that death is imminent if we don't act now.

"We're all in black, however, our cousins from West Africa, precisely Ghana [formerly Gold Coast] have white mufflers wrapped around their necks, meaning victory is not far-fetched. It means, we'll prevail in our struggle, we shall overcome, and we'll surely be leaders of tomorrow and not subservient. Thank you!"

The moderator, Mr. Alan described the debate as 'very successful'. And Uncle Sam and his entourage left the park immediately. They wouldn't stay even a minute to exchange pleasantries. He appeared livid.

❁

But the day was still young for other important activities. The African King Captain Crow would also seize the opportunity to admonish his people and offer them some advice as well.

"We mustn't forget folks that we're immigrants," he told them. "Let's strive always to be law-abiding, responsible people and eschew all manner of distractive activities. Even though we've right to demonstrate, speak etc. In everything we do let us attach moderation.

"Ladies and gentlemen, I would like also to reiterate that victory will soon come. But be reminded that victory comes not easy. There's hard price to pay. It is costly and it's risky because we have to face the wrath of the cruel and encounter the anger of the outrageous man. Nonetheless, let me ask you all, who amongst us here individually, can withstand the venom of envy? Certainly, no one as the good book says. The enemy is here to destroy us. He is like the pandemic disease bubonic.

"Lest I forget, does anyone of us here know or is aware of the next battle we've in our hands? Obviously, the response will be negative. I knew that from the get-go. It's hard to tell where the tidal waves are panning if you aren't familiar with the terrain. From the grapevine, Uncle Sam and his cronies are yet to unleash another deadly blow.

"This would be called a silent war. By its subtle nature, the battle is going to be psychological. In effect, they're going to employ what the guys have termed social challenges like accent, color, and nationality.

"Even though in the eyes of God, none of the above-mentioned stuff qualifies their definition of social limitations, it would be used against us anyway. I'm therefore sounding this caution beforehand—to be forewarned is to be forearmed. That doesn't mean we are going to carry arms and fight the enemy. No, what it means is that, henceforth, we will individually and collectively psyche ourselves up in the face of this battle.

Folks it appears the fight for survival and dignity has intensified lately. And it could get worse the coming days. I have heard about profiling but I never thought accent will also become an issue.

Yes you heard me. Accent has now crossed carpet and had equally gained entry into mainstream immigration issues. My son Otumfuo last week had a shock in his life when a lady secretary told him bluntly: "Sir, you've accent so we can't hire you."

I couldn't believe my ears so I asked his brother Osagyefo to go to the office the following week. And surprisingly he too couldn't escape the cold reception.

"Dad I was completely stupefied," he narrated.

He said while waiting at the reception Yvonne the secretary approached him and asked, "Where are you from, sir?"

"I'm from Ghana," Otumfuo told her.

Well to cut a long story short after a series of questions and filling a long application form none of my sons got hired.

So, let's close our ranks, pool our strengths together, and unite as a formidable force that way we can stand before the enemy. I also like to urge you all to stay the course and never lose focus. Yes, the going would be tough but remember no condition is permanent. God willing you'll one day find yourself at the right part of the ladder. Thank you all for coming!"

Barely two hours after those poignant exchanges between Paul Cook and Uncle Sam officials from the security agency arrested Paul and two others. The two, Billy and Marijata were freed shortly afterwards. However, the Trinidadian would spend two days behind bars anyway.

Apparently, Uncle Sam had pressed false charges against him. As a result, Paul was flogged and warned not to incite the public to cause what the authorities described as 'public nuisance'. But it remains to be seen whether the newly-baptized activist Paul and the crows would back down their planned protest.

Chapter 22

It wasn't a damp squib. Paul Cook, Captain Crow's bosom friend, had rallied the crows. They had carried out their threat of staging a mammoth protest on the streets of Tacoma, causing traffic jam. On rooftops, traffic lights, shopping malls right up to the Wright Park, the irate birds registered their remonstration.

The name of the game, "rough tactics," had become inexcusable, hence the mass protest. Once again, Captain Crow and his Walatu-Walasa group in solidarity had joined the crows. As the crowd thickened by the hour, a certain guy also stormed the park. Later, the maverick and his entourage would learn he was a regular patron. The big dude from the hood, as he was often referred to, had sneaked into the popular stand.

His huge size of seven feet and six inches and bullying antics intimidated many in the vicinity. He usually wore size 18 shoes, fifty-six waist slack to match with a 4X NLF jersey. He never smiled. He never giggled. Beneath his awful looks, were unkempt spongy beard sandwiched by wide-ranging ears. One could smell him sometimes from a distance far off even before he drew near.

Captain Crow wondered what kind of cologne or deodorant he wears.

"Very sweet scented," noted the African king. "It was nonetheless offensive."

He drew the fury of many tourists to the popular arena. The notorious fragrance had forced itself into the gorgeous afternoon breeze. The atmosphere had been polluted. So strong and so powerful that it caught the nostrils of all the patrons at the park.

But the tang couldn't stop the people from either laying face down or face up in the sweltering summer weather on the park's well-manicured green grass to tan their Coca-Cola-shaped firm skins.

While some biked around, others barbecued in the baking sun.

The conservatory in Wright Park has over the years and up to date allowed Washingtonians, especially people in Tacoma, to enjoy beautiful flowers all year round, courtesy of I. J. Knapp's Victorian-style design, which was chosen during the garden's preparatory stages. Besides, the tropical plants inside, I'm told, charmed early patrons like President Theodore Roosevelt and gave many their first chance view about exotics.

In summer times, the park's most visited patrons—kids—roll themselves downhill on the beautiful landscape repeatedly with their moms and siblings also taking part in the summersault exercise.

The mini glass museum is another spot that attract visitors. It sits opposite the senior citizens apartments, uphill over by the G Street, where one can also see the red oak tree.

"The big red oak tree you see over there has been here since 1903," Donna told Captain Crow. Donna who now wears silver hair and used to visit the park until at age twelve, when she and her parents moved to somewhere in the midwest, also mentioned the big dude.

"My husband [Bob] and I just moved back here. It's still the beautiful park I knew when I was a child."

So, no wonder to this day many come to the park despite of the presence of the offensive visitor. "Nothing has changed,"

Donna said. "The swings are still there, the landscaping is much the same, and the visitors still come to watch the geese and seagulls as they swim and swing along in the nearby pond. If you still haven't gotten the clue yet, I am talking about the aroma of Tacoma. The good old odor caused by the pulp mill!

In the "City of Destiny," as Tacoma is called, perhaps everything is possible.

"You can't get it better anywhere, smelling the legendary aroma and doing people-watching synchronizingly.

The protest has ended peacefully but remained to be seen whether something good would come out of it. Meanwhile, Captain Crow and few of his buddies remain at the park to enjoy the afternoon gentle breeze under a huge sycamore tree. Moments later, the maverick observes something not unusual——patrons feeding the seagulls, the geese etc. Not quite long he witnessed something unpardonable.

"It must have been a déjà vu," Captain Crow told Paul. "If I thought the situation at Uncle Sam's farm could get any better soon. This is a horrific scene, and it challenges my entire thinking faculty."

Guys how long is this battle going to last. Would this change ever come at all and when?" Crow asked his buddies.

"Probably not but we can't stop the fight." Paul replies. "I think in as much as the rich few continue to pontificate themselves as the political and economic gurus."

"You're right. See, some of our friends are living under severe fear. Last night, I kept thinking about what the future has in store for folks in the minority like us, the crows and the squirrels.

"Isn't this a betrayal?" Captain Crow asks. "I feel so let down and I'm pretty sure all of you do, because just a little over one hour after the huge gathering, obnoxious Uncle Sam has again released his German shepherd dog, Tarantula. He weighs 240 pounds and stands about four feet tall.

"The wild, wide beast has gone berserk looking for a prey. It's become a ritual, and he does it gracefully on purpose for sheer joy and pleasure. They say one man's agony is another's pleasure as one's trash becomes other's treasure.

"The problem is, if God does not stay home and goes out to meet Moses on Mount Sinai that means someone is in deep trouble. Evidently, it becomes even double trouble if he heads down to the upper room to have the last supper with his Apostles."

Crow's buddies have been tickled by the icon's mastery of wits and sarcasm.

Jean Claude Billy yells, "Nous voulons plus monsieur." (We want more, sir.)

Captain Crow giggles, pulls out a white handkerchief to wipe off the perspiration on his forehead. He giggles again and then launches the punch line.

"Well, if the Lord winds up in Golgotha, then it is trouble! Trouble! Trouble!

"But He will rise up! The flying birds can at least fly away in case they sight the enemy first, but not so with their neighbors, the rodents."

"Under a shady mahogany tree a small-sized squirrel with bushy tail and relatively big eyes also prowls around for some nuts. She stands on the soft pad of her hind limbs which is generally longer than the fore limbs. Her diminutive size could give her cover in the evenly cut meadow. Mama Squirrel weighs just about ten grams and her length a little over seven centimeters. "Can you imagine George Foreman in his boxing heydays facing it off with actor and martial artist Weng Weng? Disaster looms!

"Tarantula's penchant for terrorizing these innocent folks has been going on for ages. No one seems to care. Pretty soon, he would strike. He has the license to torment, to threaten, and to kill. And of course, he shows no compassion for his victims.

"I witnessed him kill one of Mama Squirrel's child last week,'" notes Captain Crow. "He tore the animal into two as blood streamed down his mouth profusely. I surely have no slightest idea as to what might happen now.

"The distance between Mama Squirrel and Tarantula [the prey and the predator] was merely twenty-five yards. Her chance of life or death was just fifty-fifty. Nevertheless, strategy was of the essence so as luck.

"Tarantula walked surreptitiously forward toward Mama Squirrel. He inched up slowly. His eyes turned red, ears cocked up, and claws erected like the lion's. Again, he stretched his forelegs to their elastic limits."

Uncle Sam watched with great excitement, but at the opposite end, Captain Crow observed the scene with great consternation. Close to a mahogany stood a tiny maple tree. Mama Squirrel had to make the right decision at the right time, else she risked being marauded by the hungry monster. She stared back at the beast. And the beast scowled her the more.

The heat was on. The plot unfolded and the action brought itself.

Bracingly, the ferocious brute took a step forward, swung diagonally to the right side then to the left. He took another step and yet another one. He sent yet another jab forward, zoomed in aggressively on the tiny squirrel like an unmanned vehicle drone to capture the pisspot poor rodent but he had been beaten to it. Tarantula had missed his prey narrowly.

Indeed, the old lion perishes for lack of a prey and the plump lion's whelps scatter abroad. Certainly the race is not for the swift!

Tarantula roared angrily and barked harder as though his boding evil would cause Mama Squirrel to come down. But from her elevated perch on the fortitude wings of the tiny maple tree, she had found a safe haven. "I can't be bothered buddy," she seemed to have told her pursuer. Its over, the thriller has ended. Yet, on top of the tree she (Mama Squirrel) shook violently.

The beast jumped helter-skelter, wagged his pruned tail, gnashed his seemingly dragon's teeth, and cursed his stars.

He had lost the game. Tarantula had lost it!

❧

But the other game had hit apogee. Tension had soured in the community where the two mavericks Captain Crow and Cowboy Uncle Sam lived.

Remember the last debate between Uncle Sam and Paul Cook?

The two had locked fierce horns again. They jockeyed aggressively to win the day. And as each day offered a new drama, the patience of Tacoma began to wane. Maverick Captain Crow, however, and his comrades would continue to lend support to their faithful friend Paul to battle hard the powers that be.

Their clarion call for a level playing field at the Wright Park had not been answered, and so they would shift gears. The rogues, they called them. Others labeled them noisemakers. But none of that would put breaks on the speeding locomotive. The crows were moving fast, at the same time, cautiously marshalling support from every corner in the city of Tacoma.

The new scheme was to engage Uncle Sam a debate at a town hall, coupled with sit-down strikes, positive defiance marches, and mass protests.

Though they knew the terrain was rough and the battle equally tough, nothing, according to the crows, would stop them. Speaking at a town hall meeting, Paul Cook noted that even though there might be fatalities, the group would never rest on their oars, stressing they knew where, "we're coming from and our destination point."

"We're like the porcupines, if you kill a thousand, another thousand will come back to fight you. Our strength is embedded in our quills. And our power lies in our Maker."

Weeks before their departure to the motherland, Paul who had then decided to travel with his friends to Ghana had a final brush with Uncle Sam. That showdown would shake the very foundation of the entire city of Tacoma, reminding its inhabitants if they retreat today, they will reload and come back tomorrow.

This followed a strong petition the group sent to the city mayor and copied Metro Parks Authority. The petition among other things asked the authorities to stop forthwith the feeding of all wild animals at the pond's side, its surroundings as well as the park.

According to the crows, the practice had not only impoverished the wild animals, but also made them become lethargic. They argued that if for some reason (in a worse case scenario), disaster strikes or Uncle Sam dies or become incapacitated or any of the patrons failed to bring food for days, they might die.

Their premise seemed to support the conclusion, but it remained to be seen whether the authorities would buy the argument.

At a town hall debate, Paul's opponent had rubbished the whole idea, describing it as outrageous and absurd. "I think your argument smacks absurdity," he told Paul. "But not only that, it's baseless and outmoded at birth."

Uncle Sam charged, "Who do you think you are street-smart guy, a geek or a nerd?"

"Did you hear him say that?" He turned to his wife standing next to him at the right flank.

"You can't even get into the water for food, and you're flexing your muscles. You've petitioned the city mayor. Who would buy into this foolish argument? Who would consider this baseless point? Don't I have the right to feed the wild animals?

"And then you, Mr. All-Knowing, had the impudent to petition the city authority to make the feeding of the wild animals a prohibition."

As the weeks went by, the crows continued their campaign across the city urging people to support the petition. And before long, their solemn appeal was granted, and patrons were prohibited to feed the wild animals.

The authorities had flyers, posters, notices, and placards mounted at every vantage point. At the Wright Park where the historic confrontation began, mini-billboards had been erected. They were visibly dotted on every footpath leading to the banks of the two ponds: "Do Not Feed Any Wildlife," etched boldly on them.

According to a release issued by the authorities, a citation would be issued for violation.

In a three-point resolution, it said wildlife can experience malnutrition, disease, and overpopulation due to human feeding. The release explained further that the animals often exhibit aggressive behavior when they become conditioned to expect food from people. It cited overpopulation as a major contributor to poor water quality and toxic algae growth, endangering public health and safety.

The release further warned that feeding of the wild animals carries a $532 penalty (TMC8.27.130), adding offenders would be dealt with accordingly.

Hours after the news hit the community, it was also reported that Uncle Sam had collapsed and been rushed to the Tacoma General Hospital nearby. The cowboy was not only devastated by the outcome, but the fact that his sworn foe had triumphed over him brought an untold shame and hardship months later.

But pride and honor had draped his opponent. To the crows, the new move called for jubilation. It brought an indescribable joy!

The civil rights activist told the *Fact*, a community newspaper, that though the group was excited, going forward the necessity to make even more sacrifices was overbearing.

"I know that man," Paul told Captain Crow. "He doesn't fight to quit. And I'm also not a quitter."

"You better not," replied Captain Crow. "We would continue to give you our unwavering support. Just remain vigilant as ever before. Let me tell you something Paul. Back in the days, throughout my activism movement, I never had it easy. Folks and

I got beaten sometimes. We were water boarded and charged not to continue our fight. But did we stop?" he rhetorically asked.

"No. Instead, we took the pain in our strides and marched the enemy boot for boot.

"Get this my people, there are some social challenges humanity can never eliminate like inequality, injustice, and poverty because society deliberately creates them, and they now have an entrenched position on the social ladder.

"However, if we choose to be lethargic and don't act, they will overwhelm us, hence our pursuit of equality and justice. I know there is still more work to be done, because people are people. People yesterday are the same people today, and they will be same tomorrow. The elders are right, 'nowhere cool' [*apuene babiara nnwoye*]. Come let's make the historic journey back to our roots."

Chapter 23

Captain Crow and his entourage had made their epic journey back home. The journey they dubbed "back to the root," had been preceded by a thanksgiving service which was held at his favorite park, the Wright Park.

A week earlier, the group had politely turned down the city mayor's plan to have a live band played for them. "We don't need any spotlight now," the maverick told the official. "Last days are dangerous," he said amid laughter.

However, day after day, the beleaguered countryside farmer sought to do everything humanly possible to relive his bitter emotions and revulsion against the man he regarded as a foe. Indeed, his (Uncle Sam's) desire to outdo Captain Crow was like a fire burning in a straw house.

Residents in the community believed the farmer's hatred against Paul Cook and his best buddy Captain Crow had even grown bigger than before as he trudged the blocks each day talking to himself. "He must be suffering from paranoia," a neighbor spoke about him. "So obsessed with nothing. After all, this man he hates so much is no longer here."

"What's his beef?" Devita questioned. "He wakes neighbors up early in the mornings to outbursts, cursing and swearing."

"For me, I think he's lost his mind," said Joan Friedburg, another resident. "This is not the Uncle Sam I've known growing up in this area. He's lost weight, lost his self-esteem, and lost almost everything he owned in the farm."

Months back, before Paul left with his friends for Ghana, every attack was physical. The two (Paul & Sam) matched each other boot for boot at town halls and play grounds. They traded diatribes and launched verbal attacks that could pass as fistic.

The old order had changed. Uncle Sam had rolled out a new set of plan to attack Paul spiritually, imaginarily, and emotionally. Simply put, the supposed battle must be won by any means necessary. To Uncle Sam, it didn't matter whether Paul was in state or out of state. And tightly, he clutched onto the straw as though help could come from there.

But in the midst of all this, he had two quick decisions to make: pack baggage and leave as a defeatist strategy or stay put in his newly acquired ramshackle kiosk and zip-up his loud mouth, after all that was the only property he had left.

The option had come down to this—either he obeyed the rules or left the community. Otherwise, he risked being forced out of his longtime loved neighborhood. What made the whole situation more precarious for Uncle Sam, and perhaps his henchmen, was the fact that officials of Metro Parks meant business this time around.

They'd deployed security agents to police the park from dawn to dusk. This was to help arrest anyone who flouted the law. It was also to enforce sanity in the whole environment and give the animals space as this would, in their own words, "help stem overpopulation."

As one loser boxer kept licking his own wounds, the other one was brimming with smiles. It was summer in the early 1970s. Veteran Captain Crow, Paul Cook, Marijata, Sundiata, Otumfuo and Osagyefo were returning home.

They'd seen the Twin Towers, visited the Disneyland, sat at the Oval Office with the world's most powerful man, and above all, toured all the fifty-two states of the United States. They had stories to tell. They had lessons to share back home.

But still overwhelmed by trauma, Uncle Sam sat on the ground to nurse his sorrows. His little girl, Zimi, swung and bounced around gleefully in an old trampoline in the vicinity unaware of the shockwave. While the mother, Monolissa Sam, watched her with little or no attention as she too kept brooding over the anguish trying to decipher as to what went wrong.

Suddenly, he stood up from the ground where he had sat for hours, and then began to walk around. He had something on his mind. He hadn't spewed out all the toxic yet. Fuming with rage the western cowboy punched the heavens with his fist .He inched up to Monolissa to engage her in a conversation.

"I suppose this Cro-Magnon man and the Board of Park Commissioners are bedfellows," Uncle Sam, insinuated. For the first time, the cowboy had refused to call his opponent by name, addressing him as primitive and palm greaser. "That guy must have greased the palm of the city officials. Else something out-of-the-ordinary might have occurred."

"Honestly, I never thought these guys would stoop so low and sacrifice justice for dollars. I mean accept dollars from this Caribbean guy and his African compatriots and side step one of their own. Again, I think I guessed right: Something out-of-the-ordinary must have happened."

"How on earth could the Metro Parks issue such a decree Do not Feed Any Wild Animals? I mean, how? It's just as absurd as it is nonsense!"

"Enough honey. Enough!" Mrs. Sam interrupted. "You might be rushed to the ER again, if you don't stop thinking about this Crow man. I'm surprise you've still not gotten over this debacle. How long will it take you to figure out why things went the way it did?"

"There's no need to fight over spilt milk. Well, it might smack like hell looking at it from your standpoint. But remember, the heavens aren't coming down now. Life goes on, regardless. You must learn to forget the past and its woes and sorrows. Again, you must remember that the sun rises but not at the same time every day."

The farmer's wife continued, "This premise doesn't match up at all to me. You are suggesting that Paul Cook must have bribed the whole Metro Parks officials for them to have come out with that law. I find the entire argument very preposterous, unfounded and baseless. You know what, much as I believe on one hand that a foreigner can bribe the whole city's officials numbering fifty. It is equally doubtful and unthinkable.

Where would he get that money to dish out?"

"That man excuse my language honey, as I understand was an ordinary custodian in this country. Better translation a janitor. And you're telling me he doled out his hard won money to the city officials?"

Hello, that isn't correct. I refuse to buy into this botched argument. It doesn't make sense to me. Unless you can convince me that Paul Cook and his cronies were into some narcotics business, but I'm afraid the security guys (FBI) would have busted his butt.

"I think the earlier you close the pages on this issue the better. Let's move on with our lives as the crows also fly home."

"I have heard you," Uncle Sam said.

"You better," replied Monolissa.

"Oh gosh I nearly forgot!"

"What is it honey?"

"I'm hurrying to the convenience store at the corner to get some jerky fish (dog food) for Tarantula. And then first thing tomorrow morning, I will have to take him to see the Vet Officer," Uncle Sam told his wife.

"Honey you had better take an umbrella, looks like the rains are coming down soon. It might pour. Here take it and don't stay long."

❧

The early bird flew by. The sun rose early too. And they all had breakfast together around a big dining table reminiscent of the last supper the Lord had with his twelve apostles. White bread, bagels, egg scrambles with peppers and mushrooms, grits, rice pudding, and oat meals, bacons, and sausages.

By ten o'clock in the morning all was set and ready to go!

Many stopped by in front of their hotel in downtown Tacoma to bid them farewell as they got onboard a minibus that transported the group to SeaTac International Airport. Their shoes sparkled like the stars in the heavens and all dressed in suits with kente-designed bowties to match; it was just as beautiful as Bonwire Kente in Ghana.

"Everywhere the crows go, they draw large crowds," a bystander noted.

They took photographs with their idols. They'd brought their pictures to be autographed. And finally, the Walatu-Walasa guys departed—going home with their boots full of pride.

Three months later, Captain Crow received a letter (on behalf of comrade Paul Cook) from Dr. Pepper Booker, a close friend of his. Doctor Booker was an Attorney at a popular law firm in Seattle, Washington. He was a man of his word who tirelessly fought for civil rights movement in the United States and championed the freedom for the minority in the Northwest region in the early 60s.

In the said letter, Doc, as the crows used to call him wrote:

My dear friend, this is to inform you that controversial Uncle Sam has done it again.

I received a letter from his lawyer last week threatening that his client wanted to sue the state and Paul Cook, regarding the prohibition of the feeding of wild animals at the Wright Park in Tacoma.

I wrote back to George Macbeth, his attorney, a day afterward stating inter alia that my client (Paul Cook) was out of state and would not be able to come to the court or appear in person for any legal proceedings. I thought that would discourage the plaintiff's lawyer in view of the fact that you've returned home. And most importantly, there's no case.

Surprisingly, three days later, he mailed to me another letter which in part read: "Plaintiff Uncle Sam has prayed the King County Superior Court in Seattle to summon defendant Paul Cook a native from Trinidad & Tobago now domiciled in Ghana to appear before it in November 24, 1973."

I think this a foolish case, and I don't know if you guys would like to travel that far to come here for the arbitration. But I suggest you come not.

Yours Truly,

Dr. Booker

❧

In his usual calm and genteel attitude, Captain Crow on behalf of the group, wrote to thank his bosom friend Dr. Booker and wished him well. As for the so-called court suit and threats by Uncle Sam, the group treated it with all the contempt it deserved.

"This is laughable," one of the comrades remarked.

They laughed over the whole legal suit and resolved never to appear before any court.

Meanwhile, Uncle Sam had sold all his property, the group learned. He had not only sold his property and the mortgaged home to pursue the so-called case, but had gone borrowing to hire one of the country's best lawyers to fight the state and Paul Cook.

Even in the midst of gloom, the controversial figure swore heaven and earth to find what he described as justice.

A lady friend who lived next door to the Sams once told Captain Crow that the conservative farmer had from infancy never loved himself. "Never heard of Uncle Sam?" she asked. "He is so vicious, and all the time, he feels embittered. It was once rumored that he belonged to the Ku Klux Klan, the white supremacist group."

"In fact I have known him since elementary school days. I knew his parents as well," Tonya Bruce added.

"Who would you say he took after, his father or mother?" Captain Crow asked.

"Interestingly, none of them. I can guarantee," she replied.

"The parents were devout Christians that I know for sure. And I think the father was an Irish and the mother was German or Italian. Uncle Sam was their only child, but he had an adopted brother from the Philippines. His name was Nimrod who died later in his late twenties. So I think he's been used to this 'I' and 'Me' syndrome. Born selfish and raised selfishly."

"Sam has always played the victim's card," Tonya revealed. "And he still does. The thing about him is that if you play into his game, you'll be in trouble. So once we learned his gimmicks, he never got any of us. Let me put it this way—we stayed safe and peaceful all the time. However, others fell into his mole hole," she said with laughter.

❧

So far as evident in the letter, the Washingtonian maverick refused Monolissa's advice to let the sleeping dogs lie. He chose to let them out, and out the mad dogs had descended the streets of Tacoma.

Uncle Sam, the man with the Aaronic beard, had resurrected the old wounds. Though he promised not to expend his time and energy on what was already lost, that ceasefire didn't last long.

Consequently, his beloved wife deserted him, the crows learned.

Lady Monolissa had eloped one fine evening; her whereabouts no one knows up to date. But some residents believed she might have absconded with a handsome young man named Bar Jesus. Zimi, their only daughter had been put under the custody of Child Protective Services (CPS).

This is how protracted litigation had left the once-loving Sams home. The peace and beauty had been ruined. And the man many in the community once feared was no longer a threat. No one felt his presence any longer, and no one even bothered about him.

By and large Uncle Sam personified someone who had no sense of shame and no remorse. For instance, he didn't show any compassion on Mama Squirrel the last time Tarantula tore the scrawny flesh of the baby squirrel into pieces. And it was that kind of symptomatic hatred that he later unleashed onto Captain Crow and his cronies.

Again forgiveness and forgetfulness wasn't part of the conservative's farmer's creed. No wonder, even when the crows had returned to their home country, he still fought their shadows.

"When would Uncle Sam learn his lessons?" Captain Crow wondered. "I thought my departure would bring total end to all the nonsense months of protracted litigation over this feeding of the wild animals rather the bogey cowboy had been running around loose in the Kalahari Desert like a wild camel in heat. I'm told when she is in heat no one can control her."

Apparently, Uncle Sam had run amok, no one could stop him not until he hits the bump again and again. It will be recalled that

six months ago, the cowboy's German shepherd dog, Tarantula,
lost his own dicey race against minnow Mama Squirrel. And as
though that wasn't enough to spare them the inevitable doom,
another defeat surfaced at their already troubled home.

Unbelievably, the maverick himself got the beating. He hit the
dead-end and lost big time. Uncle Sam lost his home; he lost his
marriage, lost custody of his only daughter Zimi, and lost his best
friend Tarantula. He lost his cattle and lost the battle.

It was believed that everybody in the Wright Park community
knew Uncle Sam and his dog Tarantula because of their notoriety.
Hence, his sudden passing caused a stir in the neighborhood.

"I didn't know Tarantula had a friend named Bell," said a patron.

"Several days or weeks had passed after his death I recall when
a lady introduced Bell to me. Cindy the owner had brought Bell
to the park prowling around," Sheila Lee narrated.

Bell was a female dog very pretty looking. She was also a
German shepherd.

Like her boyfriend, she, too, had the appetite to disturb the
peace of the little ones (the squirrels); often lurking around: At
times even chasing the birds.

She was as daring as Tarantula, perhaps worse than the
dishonorable beast.

"I like Bell," Sheila noted. "Because of her (Bell's) style of
hunting the vulnerable animals was kind of special. Patience was
her key ingredient!"

"There was an evening the pretty girl laid wait for hours
unmoved under a Ponderosa Pine tree. Apparently, she had seen
two young squirrels perching up there. She knew the guys were
hungry and would at all cost come down to find pastures. But
that expectation would fizzle out." Sheila recounted.

The skinny guys had also sighted her from the heavens; so they
wouldn't come down until perhaps the dawn of the next century.

Bell would eventually give up just like her boyfriend Tarantula
did several months ago. ." She observed.

As for the tragedy that befell the cowboy maverick and his family; residents, visitors and friends in Tacoma would for months and probably years be talking about it.

His fall from grace to grass, according to many in the Wright Park community, was perhaps destined to happen. They believed Uncle Sam dug his own trenches, and therefore, he deserved to go the way he did.

"I never understood the old saying 'no condition is permanent' until I saw with my own naked eyes when everything Uncle Sam owned went topsy-turvy," a young woman named Lisa who was walking her 13-year-old Chi Wawa dog at the Wright Park around sundown told a friend.

"You really never know what the future might bring you. This Uncle Sam man wielded so much power, respect and he had wealth in this neighborhood. Then just like a fleet everything is gone. I can't believe that but it's real," Lisa added.

"Well let me gossip a bit," her friend probably 50, appearing sneaky whispered into Lisa's ears.

"Have you heard his wife has run away?"

"Where did she run to?" Lisa asked.

"She has eloped. Yes, beautiful Monolissa is gone... she emphasized.

"I knew that woman pretty well. She is a pretty lady, big eyeballs, very friendly. "But anyway, the die is cast and it's a lesson we must all heed," she counseled.

Like the crows, the squirrels didn't worry so much about the turn of events. The reason, the game never favored them. It didn't factor into the whole grand scheme their plight and the dangers they had to face on daily basis. As he witnessed Paul in one of his encounters with Uncle Sam: Captain Crow noted that the squirrels had always risked their lives time and again in the rough terrain looking for pastures.

They had no business getting close or closer to the pond. They couldn't dare because the cowboy often had Tarantula with him.

However, the seagulls, and especially the ducks moaned day after day; in that, over the years they had food at their beck and call. "Uncle Sam is our Shepherd we shall not want…" became their anthem as they never dreamt that manna would be over someday.

The crows as earlier indicated remained coolheaded. But one thing that sort of roused Captain Crow's inner conscience was the niggling question.

"Why me and my group?" asked the maverick. "Why doesn't he sue officials of Metro Parks?" he wondered further.

"So, even when I'm long gone, the wimp is still pursuing me? I'm surprised to learn that over ten thousand miles away, the oppressor is up in arms aiming to shoot me down."

"From the wreck I learned you sought for me, a one-time wretch. Thought you could find me in the ghettos. But I was long gone, gone pass the old Santa Grotto. I had long traded my trash for treasure, and sold my old clothes for a golden coat. Along the way, I courted Wisdom and married her. We had Courage, Strength, and Obedience.

"You may call me avarice vulture because I roped in Wisdom's cousins—Faith, Peace, and Joy. Not only that, I also befriended their blood cousins—Prosperity, Longevity, Security, Blessing, as well as Love. I even had an affair with Grace, their aunt, and Favor, their aunt's sister.

"And then, as I surged on across the high mountains of Zion, down the valleys in Sau Da the land of Judah [modern day Sudan], goodness and mercy also trailed me.

"Last but not least, I carried with me my spiritual toolbox stuffed it with prayer, meditation and fasting. And as we pressed further west, we met the enemies on the highway [no, it was rather on the one-way which was my way]—Envy, Jealousy, Poverty, Covetousness, Sickness, and the entire family.

"Thankfully, we conquered them all!

"Still, I was told you were looking for me. Looking for me, when I had long shifted gears heading for Utopia?"